DEATH AT ARMADILLO

A Paul Seawright Murder Mystery

John Littrell

For Mary

ar.ma.dil.lo (är me dil -o), n., pl. -los. 1. any of several burrowing, chiefly nocturnal, edentate mammals of the family Dasypodidae, ranging from the southern U.S. through South America, having strong claws and a jointed protective covering of bony plates: used in certain areas for food. 2. hacienda in La Ruta, Mexico, built by archaeologist Maximilian Eicher: Casa Armadillo. [Sp. equiv. to armad (o) armed 9, L armatus; see ARM2, -ATE1) + illo < L -illus dim. suffix]

The MacGuffin Dictionary

CHAPTER 1

Prairie Lights

I am a detective, but not the private-eye type. My investigative skills allow me to peel back layer after layer of subjects' lives to reveal the truth about their essence. Then I write their biographies. To date, I've only written one biography, but it was successful beyond my wildest dreams.

Two years ago, my critically acclaimed biography of Freud shot to the top of the *New York Times'* bestseller list. Since that time, a debilitating case of writer's block has prevented me from writing a coherent paragraph. In the eyes of the public, I'm a success; in my own eyes, a loser.

Students flock to my university classes to learn at the feet of a celebrated English professor. Teaching awards decorate the walls of my office at home. But I conceal from others that my life is falling apart.

This evening, I'm trying to forget my writer's block, but more importantly, I'm eager to hear Prairie Lights' acclaimed speaker. I scanned the front row and felt relieved that the far-right chair was still vacant. I claimed it as quickly as possible, as I've tried to do at every public gathering since the first grade. When I sit in that specific chair, nobody can stare at the right side of my face. I suspect I'm neurotic—Freud would have known so.

While waiting for the program to begin, I reached into my coat pocket and removed a cream-colored invitation with embossed lettering. The floral design was indeed gold leaf. Holding the invitation as if it were a prized possession, I read it for the umpteenth time.

Theodore Neumann invites you to a reading
and signing of
*Like a Phoenix from Ashes:
A History of the Cinematic Mystery*
Prairie Lights Bookstore
7:00 p.m., February 14, 1980

Hand-written calligraphy at the bottom of the card personalized the invitation:

Dr. Seawright, please be my special guest at this event. I must talk to you after the program. Theodore Neumann

A round-cheeked, red-haired man adjusted the microphone. "Welcome to Prairie Lights. I'm Jim Harris, the owner of your favorite bookstore. On this freezing Valentine's Day in Iowa City, it's my pleasure to introduce Theodore Neumann, America's preeminent screenwriter. I guarantee he'll warm your film-loving hearts as he shares passages from his latest book and answers questions. Without fail, his movies—*Magic Death, Heart in the Shadows,* and *Hidden for All to See*—hold us spellbound. His revolutionary ideas about the cinema have inspired directors, writers, actors—and even critics." Jim gestured to the opposite end of my row, "Theodore Neumann, the floor is yours."

Applause swelled as a tall man stood. Smoky sunglasses obscured his eyes. The hair above his ears looked like wispy, white clouds. And while he sported a Santa Claus beard, he lacked the round belly. Impressive. *He must do his daily sit-ups.* Neumann flashed the smile of a kindhearted grandfather. "Thanks, Jim. Given your way with words, have you ever considered writing in Hollywood?" His teasing was gentle, not barbed. I relaxed for an evening of stimulating ideas. Secretly, I hoped he'd help me overcome my demoralizing failure to write.

Neumann beguiled us with anecdotes that captured the messiness of the creative process and the turmoil of transforming half-baked ideas into polished screenplays. After forty-five minutes, he grinned. "I recently celebrated my eightieth birthday. Life has blessed me with opportunities to entertain and mystify millions of people. Writing screenplays is my passion. I ask you to find and embrace your passion." He thanked us and gave a deep bow. We responded with a prolonged ovation.

"I'll take your questions," he said.

My hand shot up, and Neumann called on me; I stood and gave my name. "What do you do when you can't generate even one good idea for your next writing project?"

"Dr. Seawright, thanks for identifying yourself." Neumann addressed the audience. "Paul's groundbreaking biography of Freud is the most user-friendly scholarly work I've read in ages. I wish I had his writing talent. Thank you, Paul." He waited as the audience clapped. "When I'm stuck, I deliberately put myself in a new environment. Then I ask myself: what is so riveting here that I feel compelled to write about it? Stick around. We'll talk after the book signing. I have some other ideas to share with you."

After twenty minutes of fielding questions, he sat behind a table piled high with copies of his book. A woman poked a Polaroid camera in his direction. "May we have our photo taken together?" she asked.

Neumann shook his head. "As a working writer, I operate furtively. If I'm not recognized, I can move closer and listen in on people's conversations. I hope you'll understand."

The woman lowered her camera and smiled. "In that case, please sign my book, 'To Patty, who loves my films.'"

After the last signing, Neumann walked over and gripped my hand. "I'm glad you came." He looked around the room. "This place is too public. Let's head to the Hawkeye Bar and Grill and pick up a couple of their popular Reuben sandwiches. I'm staying at the Hotel Washington around the corner from there. We can talk in my room." I noticed his satisfied smile as we left

JOHN LITTRELL

Prairie Lights.

CHAPTER 2

Hotel Washington

Neumann paused outside the Hotel Washington's picture window. "Here's a trivia question for you. Which presidential candidate stopped here during his campaign in the fall of 1959?"

"It was either Richard Nixon or John F. Kennedy," I said. "My guess is Nixon."

"Nope, it was Kennedy."

Looking in at the lobby some twenty years later, I thought the hotel was as dead as Kennedy.

The gaunt, gray-faced night attendant standing behind the front desk reminded me of a ghoulish Charles Addams character. He bowed his head slightly. "Good evening, Mr. Neumann." When he turned his attention to me, I caught him staring at my face. I felt a familiar flash of irritation. His face reddened, and he quickly glanced at my stylish leather jacket. *Hey, jerk, you aren't fooling me.*

The elevator creaked upward to the eighth floor at half the speed we could've walked it. Wallpaper, once stylish in the fifties, hung on the walls leading to Neumann's room. The hallway's original spring green carpet was threadbare and patched. Upon entering Neumann's suite, I began choking on its musty air. Neumann pulled over two straight-backed chairs to a kitchenette table and motioned for me to sit down. He filled two glasses with tap water, and we unwrapped our sandwiches. *The man's rich. Surely, he can afford a beer to wash down the Reubens.*

Up close, deep crow's feet spread out beyond the frames of Neumann's sunglasses. "Paul, I'm pleased you accepted my invitation to talk."

"After seeing all your movies, I'm thrilled to meet you."

"And I'm delighted to meet the author of *Freud*. Your parents must be super proud of you."

Sharing much about myself has always left me feeling anxious, but maybe I could open a bit more with Neumann. "If my mom were alive, I'm sure she'd be. She died of cancer when I was in ninth grade."

"I'm so sorry to hear that. And your dad?"

"After my mom died, my dad drank really hard. He died during my senior year of high school. His doctor said his liver looked like a blistered igneous rock." I disliked the harshness I heard in my voice.

"You must have been devastated when both of your parents died within such a short time."

I hesitated. Talking about my family, like talking about myself, made me uncomfortable. "They weren't my birth parents, about whom I know nothing. Don't get me wrong, my adoptive mom and dad were kind people, but there was an unbridgeable emotional distance between us. Overt expressions of love were too much for them to share." I felt a knot tightening in my gut.

"Paul, even the death of adoptive parents can devastate a child."

"I was fortunate in one way. Shortly before my dad died, an anonymous relative established a trust fund for me. The person must have felt pity for me because I received enough that I've never had to worry about paying the bills. When I moved to Iowa City to begin my freshman year of college, I searched for a house to buy. When one I loved came on the market, I made an offer that included everything, even the furniture."

"You're so resilient. I'm glad you shared some of your personal life. But I'd also like to talk about *Freud*, your bestseller." While we ate, he quizzed me extensively about my book. While answering his questions, I fantasized that he'd ask me to help him write a screenplay from my bestseller.

Our sandwiches finished, Neumann wiped the Russian dressing from his beard and tossed the napkin into a wastebasket. "Let's move to more comfortable chairs."

After he settled into a scuffed leather, wingback chair, he reached down and lifted a green book bag onto his lap. With the skill of an entertainer, he loosened the drawstrings on top, brandished his outstretched hand in the air, plunged it into the bag, and pulled out a pack of Camels. He placed one in his mouth. Holding out the pack to me, he grunted, "Here."

"Thanks, but I don't smoke."

Like a quick-change artist, Neumann replaced his engaging warmth with a glacial expression that said only a fool would venture a smile. I kept a straight face. He slowly raised his eyebrows. "I'm not one for small talk. Tell me about the port-wine birthmark bathing the right side of your face."

The unexpected words stung like a hard slap. Most adults glance at my birthmark and then try, like the night attendant, to ignore the elephant in the room. I heard myself stammer a defensive, "Why?"

"Because I'm a writer. I look at your face, and I see a story. But don't worry, if I include it in my next screenplay, I'll shield myself by stating that this is a work of fiction and names have been —"

"I don't find that funny." Despite the coolness of the room, I felt my face burning.

"You weren't listening to me. I said, tell me about your birthmark."

"What's there to say? I was born with it, and it's still on my face. End of story."

"Stop being a dishonest coward. I called Dr. Adamani, who said, and I quote, 'Paul was the brightest doctoral student I ever worked with, and I've worked with some of the best.'" Neumann pointed a slender forefinger at me. "We both know *Freud* wasn't a fluke. So cut the screw-you-Neumann attitude and tell me what you think and feel—if that's not too complicated."

What an insufferable jerk! I bent toward him. "You want to know what I think and feel? I'll tell you! This birthmark embedded, not bathed as you put it, in half my face is a fucking nightmare. Sometimes I drown in self-pity. Other times, I feel like lashing out at people who aren't in the least sensitive."

"Got it. Do you have a girlfriend?"

"A girlfriend?" I laughed bitterly and pointed to the right side of my face. "With this? You must be blind!"

His face softened. "I appreciate your honesty. By the way, I've been awaiting your next book for quite a while. When's it coming out?"

I struggled to adjust to his sudden return to sociability. "Someday soon...I hope."

He snorted and gave me a look of disgust. "Your 'I hope' sounds like a pitiful yelp from a wounded animal. Learn this lesson in life and learn it well: hope isn't a plan; it's wishful thinking." He cocked his head and grinned. "So how far along are you on your second book?"

It took me several seconds to realize that he'd asked an easy question, but I found it embarrassing to answer. "I wrote *Freud* in record time. The IBM typewriter ball whirled crazily, and every day, I wrote a stack of pages. Now the ball glares at me like the unblinking eye of a hostile Cyclops. There's no doubt about it: I've mastered the art of writer's block."

Deep in his throat, Neumann made an unsympathetic chuckling sound. "Writer's block? As my late friend Fritz Perls, a gristly Gestalt therapist, was fond of saying, 'That's elephant shit!' What you're missing is what I talked about this evening—passion. I trust you were paying attention. When you find a spellbinding person to write about, you'll write enthusiastically and superbly."

When I'm uncomfortable, I retreat into humor. "Did I write last night or last week or the month before? No. I qualify for a black belt in procrastination." *Paul, that isn't funny, merely path-*

etic.

"Well, Paul, this is your lucky night. I'll tell you about a man who will revive your passion for writing. Ever read Max Eicher's *Maya Magic*?"

Trying to keep up with Neumann's changing topics and moods, I shook my head to clear it. "Who hasn't? It was required reading during my freshman year of college."

He reached into his book bag and produced a brittle newspaper clipping. "This is Max Eicher's 1950 obituary from the *New York Times*. I've carried this clipping about my friend for almost thirty years. Here, please read it."

> Maximilian "Max" Eicher (born January 1, 1900) archaeologist, died after a prolonged illness on November 1, in Casa Armadillo, the home he built on the outskirts of La Ruta, in Chiapas, Mexico. Eicher received his doctorate in archaeology from Yale in 1925. His cult-status book, *Maya Magic* (1933), was a pioneering study of ancient Maya rituals. Eicher was soon summoned to Hollywood as a consultant on movie scripts. He married actress Ruth Kelly in 1934. She survives him.

Neumann cocked his head. "The phrase 'prolonged illness' is the *Times'* subtle way of telling readers that a person died of alcoholism or cancer—regarding Max, it was the former." Neumann leaned in and lowered his voice. "Max's widow, Ruth, tells everyone that Max drank himself to death. Others spin a romanticized portrait of his life as a tragic quest for love that ended when he died of a broken heart. However, one person at Armadillo, Doña María, will imply that someone murdered Max."

"Murdered?"

"Interested in learning more about the man?"

"You've got my attention."

"Max Eicher and I were boyhood friends and roomed together

in Hollywood in the early thirties. We kept in touch until shortly before his death." Neumann looked toward a faded print on the far wall, but I doubted his eyes saw it. "Max was nothing if not a bundle of contradictions: simple in speech, yet a complex thinker; often forthright, but also secretive; and bound in marriage to Ruth by his devotion to Catholicism, while simultaneously starved for love."

Neumann lifted a stack of books and papers from the floor and sorted them into piles on a coffee table. "I brought a few visual aids to make my presentation memorable. The piles you see contain information about members of a newly formed board of directors at Casa Armadillo: Ruth Eicher, David Budman, Dr. Harriet Galveston, and Dr. Gerald Strupp. Two board members not represented in piles are William Farrell and Roland Westby.

From the first pile, he picked up a copy of *Life* magazine. "Ruth Eicher, Max's wife, was featured in this 1946 issue. She's still quite the woman. I suspect you've seen photos of her in Maya-style poses."

In my mind's eye, I pictured one iconic photo. "You're right. She was unquestionably photogenic." I described the photo to Neumann in minute detail.

"What a detailed image you've just sketched!"

"I have a photographic memory."

"In that case, memorize this!" He handed me the magazine. "You just described one of David Budman's most famous photos of Ruth Eicher. It was quite daring for its time. The article starts on page forty-eight."

I flipped to the page, and there was the photo. "It's a fantastic photo."

"Even more photos line the corridors at Casa Armadillo. Visitors report the photos are, in the words of your generation, mind-blowing."

Neumann pointed to a book in another pile, *Maya Magic: The Key to Contacting Extraterrestrial Beings*. "The author Dr. Harriet Galveston, a UMass professor of archaeology." Neumann caught me giving the book a disapproving look. "Not exactly your cup of tea?"

"Too pseudoscientific for my tastes."

"In Dr. Galveston's defense, her book is a huge departure from her usual highly regarded scholarship on the Maya. But let's move on to Dr. Gerald Strupp, the author of the books in this next pile. He's vying to be Max's official biographer. Have you read any of Gerald's biographies of famous archaeologists?"

I pounced on the question because it didn't make me squirm. "I've read his *Hiram Bingham: Machu Picchu Explorer,* but only three chapters of his latest, *Howard Carter: Discovering Tutankhamun's Tomb.* Gerald shredded those guy's reputations."

Neumann contorted his face, and his puckered lips seemed poised to spit on the two books. "The blurbs on his books leave no doubt about his intent. One reviewer declared, 'Strupp bares the truth in his exposé of Hiram Bingham,' and this one proclaimed, 'Strupp unearths the real Howard Carter who lay buried beneath his lies and misrepresentations.'"

Finally, Neumann and I were on the same page. I began to relax.

Neumann slapped the table, and I jumped. "If Ruth chooses Gerald to write Max's biography, he'll suffer the same character assassination as Bingham and Carter." Neumann rapidly drew a finger across his own throat.

"You could say that Max's ass would be grass, and Gerald a lawnmower." *Damn, the words were out of my mouth, and I'd said them.*

Neumann groaned. "Thank goodness you didn't write metaphors like that in *Freud."*

"My editor insisted I take them out."

"I sing praises to your editor; by all means, keep the same one. But that aside, I've studied your book. It's awe-inspiring. After thinking it over, I've concluded that you're the best person to undertake Max's biography."

I felt my face turn red and looked down. "I'm stunned by your confidence in me. But since you were good friends for all those years, why don't you write it?"

"Because I'd have to travel to Casa Armadillo in a remote part of Mexico." He thumped his chest. "My doctor forbids me to fly. I took a bus from Hollywood to get here. While your writing muse is working against you, my body is working against me." He ruefully shook his head.

I sat back in my chair. "It's a tempting offer, but it's the middle of the semester, and the University of Iowa expects me to teach my writing and literature classes. Besides, I need to spend every minute writing my next book if I'm ever going to get tenure and advance in my profession." I didn't mention that last week, my department chair threatened me: either publish or perish. I smiled at Neumann and said, "However, I'll give your offer serious thought."

"Not good enough. You're my first and only choice. I guarantee that Max's biography will be the most important book you'll ever write. Given your success with *Freud*, I'm sure that if your parents had lived, they'd have been very proud of you."

Neumann drove a hard bargain. I love academia, but at the same time, I knew my life needed a jumpstart. Signing on to write Max's biography offered an enormous opportunity, but one with an uncertain future. But as I soon found out, Neumann wasn't finished.

"In this last pile, we have some undeniable treasures. Peek at this first edition of Max's *Maya Magic*. Note the inscription on the first page."

I read aloud, "To Theo from your life-long friend, Max." I looked up at Neumann. "I bet this is worth a small fortune."

"Around four-hundred dollars."

Finally, we were discussing academic topics, and I felt more comfortable. "*Maya Magic* generated heated discussions in an undergraduate anthropology course I took in the sixties. I loved the book, as did other students. But our professor ripped it to shreds. She said, 'Some scholars even believe Max was on drugs, and his purported findings were visual hallucinations. The book is riveting fiction, but fraudulent science.'"

Neumann cocked his head. "Was she right?"

"We'll never know."

"Wrong, you'll know after you complete Max's biography." He gave me a thick manuscript of yellowed paper. "In contrast to the autographed copy of *Maya Magic*, the worth of these pages is incalculable." The top page read, *Max Eicher's Memoirs*; the date was September 27, 1950. "He must have suspected he was dying because he sent this to me just before his death. It isn't the full story of his life. More like detailed recollections of his interactions with four women. As soon as you decide to write his biography, it's yours."

Neumann waited as I skimmed the unbound pages and read some passages at random. "This is priceless. Who knows about it?"

"You and I."

"Any biographer of Max Eicher's life would kill to possess this."

"A definite possibility, especially if the biographer is Dr. Gerald Strupp."

I thumbed through the pages. "I'd love to read this. Do you have a photocopy I could borrow?"

"Take both the book and the manuscript. I trust that you won't lose anything this valuable."

Don't be so sure. I've squandered two years of my life while sitting at a typewriter and staring at blank pages. "You have more faith in me than I have."

"I'm sure I do." He placed a business envelope in my hands. "Go ahead and open it."

I lifted the flap and drew out a brown strap of crisp fifty-dollar bills. "What's this about?"

"Five-thousand dollars to cover your expenses and then some." He took back the money and placed it in the envelope. "All yours when you decide to go to Armadillo, but not before. I'll call you early tomorrow morning for your answer."

Part of me felt guarded like a politician accepting a bribe. Another part felt elated like a lottery winner. "I appreciate your offer, and I'll certainly think about it. I'm lucky to have met you."

"Luck and hope are the same. Don't count on either one."

Walking home against the biting wind, I tried to make sense of the evening. I was ecstatic that Neumann had selected me to write Max's biography. Nevertheless, his mercurial behavior was deeply unsettling. Half the time, I felt close to him; the other half, the object of his scorn. I was sure of only one thing. I couldn't wait to read Neumann's copy of Max's *Memoirs.*

CHAPTER 3

"Yes Or No?"

I finished reading Max Eicher's Memoirs at three in the morning. I conceded that Neumann was right; the manuscript fueled my imagination. Wide awake, my mind raced from idea to idea. After an hour of chasing ideas, I fell asleep.

The phone's relentless ringing roused me from a deep sleep. I blinked, rubbed my eyes, and looked at the clock—six o'clock in the morning. I propped myself up on a pillow, pulled the covers around me to stay warm, and picked up the receiver.

"Are you going to Armadillo? Yes or no?"

Why was Neumann calling at this hour? I struggled to be civil. "Mr. Neumann, I have my career to consider. Besides, my department chair would never approve a week's leave of absence in the middle of a semester."

"I'm telling you again—cut the elephant shit! Three weeks from now, your midterm break begins, and you're free to go." *Impressive! Neumann gets an A+ for doing his homework.*

Speaking slowly and enunciating each word like a hypnotist putting a subject into a deep trance, Neumann asked, "Are you going to spend the rest of your life ignorant of who you are and who you can be?"

I bolted upright. Last night in his hotel room, Neumann offered me the chance to author Max's biography, which made for a high opening ante. Now, Neumann had substantially upped the ante by encouraging me to say yes to the opportunity to test myself in unexplored territory and to stretch my understanding of myself. More than that, he was bestowing on me an incredible honor: Theodore Neumann, one of the greatest screenwriters of all time, was championing my journey.

"I'm going!" The suddenness of my decision jolted me. For far too long, I'd put my life on hold. I needed to face, embrace, and live life. I dropped the receiver onto the down comforter and slapped the sides of my face, instantly realizing how much I avoided touching my birthmark.

A loud but muffled voice came from the comforter, "Are you still there?"

I snatched up the receiver. My decision was the right one. A renewed sense of purpose surged through me. "Yes, and I'm going to Armadillo."

"Excellent decision. I'm at the bus station and, in a few minutes, I'm returning to Hollywood. Sooner than later, stop at the front desk of the Hotel Washington and pick up your envelope. Have a life-changing trip."

Neumann at the bus station? Five-thousand dollars in crisp bills at the hotel desk? But how did he know I was going to say yes when even I didn't know what I'd answer? I felt jerked around like a marionette, while Neumann adroitly pulled my strings.

Eager to learn more about Max Eicher's life, I arrived at the university library as it opened at eight on Friday. Three hours later, I mumbled a few obscenities. A female student sitting in a nearby carrel eyed me warily, gathered her books, and left hurriedly. Despite my well-honed research skills, I found reviews of Neumann's screenplays and opinions about Max Eicher, but few facts.

Before turning off the lights that evening, I wrote my to-do list, which even I thought was highly ambitious.

1. Look everywhere for information about Max Eicher

2. Study Maya history and hieroglyphic writing system
3. Learn and practice some basic Spanish
4. Remember to eat, exercise, and sleep
5. Pack for staying in a jungle setting

The next three weeks flew by. I worked on my to-do list, taught my classes, avoided my typewriter, and worried if I could meet Neumann's high expectations. At one point, I reflected on my good fortune. Neumann had entered my life precisely when I desperately needed encouragement. He was well informed about my biography of Freud, arrived for his book presentation in Iowa City when I needed a kick in the butt, and presented me the opportunity to write a scholarly biography. And, Neuman gave me the money to go to Armadillo. The thought entered my mind that perhaps all my good fortune wasn't a coincidence. *Right, like Neumann planned all this so he could throw away five-thousand dollars on a writer who hasn't written in two years.*

After completing the last item on my to-do list, I evaluated my progress. No question that I reasonably achieved numbers 1, 2, and 3. *Bueno, señor Paulo.* Number 4 was only a success if I ignored gaining four pounds, exercising only twice, and sleeping but five hours a night. The last item on my list, packing, was done—unfortunately, it was now two in the morning, and three hours from now, I'd head to the airport utterly exhausted.

CHAPTER 4

The Long And Winding Road

J orge, my taxi driver, and I departed picturesque San Cristóbal de las Casas in Chiapas, before dusk, and continued to
the northeast to reach the small village of La Ruta. But given
the hairpin-curves on the wet, gravel road, why in the hell was
Jorge racing like an Indianapolis 500 driver? Sweat drenched the
palms of my hands. Luckily, impenetrable jungle and a starless
night blocked my view of precipitous drops—most of the time.
Then the taxi's headlights would illuminate an abyss with no
guardrail to prevent a yawning Jorge from launching us into the
wild black yonder. Yelling *no tan rápido* (not so fast) produced
no slowing down. I reluctantly concluded that accepting my
fate was the best I could do. Nevertheless, I braced myself to
minimize the ceaseless body-racking jolts inflicted by potholes
the size of melons from Muscatine, Iowa.

After an eternity, which registered less than three hours on
my watch, we entered rain-soaked La Ruta. A smattering of
streetlamps illuminated many abandoned homes that told the
story of how San Cristóbal and Mexico City had lured away local
inhabitants with offers of pesos and jobs. We quickly passed
through the town, and thirty seconds later, we reached Casa Armadillo. Back in Iowa City, I'd envisioned Max's home as Xan-
adu, a fictional estate complete with Gothic spires, as shown in
the opening scenes of *Citizen Kane*. But now, I blinked several
times in disbelief. Illuminated by two spotlights, Armadillo

was a squatty, stone fortress in the heart of a steamy jungle.

A foundation of hewn, lichen-covered stones rose three feet from the reddish soil. Above the stones loomed a twenty-foot wall, its rust-colored stucco still somewhat visible beneath the tropical mold. The balustrade on the top of the wall looked like a rickety silhouette. Six steps, located dead center on the front wall, ascended to an ornate wooden door crowned with a fan-shaped halo of cream-colored brick.

Two questions troubled me. Was I a fool to trust Max's *Maya Magic* and *Memoirs*? And what possessed me to tell Neumann that I'd write Max's biography?

I paid Jorge and climbed out of the taxi. Trying to open my umbrella and juggle my suitcase, I braved the drenching rain. At the top of the lichen-slick stairs, I put down my bag. Numerous times I lifted and dropped the tail of the brass armadillo door knocker, all the while hoping someone would come soon.

The door creaked open to reveal a short Maya woman. She squinted at me. "Quick, come in. Are you Dr. Paul?" I nodded, yes. "In my heart, I thank you for finally coming to Armadillo." I looked at her in astonishment. She turned and bustled down the hall, calling back, "I'll tell David you're here."

Presently, a tall, dapper man appeared and grabbed my suitcase. "Oh my, Dr. Seawright! You're sopping wet." But he wasn't quick enough to suppress a look I knew from countless encounters with strangers. I reciprocated by giving back a look, but this time, mine wasn't one of anger, but amusement. I fought the urge to laugh at the anachronistically dressed man who wore an elegant navy-blue suit with wide lapels and a blue-and-white checked shirt. A hand-tied silk bow tie perched at his collar. Red polka dots danced on the cobalt fabric. *Oh, my gosh. The White Rabbit from* Alice's Adventures in Wonderland *is here to receive me.*

He hurried ahead of me through the vestibule before wheeling around. "You must think I have no manners. Welcome to Casa Armadillo. You just met Doña María, the best cook in Mexico. I'm David Budman, resident photographer, general manager, and tour leader—sometimes referred to, affectionately or disdainfully, as The Gofer." He ran his fingers through his graying hair as if scurrying to the door had mussed it.

"Pleased to meet you, David."

"We're delighted you're here. Ruth Eicher has been eagerly expecting you."

At the reception desk, David took my passport and recorded pertinent information in the guest registry. "My goodness, you're only twenty-nine." He adjusted his bow tie. "I'm sorry for the surprised look I gave you at the door. I was expecting a considerably older man." I gave him credit for quick thinking to cover his uneasiness with my face.

David continued his spiel. "I see you've paid in advance for your room and board. Guests pay for their alcoholic beverages. We serve lunch promptly at one with dinner at seven—Max and Ruth never adjusted to the later mealtimes in Mexico. Be ready for my tour of Armadillo at nine tomorrow morning. I'll stop by to get you and the others." He looked into the courtyard. "As you see, at this hour of the night, Armadillo is quite dead." He was right; the place was as quiet as a morgue at midnight.

David handed me a key. "Each room and its key have three identifiers. In the case of your room: a celebrity's name, Cole Porter; an Arabic numeral, four; and a Maya numeral, four dots in a row. Most guests prefer to use celebrities' names."

We walked through a corridor protected by covered walkways. I could barely make out the wet Cyprus branches standing like tall sentries outside Armadillo's thick walls. Magenta bougainvillea cascaded from terra cotta pots atop the balustrade, softening the stark, cobblestoned atrium.

David pointed toward an interior wall. "Over there is one of my photographs of Ruth."

Before traveling to Mexico, I studied the reproductions of Ruth's photos in *Life* magazine. One photo showed a frontal portrait of a Maya woman. I recognized it as an image borrowed from a rare, ancient Maya codex, a book written in hieroglyphic script on bark paper. Superimposed on the image of the woman's head, David had placed Ruth's profile. The result was a Picasso-like cubist shot of a head seen simultaneously from the front and side.

"I've been amazed," David said, "that my photos speak to so many people, even the critics." In my mind's eye, I could see the information written on a page in *Max Eicher's Memoirs*:

> Ruth encouraged David Budman to photograph her. Thanks to his photos, she achieved the fame that had eluded her as a movie actress. And thanks to the power of the mass media, millions of people worldwide are mesmerized as I once was. Poor souls.

David ushered me into my room. "You must be exhausted." He waved his arm with a flourish as though he was an attractive, young assistant on a quiz show. "Hope this is to your liking." *What's not to like?* The pomegranate-orange walls radiated warmth. The woven rugs, showing the wear of many years, provided a comfortable, lived-in feeling. One discordant element was a faint whiff of mildew, although mild compared to Neumann's hotel room back in Iowa City.

"David, did Cole Porter stay in this particular room?"

"He certainly did. We have the register that shows he stayed here a week in early 1937. In a marketing ploy worthy of Madison Avenue, Ruth began naming rooms after the celebrities who stayed in them. Close to the time that Porter visited, Ernest Hemingway and F. Scott Fitzgerald vied for room naming honors."

"Quite a star-studded guest list," I said.

David struck a pose, leaning against the doorframe. "Many other celebrities visited—Greta Garbo and Clark Gable. The anthropologists Margaret Mead and Gregory Bateson shared a suite. And I'd be remiss if I failed to mention Diego Rivera and Joan Miró, who contributed an original drawing in their respective rooms. Look around and see if you can spot Cole Porter's playful addition."

I need some sleep, not a game of hide-and-seek. I glanced around the room and shrugged.

David pointed. "Take a close look at the wall above the bed's headboard. That's where Porter wrote the title of his song 'Let's Misbehave' and placed his signature below. It's faintly written in pencil."

I examined the half-printed, half-cursive signature. "It appears authentic."

"Be assured it is," David said. "Last year, the renowned art dealer William Farrell, who Ruth recently named a board member at Casa Armadillo, authenticated it. He assured us that it's worth quite a bit." David gave a boyish smile and added, "By the way, guests aren't allowed to bring erasers into this room."

My ears had pricked up when he mentioned William Farrell. I remembered the section in *Memoirs,* where Max characterized Farrell, a visitor to Armadillo, as the embodiment of a sleazy businessman. I took a chance and said, "I'm surprised Ruth allows Farrell to enter Armadillo."

David wrinkled his brow. "What do you mean?"

I was sure he understood me. I pressed on. "Someone once speculated that Farrell would remove Porter's contribution from the wall with a hammer and chisel and later sell it back to Ruth for a minimum of four figures."

David alternated between a smile—at my caustic depiction of Farrell—and a grimace—for my even suggesting that someone might steal such a priceless object. Then he reverted to his thoughtful self. *Did I just see David momentarily betray his personal feelings?* "Any questions?"

I looked around the room. "I'm curious. Why was I given a room with two single beds?"

"All the rooms at Armadillo have two beds," David said, his eyes twinkling. "I hope it's not an inconvenience." He gave a sheepish smile. Considering Max's reference in *Memoirs* to the popularity of trysts at Armadillo, the thought of clandestine lovers reduced to rendezvousing in single beds amused me. But not for long. David left, and I immediately fell asleep.

CHAPTER 5

Armadillo 1930

I slept hard, and it was eight-thirty before I awoke. After showering and shaving, I opened my door and saw three men in the courtyard. Oh, no! I forgot about David's tour. So long, breakfast.

"Good morning, Paul," David said in a voice way too chipper at this early hour. "Glad you can join us for a tour of Casa Armadillo. Gentlemen, this is Paul Seawright, the best-selling author of *Freud*. Paul, these two gentlemen are newly appointed board members. Roland Westby is a noted architectural preservationist."

Roland raised his glance no higher than my shirt's top button and, exhibiting the warmth and charm of a warthog, said, "Pleased to meet you." His handshake was lifeless. His only sign of being human was the sweat on his brow, most likely caused by his wool Brooks Brothers' suit. *Thank goodness, I packed sensibly for Armadillo.*

"This other gentleman is Father Lester Sheehan, a professor at Notre Dame. His specialty is Catholic Church art in Mexico." Sheehan wore a black cassock shirt with a white collar. He towered over us. I imagined him as the most massive lineman on his high school and college football teams. As he reached out to shake my hand, I winced, sure he'd mangle it. He saw the look on my face. "Don't worry. I only crush players on opposing teams. I assume we're on the same side. By the way, everyone calls me Father Lester."

I looked up at his rounded face sporting a trimmed beard. "Do you ever go by Les?"

He smiled warmly. "I never use that nickname. No sense in telling people I'm Father Les."

An awkward smile took possession of my face. "Wise decision."

Failing to appreciate—or understand—the joke, Roland looked ahead blankly.

We strolled through the first courtyard. In the morning light, I noticed the contrast between Max's descriptions of Armadillo's prime and present condition. In his account, Armadillo bustled with celebrities and overflowed with energy. Now, it resembled a wasteland of crumbling adobe frequented by few visitors. I felt an aching melancholy as I surveyed what remained of Max's world.

David pointed toward one corner of the courtyard. "This way to the chapel."

Father Lester clapped. "Now, you're talking."

David flipped on the light switch near the door. As though on cue, Father Lester waxed enthusiastic about the chapel's architecture. "This place desperately needs to be restored, but it's an absolute gem! The white paint gives the interior an airy feel. These slender, ornate Corinthian columns remain some of the finest in all Mexico. Just look at their gold leaf details!" Father Lester couldn't stop. He praised the eighteenth-century paintings that adorned the walls. "For all my academic life, I've studied Mexico's religious art. Several of these paintings are among the most magnificent ones I've ever seen. Look, the faces of the cherubs are of Maya children." He was nearly in tears.

"We believe that Max acquired most of these paintings in the late twenties. During the same period, he collected the wrought iron crosses now hanging in the corridors. He picked up religious art for a song during Mexico's anti-clerical era."

Father Lester placed his hands over his heart and gazed

around the chapel. "David, I promise I won't move my bed into the chapel, but if you want to find me, I'll be here."

As we walked past the pews to the back of the chapel, Father Lester cried out, "Look at the Madonna and Child painted on the door of the confession box! That's the finest work of art in the chapel." The painting's background depicted a Chiapas landscape from a much earlier time. In the foreground, the Madonna sported a Frida Kahlo-like unibrow and held a chubby child with a face that resembled Diego Rivera's. "Who was the artist?"

David beamed as though the chapel belonged to him. "We haven't yet identified the artist. We know the confession box was painted during Armadillo's construction, sometime between 1928 and 1931."

Father Lester swept his arm in a half-circle. "A critic of Johann Wolfgang von Goethe's house in Frankfurt once said that craftsmen restored the building with loving care and damn-the-expense craftsmanship. We'll need to do the same with this chapel —assuming we can raise the money."

Speaking to no one in particular, Roland pointed up. "The ceiling shows signs of severe water damage."

We left the chapel and walked along a short corridor to the second courtyard where David pointed out a three-foot-high pedestal. On it rested a crudely fashioned armadillo with layers of slapped-on plaster. "That's Max's only sculpture." A metal plate on the pedestal read:

Armadillo 1930
Max Eicher

I winced. "I'm sorry to say, but this reminds me of the worst of the WPA projects. It's a hideous hybrid of Art Deco and Soviet realism. I can understand why Max quit after one try as a sculptor."

David grimaced and said, "We keep it for its historical value."

Roland glared at the two of us. "It's imperative that you not discarded it! It may not be to your tastes, but it's an essential feature of Casa Armadillo."

"Still, Roland, you have to admit," I said, "if Max Eicher hadn't achieved some degree of fame as an archaeologist, history's dustbin would have claimed his sculpture." Roland turned abruptly and walked away.

As Father Lester passed by the armadillo, he patted its shell and said, "Down, boy, down." I bit my lip to keep from laughing. Father Lester was a scholar with a sense of humor. I liked him already.

We passed through a corridor and entered a second courtyard. David continued his patter. "Max and Ruth married in Hollywood and came here in 1934. And while the infamous parties in *The Great Gatsby* are fictitious, Armadillo's parties were real. The A-list celebrities agreed that Ruth was 'the hostess with the mostess.' Together, she and Doña María collaborated to offer delicious meals and serve the most fashionable drinks. If you look around now, the charm of Armadillo's rooms has faded, but when Ruth decorated them in the thirties, they represented the height of chic. From the mid-thirties until Pearl Harbor ended it all, Armadillo was *the* place where celebrities gathered. Ruth even hosted exotic costume parties where guests wore native costumes from the surrounding Maya villages. But back then, getting here wasn't easy—"

"It's not easy even now," Roland said. "Luckily, we arrived just in time. The forecast predicts several days of heavy rain. I worry that we won't be able to leave because of washed-out bridges and impassable, muddy roads."

David smiled. "Casa Armadillo isn't the Hotel California. You can check out any time you want, and you can always leave— provided the roads are dry. But as I was saying, back then, getting here wasn't easy. To accommodate the influx of guests, Max hired men from La Ruta to clear the dense jungle so that small airplanes could land. After his death, as nature is wont to do, the jungle reasserted itself."

Based on my readings of Max Eicher's *Memoirs,* I seized the opportunity to ask about one of Max's loves. "Didn't the heiress

Maurine Madanes' plane land here shortly before Max's death?"

David pondered my statement before speaking. "Ah, yes. Visitor's questions always get around to the topic of Maurine. She stayed for the last two weeks of August 1950. While she was visiting, Max began drinking a lot. After she left, he hit the bottle even harder. I was shocked by his drinking because I'd never seen him drink a drop. During that period, I once overheard him screaming at Ruth, but luckily for her, he didn't carry on for long. On November 2, 1950, she found his body in the library, an empty mezcal bottle nearby.

"Alas, alcoholism claimed another brilliant mind. We tend to think of alcoholism as a slow, progressive disease, but Max died in record time. As you can see, I'm not one to avoid unpleasant facts that might contradict romanticized tales about Armadillo."

As I thought about the drinking that took my dad's life, I fought the urge to get lost in that story rather than David's. But to write Max's biography, I made a mental note to ask others about Max's drinking. *Now pay attention to David's story.*

Another corridor took us to the third courtyard, filled with bedsheets and clothes drying in the sun. After David lifted a thick wooden bar, we exited through Armadillo's thick, mahogany back door and walked along a path through lush vegetable and flower gardens. In my best interviewing voice, I asked David, "I'm curious. How did you happen to come to Armadillo?"

Roland rolled his eyes and said sharply, "I'm not sure your question is relevant to Armadillo's history."

David disregarded Roland's rudeness. "I grew up in New York. My father knew Alfred Stieglitz and showed him some of my early work. Stieglitz took me on—privately, he called me his protégé—and exhibited seven of my photos in his gallery, An American Place."

"What an honor!" Father Lester said.

David smiled. "My parents knew prominent people who allowed me to photograph them. I've never been very comfortable socially, but I'm in my element when I'm behind a camera. I followed Stieglitz's advice when he told me to go to Casa Armadillo, where the movers and shakers gathered. I was twenty-two when I arrived here in 1936, and this became my permanent home. Max was most gracious in sharing his photography studio with me."

Here was my chance to learn more about Max. "You knew Max for many years. What was he like?"

Roland sped up and took the lead, while Father Lester and I slowed to match David's pace. "Max was a detached observer. He always seemed to be someplace else. I'm sure his marriage depressed him. Nevertheless, he mixed with the guests and knew how to entertain them with card tricks and great stories. Physically, he was in this world, but he seemed to live in another place."

"I'm still trying to find old photos of him," I said. "Any filed away?"

"It's true that I've taken photos of a who's who of the luminaries who came here. Yet on my first day at Armadillo, Max saw me carrying my camera. I vividly recall his first words to me, 'Never take a photo of me without my permission. Observe this one request, and we'll stay friends.'"

"Any photos of him in the background?"

David shook his head from side to side.

For all his show of aloofness, Roland had been listening. "David, I need access to your historical photographs of Casa Armadillo. They're invaluable in my assessment of the structure of the building."

Ignoring his interruption, I kept my eyes on David. "I can understand how Armadillo drew you here, but what's kept you here all these years?"

David looked shaken and sank onto a bench nearby. Father Lester and I sat on either side of him; Roland stood fidgeting a short distance away.

"You want to know what has kept me here all these years?" David asked aloud as if grounding himself. "You're the first person to ask me that." His eyes glistened with tears. "When I arrived, I fell in love with Ruth, a charismatic and astonishingly beautiful woman. It took me years to realize I wasn't in love with Ruth, the person. I'd fallen in love with her image. And that's what I've given the world in my photographs. Just like Max's *Maya Magic* and Ruth's Hollywood contacts brought stars to Armadillo before World War II, Ruth's images brought tourists after it was over. They clamored to see her in person. But by the sixties, potential visitors discovered exciting new beauties and places. Ruth and Armadillo became old news. I could see how the changing times broke Ruth's heart."

"Thank you, David. I know our time's short right now, but we can talk more about this later." He nodded his agreement.

In a harsh voice, Roland said, "I'm heading back. Thanks for the tour...." His pause indicated he'd already forgotten David's name. The three of us watched as Roland scurried away.

Leaving the gardens behind, we walked down a narrow path hacked out of the jungle. At a fork, David led us to the right. Several minutes later, we entered a small clearing containing a bench and a simple headstone. "Oh, look," Father Lester said, "they carved the words using Spacerite Modified Roman font."

He saw my confused look and added, "I once studied the history of monument typography. It comes in handy when I'm conducting graveside services. I can look at tear-stained faces for only so long. Focusing on the typeface got me through a lot."

He and I knelt and struggled to read the lichen-covered inscription.

Maximilian "Max" Eicher

January 1, 1900 ~ November 2, 1950

Archaeologist and Author of *Maya Magic*

Devoted and Loving Husband of Ruth Kelly Eicher

The first three lines spoke the truth. But honesty about the dead is at the mercy of the living. Ruth showed none when she authorized the fourth line's blatant lie.

I stood and surveyed the setting. Max's body lay at rest in an area that I christened "The Garden of Earthly Neglect." Max's close friend, Theodore Neumann, would have been furious that Max's final resting place was tended so shabbily.

Father Lester read my thoughts. "David, it's a shame someone doesn't take better care of this clearing." We all nodded.

Changing the subject, Father Lester asked, "Why is Armadillo located here? It's many miles from the nearest Maya ruins. It doesn't make sense for an archaeologist to build his home so far away from a worksite."

David's face brightened. "Max told me that he hated fraternizing with other archaeologists because they never looked up to see the big picture. To that extent, I believe Armadillo suited him well."

"I've been thinking," I said, "about your photos and what you said about the favor visitors who stayed here. You've photographed so many of them."

"I've got file cabinets full of prints and negatives."

"Have you thought about publishing a photo book featuring them?"

An impish smile crept across his face. "I've dreamed of a book like that, but I don't think people would find it very noteworthy."

"David, a book like that would be a treasure," I said. "I'd buy a copy."

"And so would I," Father Lester added. "A lot of people would."

David smiled. "I'll think about it."

I was satisfied that both Father Lester and I'd successfully planted a seed.

On our return to Armadillo, we reached the fork in the paths. "When we walked to Max's grave, we turned right. Where does this other path lead?"

"To another clearing. We can visit there later."

"Let's go while we're here." I started down the path.

Father Lester and David struck up a conversation, following

me at a sluggish pace.

CHAPTER 6

A Stone Altar

A three-foot-high, six-foot-long stone altar with a gently sloping convex top dominated the weed-covered clearing. A body lay on it, wearing nothing but a layer of dazzling blue pigment. Immobilized, I stared at it.

I yelled to my companions, "Don't come any closer!"

They stopped some distance away. Father Lester held David, whose face was drained of color, from collapsing. Neither uttered a word.

"Who is it?" I called back.

David swallowed hard and answered in a voice tormented with anguish, "William Farrell, the art dealer."

I hardened my resolve and stepped forward. Behind me, I heard Father Lester offer comforting words as David threw up. I felt the same urge but kept moving. William's ankles and wrists were bound with rough hemp ropes. A heart, the size of a large fist, lay in a stone ceremonial bowl at the foot of the altar. Flies crawled all over the heart; maggots weren't yet visible. I saw a gaping hole in William's lower chest. My whole body jerked. The blood surrounding the wound appeared reddish-black on the blue paint—more flies clustered on the opened flesh.

I felt faint. I filled my lungs with air and slowly exhaled. What was my next step? I needed to move William's body to a secure place where insects and animals wouldn't scavenge it.

I looked behind me and saw David on all fours. From where I

stood, I couldn't hear Father Lester's specific words, but his tone sounded soothing. By default, I was in charge. In his *Memoirs,* I remembered that Max had described Doña María, his cook and housekeeper, as a pillar of strength. "Father Lester, I'll guard the body. I need you to do four things. First, call the police."

"La Ruta doesn't have any police to call," said David, his voice weak.

I began again. "In that case, Father Lester, take David back to Armadillo. Next, tell Doña María we found a body and ask her to come with a stretcher. Finally, hire two strong men in La Ruta to move this body. Tell them we'll pay well."

"I know the men in La Ruta," David said. "I'll deal with them." With Father Lester holding onto David's arm, the two left the clearing.

The flies' incessant buzzing pierced the silence. I cursed them but knew it was my way of denying the agony I felt. I forced myself to look at William's face. His eyes stared accusingly. *Don't look at me like that. This is your doing—not mine.* When I looked closely at the bright blue paint, I noticed it ended precisely at the contours of the lips. Similarly, the color came within a quarter of an inch from where each eye socket began. The killer was an artist whose painting on William's body was a grotesque work of art.

A shiny object drew my eyes. Several links of a gold chain dangled from William's mouth. I half-closed my eyes, pried open the stiff jaw, and pulled. Additional chain links emerged from his mouth before an oval-shaped gold pendant appeared. I wiped it on the grass. It was a delicately sculptured armadillo, an inch long. I rubbed the pendant between my thumb and forefinger. The armadillo's raised bands textured the top. On the flat backside, I felt three raised dots. The dots were puzzling. Without thinking, I pocketed the pendant and chain. Only later did I berate myself for tampering with the evidence and obliterating possible fingerprints.

I knelt, slowly inhaled, and examined the ropes binding William's ankles and his wrists. No complicated sailor knots here, just a half hitch. Two additional ropes, each six feet long, were attached to the binding ropes, respectively. I speculated that there were two accomplices: one stood near William's head, and the other near his feet. Both held their ropes taunt to prevent William from protecting himself by swinging his arms and legs in an arc toward his chest. But, since there were no signs of a struggle, he must have cooperated as someone painted his naked skin. Was this the victim's sick idea of a turn-on?

When I inspected his lower chest, my stomach reacted with a painful spasm. It appeared that a sharp instrument had cracked open the sternum, after which the killer had somehow separated the ribs. I couldn't tell if they were arteries or veins, but the cavity contained what looked like snipped pieces of thin black spaghetti. Feeling faint, I knew I should breathe more deeply, but when I did, the vile stench increased my gagging.

Finally, I spotted the strangest aspect of the corpse. William's penis wasn't painted blue. Was he sexually aroused when his killer plunged a knife into his heart? That might account for no struggle. Even from the little I knew about the man, I suspected he'd have relished an evening of debauchery. But becoming a human sacrifice during the ritual wouldn't be the climax he anticipated.

I heard Father Lester's voice behind me. I turned and saw Father Lester and Doña María. She was looking at William and slowly shaking her head back and forth. On her back, she carried two, eight-foot poles, a large canvas awning, and a small bag. She moved to the altar and placed her load on the ground. She rolled the canvas around one pole several times and nailed it in place, then repeated it with the other pole, forming a three-foot-wide stretcher.

As she worked, Father Lester inspected William's body. "Dear God, someone hated this guy. I haven't seen a wound this bad since 1969." When he spotted the puzzled look on my face, he added, "I served as a chaplain in Vietnam."

I struggled to find the right words and said, "It's the worst I've seen." The truth was I'd never seen anything even remotely so vile and repulsive.

When Doña María finished, she studied the body. If she reacted emotionally, I didn't catch it. She looked up at me and said in a voice I strained to hear, "The men from La Ruta will come soon."

"Where should we put his body?" Father Lester asked her.

"In a storeroom at the back of Armadillo," she said. "The temperature is cool, and it's far from where people stay."

"Doña María, while we wait, may I ask you some questions?" She consented but seemed impatient. "Do you know where William was last night?"

She told me that at ten o'clock every night, she locked Armadillo's two outside doors. The night bell for the front door rang in both the entrance office and her room. "Last night the bell in my room rang very late. William was back from La Ruta. He wore a smile and showed all his teeth. I stayed my distance from him because I saw he drank too much. He went to his room."

"What time did you let him in?"

"I know it was very dark. People were sleeping."

"As a person, what was he like?"

Doña María paused before responding. "William was an evil man. Women were never safe when he visited Armadillo."

"What did Max think of him?"

"Max tried to keep women safe, but Max couldn't be everywhere."

"And what was Ruth's opinion of William?"

"Ruth is strong, so he doesn't bother her. He comes to Armadillo almost every year to cheat our visitors. I kept my daughters far away from him."

"Your daughters?"

"Itzel and Sacniete. No mother wants to see her children hurt." We heard footsteps. "Look, David is coming with the men."

"Sorry that we took so long." David avoided looking at the body. "I made a mistake. I told the men how William died. No one wanted to come. An elder in La Ruta told the men that anyone who died on a sacrificial stone would be taken away by the Armadillo spirit god and left in a place deep within the earth. I offered lots of money before I could get these two older men to come. Ruth will be furious at the high price I had to pay."

I looked at the five people with me. *I might be facing a killer—or killers.* My legs quivered.

In a language I knew wasn't Spanish, likely a dialect of the Maya language family, Doña María directed the workers to the stretcher. Taking advantage of the ropes around William's wrists and ankles, the men avoided touching his body as they placed him onto the canvas. I was relieved that they avoided incurring the spirit god's alleged wrath and hoped everyone else was as lucky. But in my mind, successive images of William's blue body were projected rapidly as though from a Kodak slide carousel.

Doña María picked up the ceremonial bowl that held William's heart and left to convert the storeroom into a morgue. David, Father Lester, and I followed the two men carrying the stretcher.

Boxes of household supplies lined the storeroom. Doña María took a sheet and laid it on the stone floor, then directed the men to lower the stretcher beside it. The men used the ropes to move the body onto the sheet, then quickly left.

While Doña María covered William with a light blanket, Father Lester made the sign of the cross and muttered a few words. With her hands clasped, Doña María spoke rapidly in Spanish. It seemed like a prayer, except I didn't hear her say *Dios*, the Spanish word for God. Several times, I recognized *el diablo*, the devil. She finished and crossed herself. Her face radiated the saintly glow of a woman at peace with herself. Back at the altar in the clearing, I'd felt quite agitated. In Doña María's presence, an unexpected sense of calm enveloped me—but it was the calm found in the eye of a hurricane.

The door to William's room was unlocked. I slipped inside,

closed the heavy drapes, and flicked on a table lamp. At first glance, everything appeared arranged in an orderly fashion. On the dresser were stacks of Mickey Spillane's paperbacks, featuring the hardboiled detective Mike Hammer. William had neatly draped his clothes over a chair. I located a billfold containing a thick wad of pesos and five credit cards in his pants pocket. It was apparent that the purpose of his sacrifice wasn't a robbery. The billfold's inner pocket held a piece of paper with Janice Appleton's Milwaukee address and phone number. I guessed a girlfriend, ex-wife, or married sister.

The dresser held shirts in the top drawer, underwear next down, socks in the lowest. Hidden under the socks, I found a journal. I flipped to the last entry and then backtracked a few days:

February 27. Mexico City. The ambassador's wife from P___ was oh-so-hot in bed. I made a small fortune selling her a fake Jackson Pollock. She was like most of my clients. Give them the famous name before showing the work of art, and they abandon all rationality.

March 1. Oaxaca. The T___ sisters were athletic, and they winded me. Must do three ways more often to keep in shape.

March 4. Armadillo. R___ was her usual icy self. She's one temptation I can easily avoid.

March 5. Armadillo & Tuxtla. I volunteered to pick up H___ in Tuxtla. I used my standard routine, "I'm hot and thirsty. Let's stop for a drink." I slipped a knockout pill in her drink. I was set to have my way with her, but I lost all interest. She didn't have an ounce of fat on her, and that turned me off. I love the Rubenesque bodies of women from Central and South America. Nearing the end of the drive to Armadillo, H___ woke up slightly dizzy. I told her it was the heat. I

dropped her off at Armadillo's front door. Soon she'll
find my business card in her underpants and conclude
I screwed her. Now that turns me on.

The three final entries were all dated March 6—last night. It
was also William's last night.

March 6. Armadillo. While I was picking up H___ in
Tuxtla, S___ arrived at Armadillo. She's the hottest
woman I've seen in ages. I must have her one way or
another. But tonight, I'm skipping dinner because I
prefer the pleasures of the flesh, like the woman I'm
meeting tonight on the plaza in La Ruta.

March 6. Update. I was going to drive the short distance
into La Ruta, but my car wouldn't start. Some idiot
stole the battery. I bet vengeful H___ is the saboteur.

I'd just arrived at Armadillo, but I presumed that William's *R*
stood for Ruth, and *H* stood for Harriet. I didn't know who *S* was,
but I felt sorry for her. The final entry in William's journal read:

March 6. Second Update. I've arranged another irresistible treat for myself. Tonight is my LUCKY night.

I slammed the book shut but caught myself before I threw it
to the floor. Why, in this godforsaken place deep in the jungles
of Chiapas, was I trying to figure out who killed this monster?
Neumann expected me to write Max's biography, not play an
amateur detective.

CHAPTER 7

An Excerpt From Max Eicher's Memoirs: *Ruth Eicher*

Maya Magic *became an instant bestseller in 1933, and Hollywood invited me to be a script consultant. Arriving for the job, I considered myself quite a hotshot.* Silver Screen, *a Hollywood tabloid, heralded me as "The Maya Mystery Man." The lead article gushed, "Max Eicher stands six-foot-two and has Germanic, slicked-back, light-blond hair. And, oh my, he possesses the looks of a leading man. Move over Clark Gable." I admit I fudged my height a bit.*

Irving Ripstein, a bigwig over at Columbia Pictures, summoned me to talk about jungles for his next movie, Joseph Conrad's Heart of Darkness. *After I explained that the jungles of the Congo Free State in Africa weren't the same as those in Central America, he waved his arm dismissively. "Max, you're nitpicking. Audiences don't have a clue if a scene is shot in a real jungle or on a studio lot." In retrospect, I thank Ripstein for teaching me the truth about Hollywood—nothing is what it seems. Unfortunately, I failed to grasp that concept before it was too late.*

While in Hollywood, I shared a modest bungalow with Theodore "Theo" Neumann—my boyhood friend and an aspiring screenwriter. Do not get me wrong—it wasn't that kind of relationship. He and I held similar opinions about movies, women, and life. We frequented studio parties held for the wealthy and beautiful but typically attended by the aspiring-to-be-rich and merely attractive.

Women flocked to us at parties. To say we loved the adoration is an enormous understatement.

I first encountered the unrivaled Ruth Kelly the night I attended a cast party in a producer's Hollywood mansion. I stood next to a buffet table laden with plates of melt-in-your-mouth hors d'oeuvres and a large punch bowl containing a brew called Satan's Whiskers, whose kick helped everyone forget there would be a tomorrow. I stood trapped between Red and Platinum, two women who early on had stationed themselves near the limitless booze.

I scanned the room for an escape route. Noticing my impending departure, Platinum seized my arm, squinted her eyes, and pointed across the room at a stunning woman. "Take a look at Ruth batting her eyes at Jacob Lazear. He's old enough to be her father."

Red grabbed my other arm and muttered in an alcohol-infused breath, "She means her grandfather."

"If anyone can get Lazear up, Ruth can."

"If his shriveled thing gets up, we'll call him Lazarus." Red cackled at her own joke.

"Ruth's making a huge mistake killing those old guys because dead men don't cast girls in movies."

I nodded from time to time as they prattled on. My heart wasn't in the conversation because I was busy gawking at the subject of their gossip. Ruth wore a clinging black satin dress held up by straps of alternating strips of fabric and silver sequins. Her ample cleavage was on full display. On one wrist dangled a bracelet with large dark stones set in silver. Marcel-waved, jet-black hair framed her round face. She offered a look of wide-eyed innocence while her full, pouting lips hinted at a seduction talent.

Likely hearing the two women's loud, catty remarks, Ruth twirled around and caught me watching her. She flashed a flirtatious smile, took leave of Lazear, and sashayed over.

She opened the first and only round of the match with my inebriated captors. "Hello, girls. Who's the good-looking man you're hiding?" She looked into my eyes.

"Max Eicher, at your service," I answered.

"Say, I've been reading about you lately. Beats me why they didn't

include a picture of you. Come closer and let me take a look. Well, bless my soul! You're candy for my eyes."

Before Red and Platinum could mount a counteroffensive, Ruth moved decisively. "Sorry, ladies, you're no longer needed here. Go powder your ruby-red noses in the little girls' room." She reached out and gripped the elbow of each, twirled them around, so they faced away from us, and then half patted, half pushed their fannies. Within seconds, Ruth had bested her potential rivals.

The two looked back with smiles that assassins might flash before striking. Platinum slurred, "Bye-bye, Ruth" and hissed a guttural sound. Much later, I became conscious that the sound had been the word "less."

Having dispatched her rivals, Ruth turned her full attention to me. Given the scene I had watched, I was amused but tongue-tied. She wasted no time initiating her come-hither campaign. "Max, I'm Ruth." She lifted the bottom of my tie and said, "You sure know how to pick them." I admit I prided myself as a lady's man, but in her presence, I felt like an awkward, eighth-grade boy who had been asked to dance by a sophisticated tenth-grade girl. She continued to compliment me, and before the advancement of a conquering woman, I took a step back. Blocked by the buffet table, I lost my balance, grasped for support, and thrust my arm deep into the punch bowl.

"Oh, my dear. Here, let me help." She gripped the sleeve of my jacket and escorted me out of the room, led me up a grand staircase, and walked me down a hall. She opened a bedroom door and towed me inside. In the adjoining bathroom, she helped me out of my jacket and began unbuttoning my shirt. I protested, but she silenced me. "For goodness' sake, your shirt reeks of that ghastly concoction. I'll wash it out, so it won't leave a stain."

As I stood bare-chested before her, she kept up a steady monologue while she slowly rinsed my shirt. Her eyes continuously looked me up and down. I felt bewildered. I protested she shouldn't be bothering with my shirt, and I should go home. She countered. "Are you going to let a little accident ruin our evening? I want to talk to a real man. From all the reports, you have quite a story to tell." We talked into the early morning hours.

From my perspective, Ruth wasn't just the most beautiful woman in Hollywood but also the most intense. Her chocolate brown eyes showed she understood me, yet they also teased me coquettishly. Loving the attention, I told stories about Armadillo, the residence I had built in a remote region of Mexico while writing Maya Magic. She was fascinated with my descriptions of Armadillo and asked endless questions about it.

On that first evening, other than saying she'd been in Hollywood since 1926 and played major roles, she divulged little about herself. I scarcely noticed because I was the center of her attention. I foolishly assumed I had captivated her with my tales of an exotic world and that my deep-set, trance-inducing eyes had contributed to the effect. I knew this for a fact because that is what she repeatedly told me. For my part, I was quickly falling in love.

A week later, after an evening of dancing, we returned to my place. I told Ruth that Theo wasn't coming back until tomorrow.

She said, "In that case, make yourself comfortable, and I'll add ecstasy."

I sank into the sofa with a dreamy look on my face. Ruth drew the shades and turned off the lights, except for the floor lamp with the chintz shade over which she draped a white silk scarf. She tiptoed across the room to the phonograph and put a record on the turntable. A popular melody of the day, "Anything Goes," floated in the air. She stood in front of me and mouthed the lyrics of the song, while she unhurriedly kicked off her shoes. She pulled her dress high enough to unclasp the garters securing her silk stockings, then slowly removed them one by one. She held them up, and the lamp cast their shadows across her swaying body while she continued mouthing the lyrics. The straps of her dress slid from her shoulders, and her gown dropped to the floor. When the music ended, her last garment had joined the others.

She lifted the needle from the record and started it again. She lay down on the rug and beckoned me to join her. "Max, I have a special present for you. She went down on me, and ended by saying, "that seals our wedding plans."

"It sure does," I said as I wore a stupid-looking grin.

She whispered in my ear, "Max, they say that if a married couple places a penny in a jar each time they have sex during their first year of marriage and then remove them one by one afterward, they'll never remove them all. I hope it's never that way with us."

I laughed hard. "There may be fools in the world for which that holds, but when I give my heart, other parts of my anatomy will follow." She laughed in her high, schoolgirl giggle that I found endearing —then.

Two weeks later, in a small Catholic church, we were joined in holy until-death-do-us-part matrimony. Shortly after, we left for Armadillo.

At the end of our first year of marriage, our jar contained not one penny. That's because I didn't count the fellatios before or after we were married. She always gave reasons we couldn't have sexual intercourse: headaches, the wrong time of the month, she wasn't in the mood. For her, they were legitimate reasons.

The following paragraphs summarize truths I learned about Ruth after she and I married.

In the silent film era, Hollywood producers sought out Ruth for her acting talent, with which she was blessed. She was an up-and-coming star in silent movies, and if her luck had held, she might have rivaled Clara Bow and Lillian Gish. But Ruth's luck ran out when talkies killed the silent era. Unless you were on the receiving end of her charms as I was, Ruth's voice was nerve-jangling. She possessed a little girl's voice trapped in a drive-men-wild body—not a voice for the talkies. Eventually, I learned she obtained her small movie roles —all non-speaking parts—by way of the casting couch. Her career in the talkies failed to take off the way her clothes did.

I realized that once Ruth spotted me, she'd begun a campaign that wouldn't stop until she achieved what she desired—to escape Hollywood and establish herself as Armadillo's head honchō. In other words, her marriage to me was just a means to an end—a place where she was a big fish in a small pond.

Perhaps someday an aspiring author will write a movie script of our relationship:

> *Young archaeologist on the rise meets an actress on the descent. To escape Hollywood and her fading career, she seduces him with flattery. Longing for love, he believes her words and is blind to her cold heart. She flourishes at their hacienda in the jungle; he longs for release from marriage but finds no escape.*

But as I reflect on this movie script, I realize it is funereal, and no amount of rewriting will make it marketable.

CHAPTER 8

A Kiss

The suitable course of action was to notify William's next of kin. But before calling, I needed to meet with Ruth. While David managed Armadillo's day-to-day operations, and Doña María was responsible for cooking and cleaning, Ruth held power. I feared that failure to consult Ruth would incur her wrath. And while she couldn't tear out my heart, she could rip to shreds my chances of writing Max's biography. Besides, I'd delayed long enough. I couldn't afford to have her think that I was ignoring her.

A 3-by-5-foot photo of Ruth dominated the wall to the right of her door. A photo by David Budman. I studied it before knocking on Ruth's door:

> Ruth stands nude at the apex of a Maya temple. She spreads her legs wide and reaches out her arms as if inscribed in the circle of da Vinci's *Vitruvian Man*. A concealed spotlight from behind silhouettes her against an ominous black sky that threatens to crush a shameless woman. Her body's contours glow like the embers of a dying fire.

I stood there, embarrassed and flustered as though I'd been caught looking at pornography in a public setting. While photos of Ruth in the other corridor gripped me with enthusiasm to discover more about her, this photo was a visual assault.

Reading Max's description of her iconic images was one thing, but quite another to see and feel the power of her demonic allure. How, given all the women in the world, could Max have fallen in love with and married this creature? What was he thinking? These were just a few of the questions I intended to answer.

I knocked, and a woman appeared in the open doorway. I stared in astonishment. There was no way the person in front of me could be the iconic woman in David's photos. She was close to seventy, an age I associated with grandmothers, but that wasn't what disturbed me. Her dyed black hair contrasted harshly with her alabaster skin. Heightening the ghoulish effect were black penciled-on eyebrows and heavily rouged cheeks. She wore an ankle-length, navy-colored woven *huipil* with a round neckline. Just looking at her Spratling silver necklaces, earrings, and rings, I felt weighed down. *Why doesn't she collapse under the weight of all that jewelry?* She squinted her eyes as though trying to bring me into focus. I'd heard her described as a queen mother who commanded respect, but time had been cruel.

"Mrs. Eicher." I surprised myself when I gave a slight bow. "I'm Paul Seawright."

"Paul dear, don't stand there as if you're unsure that you're welcome. Come inside and join me." She gripped my sleeve, pulled me forth, and placed her hand on my arm. "Please, call me Ruth. I'm glad you've come to see me. You indicated in your letter that you're interested in writing my late husband's biography."

"I hope to get your approval if I write it."

"I'm delighted we have another contender—and a handsome one at that." Then, as if an afterthought, she added, "I trust you like competition."

"I like healthy competition." She seemed pleased with my reply. *Just keep playing along.*

"As you may have heard, the biographer Gerald Strupp is seeking my approval to write Max's biography. You'll find him a formidable rival." She raised an eyebrow. "He calls himself a Darwinian; his favorite game is Survival of the Fittest. He's skilled at exploiting his opponents' weaknesses. I can personally attest to his sneaky ways."

Our conversation—more like a monologue—grew uncomfortable. It was time to introduce some levity. "Fear not, Lady Eicher, I can hold my own against any man. I faithfully do Royal Canadian Exercises thrice a week."

She didn't smile at my attempt at humor. On the contrary, she released my forearm and wrapped her hands around my bicep. "You're a fine specimen of manly fitness." Her touch felt both seductive and unnerving. I remembered reading Max's description of how Ruth seduced him: "When Ruth unleashed her offensive attack, I didn't know what hit me." But even given his advanced warning, I winced and took a step back—not unlike Max backing up from her advances and inadvertently plunging his arm into a punch bowl.

"Don't tell me you're shy. Come, I'll give you a tour of my apartment."

Photos of her filled the living room walls. "David's an amazing photographer," she said. "One of the best in the twentieth century." It was one thing to be alone with Ruth, quite another to be in her company and also surrounded by erotic photos of her.

"He's a genius with a camera," I said. "He captured your essence."

She winked at me. "I'll determine if you're the best person to write Max's biography, but I'm also curious, why a book about him?" She continued to clutch my arm.

I recognized a minefield ahead and stepped carefully. "I was contacted by a screenwriter, who praised my biography of Freud. He wanted me to find out all I could about Max." I deliberately didn't mention Neumann's name.

Ruth's leering smile wasn't helping me relax. "If there's a book, there might be a movie. That's a lot of money that might benefit Armadillo."

"Perhaps enough to make some people happy." I congratulated myself on uttering a banal statement that she could interpret the way she wanted.

"Paul, I wanted to read your bestseller before you arrived," she said, "but I couldn't find a copy in La Ruta." She let out a piercing laugh, and I understood why, when talkies replaced silent movies, her career as an actress crashed like the 1929 stock market.

Ruth swiftly shifted gears. "My beloved Armadillo is a disaster. Everything is falling apart. To help restore this place, I've invited some prominent movers and shakers to be on my board of directors. Tomorrow, they'll present their fund-raising proposals to restore Armadillo to its former glory. They'll need to come up with a boatload of money." Ruth flashed a coquettish smile. "But despite just meeting you, I like what I see. Paul, will you join our board? You'll meet influential people who appreciate Max's work and might help you gather material for his biography."

"I'd be honored."

She winked. "I take pleasure in making people feel good. Especially an eye-catcher like you."

She gently stroked the back of my hand and led me into her bedroom, a shrine to Art Deco. The rug in front of the fireplace displayed geometric designs with bold colors. Pillars of precisely cut mahogany framed the fireplace's symmetrically shaped tiles. Above the mantel and dominating the room hung Ruth's portrait. The darkened painting showed the toll inflicted by smoke from evening fires and countless cigarettes. It struck me as a metaphor for the building's physical condition. And hers.

"Don't you think that Katherine Davis, a good friend of Max and me, did a marvelous job of capturing my insatiable spirit."

Spirit was an interesting choice of words; sexual appetite would have been more precise. In the Art Deco-styled painting, Ruth languishes on silk sheets; her full breasts seemed to relish their freedom from the sheer, chiffon peignoir. "Capture your spirit? Absolutely. I see a woman teeming with life."

"You have a remarkably good eye. I'm pleased you're not offended by the human body au naturel."

"The photo just outside your apartment offers considerable au naturel." I should've stopped there, but I added, "I believe I can handle it." *Mistake!* I made a mental note never to utter double entendres in Ruth's presence. They might encourage her to charge ahead on a seductive quest. Not that she needed encouragement.

She squinted at me and smiled. "Then, we see eye to eye." She waved her hand in the direction of a massive Art Deco bed, overrun with silk pillows. Considering the bed was twice the size of mine in Iowa City, I marveled at how they squeezed it through the doorway. "I find it more comfortable sharing private thoughts in an intimate setting." She stroked my arm again, giving my wrist a good squeeze.

I said nothing, but I began plotting my exit strategy. *I've got to get out of this place.*

"Tell me, young man, what gives you pleasure?"

"I relax by reading murder mysteries." Her nonverbal reaction conveyed that wasn't what she wanted to hear. "With your permission, I'd like to interview you to learn more about Max."

"I'm not sure about Max, but I can share more of myself with you." She leaned over and planted a lingering kiss on my birthmark. The placement of her kiss told me that nothing would stop her from trying to add me to her list of conquests.

Ruth's far-too-warm welcome was affecting my ability to think clearly. Suddenly, I realized that I'd failed to tell her about William's death. I shared details of what we found at the stone altar.

"I've known William for years," Ruth said. "I'm surprised someone didn't kill him sooner than this."

My god, she's utterly devoid of empathy. Could she be Spock's sister on Star Trek? "I was led to believe you were his friend."

"Listen, sweetie, the man didn't have friends, but he made

enemies."

When I suggested we call the police to report the murder, she looked at me as if I couldn't write my name, let alone a biography. "Call them if you want, but they won't drive three hours from San Cristóbal on possibly washed-out roads to see someone with his heart ripped out."

Ruth was equally indifferent to my desire to notify William's next of kin. "If you call her, tell her he died in a bordello after losing his heart to some young thing. It's not the truth, but it captures his essence."

Having obtained Ruth's permission to call Janice, I tackled a new topic. "We need to find out who killed William."

"I haven't given that much thought. Still, a killer running around Armadillo isn't a good way to attract tourists." She reached for a cigarette, lit it, and blew the smoke upward. "Say, with your rugged good looks, you look like a detective. Why don't you track down William's killer?"

"I'd rather not spend my time playing detective. I came to Armadillo to gather material for a book on Max," I said.

"Put the biography aside. At tonight's opening dinner, I'll announce you're a new member of the board and the person in charge of finding a murderer lurking around Armadillo. Besides, if you're looking for William's killer, you'll have to consult with me. But I'm warning you not to finger the person who comes up with the best moneymaking plan. I can't afford my biggest donor to spend life in prison. Nobody in a Mexican prison lives long." She laughed as though dying in prison was hilarious. Things occurred in cells that were far worse than death, but I kept quiet.

"I've enjoyed meeting you, but now I'm off to give Janice a call."

"Please don't leave yet."

"I want to make the call before lunch."

"Be sure to consult with me frequently." Her words suggested she was making a request, but her tone conveyed a command. "Promise you'll stop by soon—very soon."

A promise was too much. I gave a slight smile and nodded my head. I hoped neither signaled a commitment but suspected nothing I did would deter her. To avoid another kiss, I justified a quick exit by mentioning my long and exhausting journey over the last two days. Within seconds, a closed door stood between us.

Supposedly, Max was the subject of my next biography, but what if I'd picked the wrong person? Ruth was an exhibitionist, a seductress, a narcissist—themes readers would find titillating. And while Max's presence, like hers, reverberated throughout Armadillo, he seemed inaccessible, all but invisible. I wouldn't recognize him if he were standing in front of me. While exploring sources of information to prepare for Armadillo, I ran across numerous photographs of Ruth, but none of Max. His high school and Yale yearbooks mentioned him frequently, yet white spaces appeared where photos of him should've been. Was I writing the biography of a ghost?

On the way to the office to call Janice, I reflected on Ruth's insistence that I investigate William's death, which was the last assignment I wanted. Dealing with Ruth was a tightrope walk. Being too compliant, and a man-eater would devour me. Being too assertive, and Ruth would send me home with no material about Max. I resolved to do the detective bit but keep my focus on writing Max's biography.

I dialed the number on William's business card. Some time passed as it took several operators to help me complete my call. I identified myself and established that Janice was William's sister. "I'm afraid I have sad news to convey about your brother, William Farrell. He died last night."

There was a short pause on the other end of the line, followed by the phone connection crackling. Silently, I implored the weather god not to wash away the telephone lines. I didn't catch what Janice said next, but it sounded like, "…bad news?"

I repeated my words but stopped when I realized that she'd said, "What's the bad news?" Taken aback by her indifference, I wasn't sure how to proceed.

"Okay," she said, "give me the details."

"He died of a knife wound."

"That figures! Did a betrayed husband kill Bill?"

"You didn't like your brother."

"I don't know you, but I'll bet you didn't bang your sister when she was fourteen and leave her with a screaming baby. I'm glad Bill's dead."

I told her about the human sacrifice but omitted that his heart was cut out. She listened in silence. I added, "If there is anything I can do to help, I'd like to."

Briefly, she sounded as though she were crying. "I've got no money, and Bill never gave me a cent. The whole family hated him. Cremate his body and scatter the ashes at the base of a flowering plant. Make him finally contribute something beautiful to this world." She paused for a while and asked, "Did you know him?"

"No, but the people I've met who did certainly weren't sad."

"Thanks for your call. You've given me the perfect reason to celebrate. If I die tonight, it will be from an overdose of happiness."

CHAPTER 9

An Excerpt From Max Eicher's Memoirs: Katherine "Kate" Davis

*I*n late August of 1949, Katherine "Kate" Davis—an up-and-coming New York artist, and a real looker—showed up at Armadillo. She had written Ruth and David to tell them that she was impressed with David's photos of Ruth. She asked for the opportunity to paint Ruth's portrait. Naturally, Ruth invited her.

Kate immediately gave generously of her time and attention. She began preliminary drawings that she eventually integrated into her portraits of Ruth. Kate collaborated with David in developing photographs. Three times a week, she taught basic English to children in La Ruta. And I met with Kate to discuss my work in deciphering Maya glyphs. She was intrigued by the artistic way each glyph was constructed.

I was attracted to Kate. At five-foot-ten with blazing red hair and an infectious smile, she radiated life. In turn, I was awakened to life's joys. One afternoon, about two months into her stay, Kate and I sat in the library trying to interpret a set of glyphs that Doña María had drawn from a stela. Without looking up, I said, "You might be interested in some extraordinarily well-preserved Maya drawings I discovered."

"I would love to see them."

I kept my head down. "This is embarrassing, but they contain scenes that would be judged pornographic." I waited. In my peripheral vision, I saw her fidget, but also smile.

When she spoke, her words exploded with a staccato rhythm. "Excuse me. I'm an artist. Are you going to show me the drawings or not?"

I paused. "They're stunning, but I'm not sure I could show them. They're most unladylike—although they indeed contain ladies."

"I've taken lots of life drawing classes, Dr. Maxie. I can't be shocked."

Her way of saying Dr. Maxie charmed me. "In my opinion, these drawings are the Maya equivalent of ancient India's Kama Sutra. If the popular press saw them, they'd dub them The Maya Sex Manual."

"And you believe I shouldn't see them? Why? Because I'm a delicate flower, and you need to protect me? Men are so full of conceit about how they're the stronger sex. I insist you show them to me."

I looked her in the eye. "This is even more embarrassing, but ever since I found them, I've wanted to try a few incredible positions. Ruth's participation is completely out of the question. I pledged to myself I wouldn't show them to a woman unless she was comfortable with the idea. But listen, even as I'm saying this, it sounds absurd. I'll never bring up the subject again. Sorry if I made you feel uncomfortable and—"

I had not finished before she was standing in front of me and looking down. If I had worn a tie, she would have grasped it and yanked me up. Instead, Kate placed her forehead against mine and enunciating each word, said, "Dr. Maxie, you're infuriating. I'm ready to try any of those positions with you. I'll even invent some the Maya never dreamed of in their cosmology."

"Aren't you a bit—"

"I'll go you one better. When your lean body is contorted and writhing in pain and your face is as red as my hair, I'll have wrapped my body around yours and enjoyed myself immensely."

Feigning total intimidation, I proposed, as meekly as I could muster without breaking into hysterical laughter, one last challenge. "Forget everything I've said. I would want to photograph us doing the positions, but I suspect, like most women, you're somewhat sensitive about your body."

I tensed in anticipation of a slap. Instead, Kate spoke in a slow, husky voice. "In the photos you take, my body will be the Eighth Wonder of the World. We can start now, but I suspect you're all bluff about appearing in the buff."

I was ecstatic over the prospects of Kate and me posing in Maya positions. "If you're willing to pose with me for six of those positions, then I'll show you the copies Doña María has drawn. However, you must promise never to reveal their existence to anyone. Promise?"

"Dr. Maxie, I do solemnly promise."

The next afternoon, I locked us into my photography darkroom. Kate immediately began undressing.

"Whoa! It's going to be a while before I get the cameras and lights set up. You can keep your clothes on until then."

"Not a problem. As an artist in New York, I posed in the nude for life drawing classes at the Art Students League. I feel free without clothes on."

In a mock toast, I held up a chemistry beaker filled with a developer. "Then here's to freedom."

From a cabinet, I removed two wooden Chiapas masks, which featured long-beaked noses, giving them a Maya appearance. We wore the masks to ensure that if the photos ever surfaced, we wouldn't be blackmailed.

That afternoon, we performed as sexual gymnasts while posing as if to illustrate a contemporary, under-the-counter Maya calendar. After our intimate photo shoot, I whispered in Kate's ear, "You're much more exciting than Ruth."

I barely saw her hand before she slapped the side of my face. "Don't ever compare me to any other woman. I don't care if I'm your second or your two-hundredth woman. I've just had the time of my life, and much to my surprise, you had the stamina to keep up with me. But you make one more comparison, and you'll never touch my body again. Understand?"

Never again did I verbally compare her to Ruth. But in my mind, I continued making comparisons. And no surprise—Kate won every time.

Two days later, I finished developing the photos, and we studied them. Kate triumphantly pointed out her body equaled or surpassed the women in Titian's Venus of Urbino and Modigliani's Reclining Nude. She was right. I paid the local metalsmith to replicate Doña María's pendant and presented it to Kate. She loved it.

The end came too soon. In January—several months before her stay at Armadillo was scheduled to end—Kate shocked me. "Dr. Maxie, I'm leaving. We've spent a grand time together, but I'm feeling homesick for New York."

Nothing I said could persuade her to stay. On the day of her farewell, I slipped her a securely sealed manila envelope containing glossy prints of our Maya poses. I stored the negatives in a secret place away from prying eyes.

Seven months later, Kate sent me an envelope. In her letter, she announced that she had taken a detour en route to New York and stayed with her aunt in New Mexico. Now she was heading home to New York. I looked at the postmark: Santa Fe. That was curious; she never mentioned an aunt or Santa Fe.

Also enclosed was the sheet music for the song "Always True to You in My Fashion" from the musical Kiss Me, Kate. The lyrics captured her flair of being faithful to a man, but always, in her fashion. On the score was a penciled note:

> Dr. Maxie,
>   Thanks for making my hormones hum during my stay at Armadillo.
>
> Hugs and kisses,
Kate, the Eighth Wonder of the World

Ah, what I wouldn't give right now for Kate's hugs and kisses—and everything else she offered.

CHAPTER 10

Maya Magic

Why was I exhausted so early in the afternoon? The problem didn't need a detective to solve it. I'd taken a tour of Armadillo led by the talented and eccentric David, chanced upon William's sacrificed body, escaped from Ruth's seductive onslaught, and listened to William's sister rejoice upon hearing the news of his death. Having missed breakfast, I was hungry—time to grab a bowl of soup before digging deeper into Max's elusive story.

The door to the dining room was locked. I noticed a woman with her back to me, sitting on a bench in the courtyard. After my February meeting with Theo, I searched for information about each Armadillo board member. Based on my findings, I guessed that the woman with the big, bouncy Farrah Fawcett hairstyle must be Harriet. I sat down beside her.

"Hi. I'm assuming you're Harriet Galveston. I'm Paul Seawright."

She turned to look at me and cried out, "Oh, dear me!"

Life has given me plenty of practice shrugging off people's reactions to my facial birthmark, but hers was too flagrant to ignore. "Cut it out!" I try hard not to react overtly, but the pain inflicted by her remark elicited my curt response.

"I'm sorry," she said. Her face showed remorse.

"And I'm also sorry I said what I did. It's humiliating to have people constantly look at me as if I'm a freak."

"You're right. I shouldn't have reacted the way I did. And yes, I'm Harriet. Are you the Seawright who wrote *Freud*?"

She'd lowered the barrier her opening exclamation had erected in seeing me for more than a birth-marked face. "The same. I'm at Armadillo to write Max's biography."

"Good luck in taking on Gerald Strupp."

Hers was the second warning within two hours. "Meaning?"

"I'm an archaeologist, and I've heard lots of scuttlebutt about him. It's a brave person who challenges him. You look fit, but he plays dirty. I suggest you avoid Armadillo's shadowy corridors, or you might feel the blade of a knife slitting your throat."

After dealing with William's body, I was sick of knives. We chatted for a while about the weather and the rough road getting here before I broached the topic of what she knew about Max.

"*Maya Magic* and I go back a long time," she said. "I read Max's book as an archaeological graduate student in the mid-fifties— I guess that dates me. But lately, I've come to understand it in a very different way." She tapped her fingernails on the bench.

"Go on."

She squinted at me. "I'm guessing you get your fair share of strange looks."

"You got that right."

"Well, so do I. Especially when I mention *Maya Magic* and extraterrestrial beings in the same sentence. People look at me like I'm a crazy woman. By the way, you aren't a bloodsucking reporter for the *National Enquirer*?"

"No. But I assure you that I'm not Gerald Strupp. I'm not here to destroy anyone's reputation. I try my best to write an honest biography."

"Honest ones can still hurt people."

"Have you read *Freud*?"

She paused before she spoke. "Okay, you're right. As a biographer, you were very evenhanded. Given his views about women, I'd have roasted Sick-Man Freud alive." She chuckled.

"My book revealed a lot about, as you put it, 'Sick-Man'

Freud, but it also reveals much about me. I care about people."
I pointed my finger toward the right side of my face. "I know
what hurt is, and I try never to inflict it—consciously or unconsciously."

"I'm sorry for what I said a few minutes ago."

"Thanks." I paused to relax. "What do you think of William
Farrell?"

"He's a monster. He raped me two days ago in Tuxtla, but in
the version he shares with others, it was 'a consensual rendez-
vous.' I wish he were dead."

"Last night, your wish came true."

She lightly punched my arm. "That's not funny."

"This morning, David gave his Armadillo tour. In a clearing
not far from Max's grave, I discovered William's body on a Maya
sacrificial altar. Someone ripped his heart out."

Her face displayed a kaleidoscope of emotions. Disbelief followed shock and morphed into bliss, which was replaced by
serenity.

"Thank goodness. Now the women at Armadillo will be safe."
She leaned forward. "I only regret that I didn't get to him first."

"You're saying you didn't kill him?"

"Look, Doña María is opening the dining room. Enjoy lunch.
I'm off to share your good news with others."

After Harriet left, I remembered something I'd forgotten to
tell her: William confessed in his journal that he hadn't raped
Harriet.

CHAPTER 11

Surrounded By Flowers

D ominating the dining room was a wooden table—twelve straight back chairs with leather-upholstered seats lined each side. An ornate thirteenth chair occupied the far end. I was the first diner present, so I took a chair halfway down the table. Precisely at one, Ruth made her entrance. She wore a white blouse accented with a sizeable Pre-Columbian jade necklace and a white ankle-length skirt. She grabbed the arm of a young woman just entering the room and escorted her toward the table's head. Ruth took her place behind her ornately carved chair and directed the woman to sit to her left, adding, "And take off that hat."

The woman removed a stylish broad-brimmed hat and placed it on the back of her chair. She had on an explorer's shirt of fine cotton, khaki trousers, and a simple chain necklace. I tried to avoid staring at the strikingly beautiful woman with soft blue eyes and full lips. I found her devilishly sexy.

Two women in *huipiles* with red, green, and yellow designs emerged from the kitchen and placed bowls of soup in front of the three of us. I sipped a spoonful of the *caldo tlalpeño*, a chicken and rice soup filled with onions, garlic, chickpeas, tomatoes, cilantro, and avocados. I finished my soup in a dreamlike state.

As inconspicuously as possible, I listened in as Ruth and the young woman engaged in deep conversation. Ruth talked about her efforts to restore Armadillo to its former glory. The other woman spoke about the plight of the Lacandon people and their decimated rainforests. She declared, "Trudi Blom at Casa Na Bolom deserves accolades for saving some of the Lacandon's forests from commercial interests that seem intent on destroying them."

In a voice that echoed off the walls, Ruth declared, "Trudi can go to hell! Just hearing her name makes me sick." I remembered that Max mentioned in *Memoirs* how Ruth and Trudi met in the early forties and soon became the best of enemies. Suddenly, Ruth looked over at me and said, "Please come and sit next to me."

I took a seat to her right. In the company of the two women, I felt uncomfortable. Ruth intimidated me, but in the presence of the young woman, it was as if she was The Beauty, and I was The Beast. Ruth turned to her companion. "Let me introduce Paul Seawright, the handsome young man who plans to write Max Eicher's biography."

The beautiful woman reached out her hand and said, "*Buenas tardes. Soy* Sandy Martin."

I tried to stay nonchalant, but instead, a wave of shyness swept over me. I haltingly returned Sandy's greeting in Spanish. "*Mucho gusto en conocerla.*"

Sandy gave me a warm smile. "How far along are you in writing your book on Max?" Her manner of asking conveyed a genuine interest, or maybe she was tired of talking to Ruth.

"I've just started collecting stories from people who knew him." *Getting started is pure understatement.*

"Glad you're writing about Max," Sandy said. "He needs a good biography."

"How do you know about him?" I asked.

"I'm an archaeologist. Two weeks ago, I reread *Maya Magic* and was again enthralled. I decided it might be a great midterm break to visit the source of Max's inspiration."

I was finding Sandy more impressive by the minute. "What a coincidence, we both love *Maya Magic*. I'd like to hear your thoughts about it."

"After lunch, if you'd like, we could walk over to La Ruta's only restaurant for coffee." *Wow, Sandy isn't one to waste time.*

"Great idea." Was there something in Armadillo's water that caused the women I met to come on so strong? Both Ruth and Sandy generated a disoriented feeling in me. To get my bearings, I asked Ruth a question, "I'm curious, what was it like being married to Max?"

When Ruth paused to gather her thoughts, Sandy spoke up. "What I'm about to say are my conclusions gathered from reliable sources, and they're subject to validation by others." I surmised that Sandy was a young faculty member determined to demonstrate she was a dedicated scholar. Amused, I waited for her to continue. "Max was—"

"I'm the one to tell Max stories," Ruth said.

"I'm just filling Paul in on—"

Ruth's annoyed expression changed to a scowl. "Enough, I'm talking." Sandy's mouth hung open before she capitulated.

"Max was a gentleman and a scholar, and we were the consummate couple." I heard the double entendre and glanced at Sandy. We were both amused. Ruth looked at her empty plate and called over her shoulder, "Doña María, when are you going to serve the next course? Oh, never mind! I've lost my appetite—all this talk about that Trudi Blom woman and now Max. They're all that visitors to Armadillo want to talk about." She pushed back her chair. Sandy and I stood, but Ruth was already out the door.

Our eyes followed her. Sandy said once she was out of sight, "She's a fascinating woman—so refreshingly direct. I was that way before all the bowing and scraping of academic life tempered my natural enthusiasm." I thought Sandy possessed an abundance of enthusiasm; mine for her was growing fast.

From the kitchen, Doña María brought plates of steaming-hot chicken ringed with *mole* sauce. When she laid a plate in front of me, I whispered, "Doña María, thanks for your help this morning."

She flashed a smile that warmed like an afternoon sun and

glowed with a full moon luminosity. "*De nada.* I hope you like our food at Armadillo."

David approached the table and stood beside her. Using his tour-guiding voice, he said, "Let's have a round of applause for Doña María's cooking." Sandy and I clapped enthusiastically. "She's the lifeblood of Armadillo because she's a magician in the kitchen. Nobody leaves here without gaining a few pounds." Sandy stole a glance at her waistline. "Doña María helped Max Eicher when he first arrived in La Ruta, and she's been making Armadillo a food-lovers' paradise for fifty years."

David lowered his voice. "Congratulations, Paul. Ruth told me that she invited you to be a board member. Oh, look, a board member is sitting alone at the end of this table." Out of the corner of my eye, I'd noticed him come in minutes before. "That's Dr. Gerald Strupp, the archaeologist."

"Damn," escaped from Sandy's mouth as she pounded the table with her fist. Her face turned white as though a physician had informed her that she had one month to live. "Sorry, I bit into a hot chili."

"Are you okay?" I asked.

"I'll recover."

"You have to watch out for the tiny chilies in Doña María's cooking," David said. "She seasons all her unique dishes with them."

I peered down the table at the lanky man in his mid-forties who was rapidly spooning soup into his mouth but not tasting it. His face was gaunt, and the veins on his temples throbbed when he swallowed. His thin body was at odds with the amount of food he was consuming. In my head, I heard Freud ask me, "What diagnosis would you give him?" Without a pause, I answered, "I'm not a psychoanalyst, but I'd diagnose bulimia. I'd alert guys to avoid the men's room after this meal because he's probably retching." I regretted the imagined dialogue because, despite Doña María's mouthwatering food, my appetite vanished.

After lunch, Sandy and I walked down a corridor toward our rooms. I listened as she spoke passionately about the world around her: "The beauty of this place is incredible." "Don't you love the sweet fragrance of the flowers drifting toward us?" "Whatever you think of Ruth, she has an eye for accenting these halls in colors that enhance their loveliness."

At first, I thought her language a bit over the top, but then I decided to study my surroundings more carefully. Flowers bloomed everywhere. They shot up from clay containers and bordered the worn tile paths. They climbed trellises; they cascaded from pots hung high on textured walls. "Being surrounded by flowers like these fills me with bliss," Sandy said.

"Then, I want to be here with you."

She grabbed my hand and pulled me to her side, and we continued walking. I mentally congratulated myself on getting it right. As we held hands, my reticence faded. She'd looked at my face and hadn't commented as Harriet had.

"Here's my room," she said, "After I freshen up, we'll grab some coffee in La Ruta." She flashed a smile, and I said yes with an eagerness that took me back.

"Wait up," called out a voice behind me. "David just told me you're Paul Seawright, the author of *Freud*."

I stared at the man from the dining room. Without turning around, Sandy continued walking. She called back over her shoulder, "Tell him we're busy. You'll talk to him later."

Gerald grabbed my sleeve. "I'd appreciate talking to you now. Later, I've got writing to do."

"Sandy," I said, "I'll join you shortly."

"It's your loss if you don't."

I immediately regretted my lousy decision.

Still holding my sleeve, the man said, "I'm Dr. Gerald Strupp. Surely you've heard of me."

CHAPTER 12

A Banty Rooster

*B**est to start neutral.* "Who hasn't heard about you and your biographies?" Heard about was right. Back in Iowa City, Neumann issued a grave warning: "Gerald Strupp ruined the reputations of Bingham and Carter. He'll do the same with Max. Keep your friends close and your enemies closer." And then, as if Neumann hadn't made himself clear, he added, "Gerald is your enemy."

Gerald said nothing, but his arrogant smirk spoke volumes. I asked, "Do you have one of your books I might borrow?" As with David, all it took was a simple show of interest to unleash a torrent of information—but with Gerald, it was entirely about himself.

"My books are very academic with lots of footnotes. You've got a doctorate, so you shouldn't struggle too much. I'll lend you one if you return it. Come, let's talk in the library where it's quiet." He again grabbed my arm. This time it felt like a giant crab's pincers locked onto me. I attempted to pull away, but the crustacean held fast and dragged me toward the library while chattering about how we were fellow writers and how I'd appreciate what he had to say.

A massive stone fireplace that looked older than Casa Armadillo dominated the far end of the library. The high ceiling provided some relief to the oppressive feeling of the room. A solid, dark-stained wooden table, half the length of the one in the dining room, stretched out with seats on either side. Many cushioned chairs, whose golden oak reminded me of my own Stickley furniture, lined the walls. I suspected these chairs would survive much longer than Armadillo's stone foundation and adobe walls. Gerald steered me toward them. When I sat down, I changed my mind. At some point during the last fifty years, the cushion I sat on had collapsed and died.

"We're both fascinated by human nature," Gerald said, "regardless of how sordid it might be. While I could never be a Freudian, I credit Freud for chronicling the epic battles raging beneath the veneer of civility."

I found myself squirming—this time, it wasn't caused by the chair's cushion. I was listening to the poster child for bullshitting. Still, if we were writing about Max, it paid to find out how much Gerald knew. "I'm not a Freudian either. I wrote *Freud*, a venture in creative nonfiction, to entertain and educate."

If Gerald had heard me, he gave no indication. "A semester ago, I sat in my Penn State office puzzling about which biography of a dead man I should write next. I drew up a list of world-class archaeologists and anthropologists and began eliminating them. The remaining name on that list was Max Eicher." Gerald sneeringly pronounced Eicher with a thick German accent as though playing a Nazi in a U.S. WWII propaganda movie. "Intuitively, I know readers will find Max irresistible. His story features an enigmatic protagonist, sexy women, and an exotic setting. But you're a scholar—guess my next step."

Refusing to waste effort on a blowhard, I said nothing.

Within seconds, he pressed on. "A year ago, I sought Ruth's support for writing an authorized biography of Max. I stressed that the world needed his life story. Written, it goes without saying, by a preeminent scholar, such as myself."

Faced with a pontificating windbag, I rolled my shoulders to relax them. I just wanted to be with Sandy.

He pointed at me. "I got Ruth's attention when I told her she'd share top billing with Max. And if playing one ace wasn't enough, I added, 'I can envision a movie memorializing the story of Ruth Eicher and her equally famous husband.'"

What a narcissist. I stopped covering my yawns, but he droned on, self-absorbed and not slowing down. "I found it strange that no renowned scholar had written Max's biography. I surveyed my potential competition and learned of an amateur wannabe. I swiftly thwarted his plans."

Since Gerald wasn't aware of my interest in writing about Max, I realized I was safe now. But his attitude was ominous, perhaps because he sounded too much like a Mafia Don. If he discovered my plans, would he hire a hitman? I counted how many people knew of my intent: David, Harriet, Ruth, and Sandy. I couldn't prevent the cat from being let out of the bag, but I feared my body might end up in one. I deliberately breathed deeply and relaxed. He interpreted my head nod—in truth, I was falling asleep—as an encouragement to continue.

"I've unearthed intriguing things about this place and the people here, but before I tell you, I want your pledge of secrecy."

"Shall we prick our fingers and join them in a solemn pledge?"

My mockery fell on Gerald's tone-deaf ears. He proceeded as though I'd said nothing. "People would die to discover what I've learned. I'm telling you because I clarify my ideas when I talk them out. Besides, you're a contrast to a devious young man who interviewed me a month ago. He wanted to know all about my next writing project. I quickly figured out that he wanted to get the jump on my Max project. Before too many minutes elapsed, I kicked him out of my office. Aside from his awful dreadlocks, out-of-fashion Bob Marley shirt, and sunglasses in February, he was good-looking."

"Let me guess. You want me to be your smart, but silent minion?"

"No, more like my cabana boy—or as we might say in academia, my graduate assistant." He laughed way too hard.

As Gerald leaned back in the chair, two images flashed through my mind: my former major professor, Dr. Adamani, and my current rival, Dr. Gerald Strupp. In academia, both exercised their considerable power. But there the similarities ended. Even though my journey to value Dr. Adamani was painful, I eventually learned how much he cared for his profession and how he used it to draw forth the best in students. In contrast, Gerald's exertion of power left a broad path of destruction.

"Gerald, secrecy is necessary," I said. "I strictly observe confidentiality in my professional relationships." I didn't add that he and I weren't in that kind of relationship. After listening to informants' stories, I often felt deep sorrow because of what they'd suffered at the hands of their families. With Gerald, I felt intense sadness, not for him, but his parents.

Puffing out his skeletal chest as if ready to crow with delight, Gerald kept up his monologue. Eager to make a quick exit, I looked at my watch and attempted to interrupt him by holding up my hand. "Wow! You seem to have everything under control to make sure you complete this book."

He exhibited no clues that my summarization was a sign for him to stop. "I face two roadblocks. One is Harriet Galveston. She's aware of my biography plans and has been unrelenting in her attempts to stop me. She told Ruth that I was intent on destroying Max and all the people who knew him." He stretched out his arms as if he were being crucified. "In truth, I was flattered. I doubt Ruth will listen to her because she agrees that my biography will attract needed guests. Ruth's all about control, but the bottom line is she needs money—lots of it."

"I have to get going." I started to stand up.

"Wait. The second roadblock is William Farrell. I don't know what he'll propose at tomorrow's board meeting, but I'll deal with him."

Should I tell him William's dead? Spitefully, I decided to wait.

"Now get this, Ruth and I met a year ago. Within days, I got her permission to continue laying the groundwork for Max's biography. Receiving that good news, I felt so exhilarated that I looked around for something fun to do. Then, I remembered that Dr. S. Silverthorne, an unknown academic at an insignificant university, had written a caustic review of my latest biography—an unwarranted attack on my scholarship and me personally. By chance, an editor had recently sent me a prospectus of Silverthorne's first book to review. I skimmed it and wrote a scathing review. By crossing me, Silverthorne kissed goodbye the chances of success in a university."

My mind stopped wandering when I heard Gerald gloating over destroying a person's academic career. The taste in my mouth went sour. Up to that point, I'd been convinced he was egotistical; now, I realized he was vicious. My hands clenched involuntarily. My thoughts turned to ways I could protect myself.

"I love digging up secrets," he continued. "Either people shouldn't have them, or they should be more careful. People at Armadillo have lots of secrets. Max, Ruth, David, and William —all have secrets they'd like to keep buried. Too bad that's not going to happen."

"Maybe I shouldn't stay and have you learn my secrets," I said.

"You? You're an open book. If you possessed secrets, they'd be as prominent as...the nose on your face."

Gerald paused long enough to let me know that he meant my birthmark.

"Listen, Paul; I'm impressed with you. You'd be a great addition to the board of directors. I'll tell Ruth to invite you. If you're not a eunuch like David, Ruth's sure to value your presence—after all, you're a male."

"Gerald, I'm sorry to have to break the news to you, but Ruth's one step ahead of you. She's already invited me to join the board."

Gerald looked taken back but recovered rapidly. "Then, you'll be her fresh catch of the day, as long as you don't flounder." He snickered at his lousy pun, but it wasn't an amused laugh.

After his last put down, I'd had enough. "Gerald, you've been left in the dark. Last night, someone murdered William Farrell and ripped out his heart."

"What? Tell me everything!"

"I'd like to, but it will have to wait. I have somewhere important I have to be." In my mind's eye, I pictured Sandy as I hurried out of the library.

CHAPTER 13

Diego's Mustache

As Sandy and I walked to La Ruta, she said, "David claims that Diego's Mustache Café has the greatest coffee."

I conjured up familiar images of Diego Rivera, and in none of them was he wearing a mustache. "Are you sure he wasn't confusing Diego's Mustache with Frida's Eyebrow?" She flashed a courtesy smile.

We sat down and exchanged schooling information. I told how I'd spent my entire academic life at the University of Iowa. In turn, Sandy shared about her undergraduate years at UMass—Amherst, followed by two advanced degrees at the University of Texas. She was currently teaching at a private women's college in Texas, where she was an assistant professor in the archaeology department. Little wonder she was familiar with Max Eicher's work.

To order coffee, I practiced my high school Spanish. To my delight and amazement, the waiter delivered what I ordered. "Sandy, are there any other women staying at Armadillo whose first or last names begin with the letter *S*?"

"Now *that's* an interesting pick-up line! But since we're already together, you don't have to use it."

"No, seriously."

She thought for a while. "I believe I'm the only *S*."

"On David's tour this morning, I chanced upon William Farrell. Did you ever meet him?"

"At lunch yesterday, he introduced himself. A real creep."

"This morning, I found his body on a Maya stone altar outside the compound of Armadillo. Someone had removed his heart like the Maya did when they sacrificed people."

Sandy's face blanched. "Armadillo is already unnerving. What you said makes it terrifying! Do they know who killed him?" She turned her head away.

"No. At Ruth's insistence, I'm investigating who killed him. When I searched his room, I found his journal containing entries about past sexual conquests and ones he anticipated. In one entry, he wrote about S. If you want to know what he said, I can tell you exactly."

"I'm not eager to know but go ahead."

I recited the lines.

She rolled her eyes. "If women killed every man who thought like that, few men would be left." She paused as the waiter topped off our coffee. "You know a lot about Freud. Did he explain why men are such dolts?"

Her question reminded me of a gift I once heard about that appeared in a Neiman-Marcus Christmas catalog. A collapsible eleven-foot pole for things you wouldn't want to touch with a ten-foot pole. Right now, I wished I'd ordered one. Keeping quiet was my best course of action—so I did.

"Hey, I didn't say *you* were an idiot."

"Thanks."

Over the next hour, the waiter repeatedly topped off our coffee cups and asked if we were ready to order. On his fifth trip, I used my Spanish to order appetizers. Sandy rescued me when I ordered a whole cow. We laughed, but then followed the awkward conversational lull that occurs when people are becoming acquainted. Then out of nowhere, she asked, "What did you do during the Vietnam War?"

I felt my muscles tense, and I understood why she admired Ruth's forthrightness. Was Sandy asking if I'd avoided the draft, drawn a low lottery number, or received a deferment? Today was turning out to be my day to squirm. I readied myself. "I graduated from high school in '68. Vietnam was still claiming the lives of many Americans. That spring, James Earl Ray assassinated Martin Luther King, Jr., and race riots swept through hundreds of cities." Sandy's expression was unreadable. I paused to gulp down more coffee. "I had a Quaker upbringing; believing in nonviolence is in my blood. The day I graduated from high school, I filled out papers as a conscientious objector. To this day, I don't know why my draft board accepted me. They probably saw a photo of my face and decided not to scare the other recruits."

"Paul! That's a horrible thing to say about yourself."

"Yeah, I know. Anyway, I spent two years volunteering as a conscientious objector in a psychiatric ward before starting grad school." I was, less than three hours after meeting Sandy, telling about one of the most trying times in my life. I held my breath and hoped she wouldn't walk out on me.

She stared across the room, then closed her eyes and gasped. "My Ken took another route."

I braced myself for the worst.

"He and I met at UMass as sophomores. In the summer before our junior year, we got married."

Today isn't my lucky day.

"He was in ROTC and itching to serve. Despite my pleading with him not to enlist, he signed up halfway through his junior year. Half a year later, they sent him to Vietnam. A month after that, he arrived home in a flag-draped casket."

I carefully studied her face and saw signs of stress.

"You know how you never forget life-shattering dates? Mine is July 4, 1966. I stood beside a hole in the ground as they lowered Ken's casket into it. I spent my senior year as the grieving widow. Nobody supported our troops more than I did. I cursed Vietnam protesters as anti-American."

Gloom washed over me. We stood on opposite sides of a gorge with no bridge to unite us. A relationship I'd hoped for was suddenly impossible. While I regretted my forthrightness, I was secretly pleased with myself. I'd shared personal information about myself to a woman I wanted to know better.

Sandy lowered her voice. "Slowly, I let go of my grief and let the world back in. I watched Walter Cronkite on the CBS Evening News, and I saw the caskets coming home. Casket after casket after casket. Several years later, the final blow was that photo of a young Vietnamese girl running naked from her village after napalm had melted through her clothes and into her skin like jellied lava."

That sickening image flashed before my eyes; my body jerked back. I forced myself to listen to Sandy. "You've carried a heavy load."

She touched my arm. "Thanks. It's a burden I continue to bear. But I sense you've felt a lot of pain too. Am I right?"

Taken aback, I kept silent. I wanted to enjoy the company of a beautiful woman, not have her ask draining questions.

"Cat got your tongue? I don't get it. Half the time, you don't seem at ease around me. You won't like my asking, but I'm going to anyway. Are you straight or gay?"

"What!"

"Or did a horrible event scar you?"

"Jeez, we're out for a cup of coffee. Stop asking such personal questions!"

"No, I won't stop." She lifted her head and looked me in the eye. "Life's taught me to ask personal questions sooner rather than later. I lost a man I truly loved because I didn't challenge his joining the military. I refuse to get hurt again. I'm going to live life to the fullest. If you can't take my honesty, then let's stop being friends right now."

I released a long-held breath. "You asked if a horrible event scarred me? Look at my face? Who'd want to get close to this?" I dragged a finger across my patch of port-wine stained skin.

"Listen," she said loudly enough so that others in the restaurant turned to look. "Give me credit for looking deeper than the color of your skin. My Ken was African-American with darker skin than that." She pointed at my birthmark. "I don't care what color that is. It makes you unique. I'm willing to bet you don't have a clue how handsome you are." She stopped and blushed slightly. "Look, there's Black Power, Red Power, and Brown Power. Why not Birthmark Power?"

She was a beautiful woman, but I realized that she was so much more. "Let's call a truce. You're right that my birthmark scarred me. But in my defense, I'm working on accepting it. Less than a year ago, I couldn't say, 'my birthmark' or look at myself in a mirror. As to my sexuality, I like women all the way."

She winked. "It's in both of our best interests that you're straight."

Now it was my turn to blush. "You've been frank with me, so I'll be frank with you. Because of how I feel about my face, I've never been with a woman." *Shut up, Paul. She's going to think you've uttered yet another lousy pick-up line.*

"Who knows, this might be your lucky spring break."

The grin on my face was unrivaled by any other that I'd grinned before.

"To change the subject," she said, "there's something I don't get. You're here because you read *Maya Magic* and plan to write about Max. I loved the book too, but I'm here to relax— until you said there's a killer on the loose. You need to know that some critics discredit his book."

I relaxed. I could hold my own on academic topics; it was the personal ones I found unnerving. "You're right, the current thinking suggests *Maya Magic* was the product of a rich imagination heightened by mescaline, but in his book, Max vividly described various glyphs. And sure, scholars have attacked him for claiming he discovered them because he neither produced the glyphs nor provided any documentation. I've looked into this question and gathered some evidence that—"

"And now comes the good part?" she teased and leaned closer.

"In 1962, Ralph Ginzburg published four issues of *Eros* magazine. Attorney General Bobby Kennedy, Jack's brother, indicted him for violating federal anti-obscenity laws. But before being forced out of business, Ginzburg published erotic drawings purported to be from the ancient Maya featuring hand-colored pictures of couples making love in mind-blowing positions. The *Eros* article also—"

"Wait, let me guess. An adolescent, let's call him Paul, got his hands on that issue because he was tired of reading the literary stories in *Playboy*."

I raised my hand. "Please, no interruptions. In *Maya Magic*, Max made obscure allusions to pictures of Maya couples making love and undisclosed codices. Can I prove it? No. Only four authentic Maya codices are known to exist. If he found but one new codex, it could revolutionize Maya scholarship. Not only that, but Max's biography would be the crowning achievement of any scholar's career."

Sandy tightened her lips. "I hate to challenge your inspired hypothesis, but anyone—including Max—who discovered a codex would announce it, not hide it. Are you suggesting that he cryptically revealed his discovery in *Maya Magic* and did nothing with it during the last seventeen years of his life? If that's the case, either the codex is still around, or he destroyed it like the Spanish priests destroyed all but the few we know about."

"When you say it that way, it sounds like Max had a rich fantasy life."

"And I'm gently suggesting your imagination is rivaling his."

"Touché."

"But hear me out, Paul. If Max destroyed the codex, he's worse than the priests who thought they were rooting out a pagan religion and replacing it with God's word. Max should've known better. If he discovered and subsequently destroyed a single codex, he should receive The Millennium Vandal Award."

"I don't believe he destroyed it. I think he hid it somewhere in Armadillo."

"Hold on. You're assuming the drawings in *Eros* are real. But what if a talented graphic artist with a risqué imagination had a blast drawing them? Then he—or perhaps she—made a lot of money selling them as erotic art to a gullible Ginzburg. Hoaxes happen."

I wasn't ready to tell Sandy about Max's account in *Memoirs*.

But her doubts raised difficult questions. Did authentic, hand-colored drawings of Maya couples having sex even exist? If so, and Max and Kate took photos of themselves recreating them, where were they now? And how did Ginzburg in the early sixties obtain the drawings? I believed *Memoirs* was an authentic manuscript, but Sandy's logical analysis made a strong case for its fabrication.

CHAPTER 14

Prime Suspects

I started to Ruth's room to ask if Sandy could be my guest at the board's opening dinner. En route, I sighted Father Lester reading in a lounge chair. "Got a minute?" I asked him. "I'm collecting alibis for last night."

"Not a problem. I arrived yesterday around three and unpacked. Then I walked into La Ruta for a beer. William was in the bar and, as we Irish say, he was rat-arsed. He called me over and proceeded to tell me about his evening ahead filled with debauchery. I sized him up in two seconds and concluded I couldn't stand him. I like to savor my beer, but I downed it in record time and left.

"Last night at Armadillo, I relished one of the best meals I'd eaten in ages and met Harriet. She and I talked until ten. She's quite a Renaissance woman with depth in numerous fields. She also a zealous woman, but I shouldn't talk. My religion has also produced some doozies. Then I went to my room—alone."

"Who do you think killed William?"

"Harriet's the only one I know who had a motive. But given how worked up she was last night when we talked, I doubt she would've planned an elaborate sacrifice. She'd have picked up the closest blunt instrument and bludgeoned him to death."

"Thanks." *Damn! Now my mind had a second bloody image of heartless William.* "One last practical question. Would you preside over William's burial?

"I can't say it would be my pleasure, but I'll do it in the line of duty. Got a place in mind?"

"Behind the Maya sacrificial altar."

"An appropriate choice. I'll work with David to attend to the details."

"And I'll buy you a beer in La Ruta—one that you can drink at your leisure."

Once again, Ruth welcomed me into her lair with obvious come-on lines: "Make yourself comfortable. Would you like a drink? Tell me more about those Royal Canadian exercises you do." When I interrupted her and asked if Sandy could be my guest at the board's dinner, her words said yes, while her disgusted look screamed, "Hell no!"

I hurriedly left to find Sandy, who accepted my invitation. Walking back to my room, I felt like a lottery grand-prize winner. Once I was alone, I spread my arms and fell back onto my bed and thought of Sandy. I savored the joy of infatuation. But an irritating voice inside my head asked: *why in the world is she showing an interest in you?* I answered: Maybe my two-tone face intrigues her. My self-deprecating humor quieted the voice, and I tried to catch some shuteye. But the voice in my head morphed into gruesome images that flashed before my eyes. I saw flies feasting on William's butchered blue body, the jagged tears in his chest, the severed blood vessels, the bowl containing his heart.

Because my mind was wide awake, I turned my thoughts to possible murder suspects. Ruth and all five board members—David, Harriet, Gerald, Roland, and Father Lester—had opportunities to kill William. Doña María and possibly Sandy were also suspects.

Harriet seemed the most probable suspect because she believed William raped her. But I couldn't imagine that William, fearful of her intent, would have allowed her to bind his wrists and ankles, and lay naked on a sacrificial stone. He was a repulsive human being, but he wasn't out of his mind. Besides, Father Lester thought Harriet would have acted impulsively, not methodically.

Ruth was also a key suspect. But if William had plans to raise money for Armadillo, it didn't seem right that she'd kill him. Besides, Ruth and William had coexisted for thirty years. Why kill him now?

At this point, I barely knew Father Lester, but nothing conjured up the image of a knife-wielding priest. He said that he and Harriet talked until about ten, which gave them alibis—up until that time. But I didn't know when the murder had occurred.

As to David, if he was the murderer, then his performance of vomiting when he saw the sacrificed body was worthy of an Oscar. Besides, he struck me as the type more inclined to poison, not stab, his victim.

I'd formed an unsympathetic impression of Roland on David's tour, but that didn't make him a killer. When I questioned him, I'd have to curb my dislike and be more objective.

In stark contrast to David, Gerald possessed the ambition to stop anyone in his way. He as much as told me he viewed William as a threat in securing Ruth's approval for his biography of Max. With William dead, Gerald faced one less hurdle. Then a light bulb went on. Soon enough, Gerald would learn I was also writing Max's biography. Then I, too, would become an obstacle in his way.

As a descendant of the Maya people, Doña María knew of Maya sacrifices, and she'd access to an arsenal of kitchen knives. This morning William's dead body hadn't fazed her. She'd even carried away the ceremonial bowl bearing his heart. Perhaps this evening I should be wary of eating meat.

Finally, perhaps Sandy put on an excellent show in feigning not to know William, except in passing. She said that after their first meeting at lunch yesterday, she studiously avoided him, just like many other women. And finding someone disgusting was hardly a powerful motive for taking a life.

Besides finding the killer or killers, there was another mystery. What should I make of the gold armadillo pendant I'd pulled from William's mouth? My initial instinct at the murder scene was to tell no one about it, so I'd palmed it.

Now, I got to thinking. What was the meaning of the three dots on the backside of the pendant? Three dots in the Maya numeral system meant number three. In *Memoirs,* Max recounted how he gave a pendant to each of the women he loved and numbered the pendants by placing small raised Maya calendar dots on the reverse side of each.

Doña María received her pendant first—one dot. Ruth was given the second pendant with two raised dots. Kate Davis' pendant had three dots, and Maurine Madanes' had four. The three-dot pendant I found on William's body was Kate's. But Kate was here thirty years ago. How did her pendant, crammed into the dead man's mouth, appear at the crime scene? That didn't make sense.

I had a half-hour before the opening dinner. I showered and ran an electric razor over the stubble on my face. Since dinner promised to be more formal, I congratulated myself for having the forethought to pack a sports coat, pressed slacks, white shirt, and tie. Not that I ever wore them at the university—I preferred jeans and casual shirts. Despite my numerous attempts, the tie's length still looked like a seventh-grade boy's work—either too short or too long. I heaved a sigh, but then realized Sandy might assist me. *A good reason to visit her.*

She looked at my bungled effort and laughed. "If that's a half-Windsor, then you're the Duke, and I'm the Duchess."

"Please, I need help. I can't get the length right."

She untied my failed attempt. "Pay attention to what I'm doing." She brought the broader tip of the tie to the bottom of my crotch and allowed her hand to linger. "Like that."

"Yeah, I like that," I said.

"I thought you might. Now finish tying your tie."

I did, and the tie came out the correct length. I glanced in the mirror to judge my newly acquired tie skill. "Perfect. But I like it better when you help. The crotch technique works."

She winked at me in the mirror as she put on blood-red lipstick.

A minute later, I helped her with the small buttons on the back of her blouse. I fumbled with them but kept at it. "Never say I don't enjoy helping dress—or for that matter—undress a woman."

She waited until I finished fastening the last button and said, "And never say you've had much experience in either situation." At Diego's Mustache Café, I'd watched Sandy's face blanch. Now she watched as mine turned red.

CHAPTER 15

A Pair Of Champagne Coupes

We gathered at one end of the dining room table, which was lit by candelabras. Those in attendance wore the stylish clothes they'd packed for dining in a jungle setting. Vying for top honors were David, looking regal in his tux, and Sandy, mesmerizing in an outfit that had turned every head when she entered the room.

Reigning at the head of the table, Ruth picked up a fork and gently tapped her crystal champagne coupe. A pleasant tone reverberated through the room. She raised her glass. "I propose a toast, but you must excuse the size of the glasses—quite small. Queen Marie Antoinette, King Louis XVI's better half, used her breast size to determine the size of the glass. A mere A-cup. If the design had been mine, Doña María wouldn't be filling them as frequently." As if to illustrate her point, Ruth slowly inhaled as she arched her back.

Sandy lifted a napkin to her mouth. Out of the corner of my eye, I saw her pretending to stick her finger down her throat. I lingered between two competing impulses: laughing aloud at Sandy's miming or telling Ruth that the champagne story was a legend. But the timing was wrong for either. *What in the world was Ruth thinking?*

Ruth lifted her glass higher. "But I digress. We gather at Armadillo almost thirty years after Max's untimely death. May we forever hold his memory sacred. And let those who defile it be sacrificed in the way the ancient Maya taught us—with their hearts cut out."

Harriet's eyes and mouth flew open. Gerald's expression was deadpan except for a twitching eye, while Roland scowled at Ruth in disgust. Sandy and I looked at each other in disbelief. Perhaps, based on long experience with Ruth, David caught his breath and said, "Hear, hear." In muted voices, the rest of us repeated his words.

Father Lester leaned toward me and whispered, "Well, that was nothing if not a ghoulish narcissist toast." If Ruth heard him, she gave no notice.

"While Doña María and her assistants serve the first course," Ruth said, "I'll introduce each of you and explain why I invited each member to be on my board at this urgent time.

"I met Paul Seawright at noon, and I was impressed with his dedication and knowledge—and, I must admit—his striking appearance. He and I got along quite well, and therefore, I invited him to join the board." I noticed board members' faces tensing as if to keep their eyebrows from rising. All but Gerald nodded to acknowledge me. Ruth added that Sandy Martin was my guest. Gerald wrinkled his brow and stared at Sandy as if he were trying to solve a difficult problem.

I smiled as I observed the others seated at the table. Harriet, on my left, again exhibited a disquieting expression. I suspected she shared exasperation mixed with disgust as she speculated that Ruth was intent on reeling me in to be her latest bedtime companion. Gerald smirked and jotted down notes as if even small details might prove helpful in the future. David's face was expressionless. I speculated on Roland's pained look: was he reacting to Armadillo's spicy food, experiencing traveler's diarrhea, or realizing that his wool suit functioned as a hair shirt? Perhaps all three. Sandy, Father Lester, and I were the only ones who seemed to be enjoying ourselves.

Tapping her champagne glass again, Ruth said, "Paul's a bestselling author—"

"Me, too," Gerald said. "Three times to be exact." Ruth shot him a Medusa-like stare capable of turning him to stone; he ignored her.

Ruth turned and looked me up and down, licked her lips, and nodded as if confirming she'd made a delectable choice. "Next, I present David Budman. For years he's been my trusted confidant. He has an encyclopedic knowledge of this place. His photography, which you've admired on these walls, has always captured visitors' hearts. His oeuvre is a tribute to me, the co-founder of Armadillo. And because of David's artistry, my image will be forever immortalized."

I was stunned at how she twisted the facts. Max had built Armadillo several years before he met Ruth in Hollywood and brought her here as his bride. If Armadillo had a co-founder, it was young María. She'd revealed to Max the foundation of the Maya temple and helped him build Armadillo. Remembering I'd only read Max's version, I consciously relaxed so I could listen to how others understood events. It again occurred to me that *Max Eicher's Memoirs* might be unreliable as Ruth's and David's versions.

I popped back from my reflections in time to hear Ruth say, "David located the board members and arranged for their stay. I appreciate his efforts in bringing us together. And aren't his pictures the best?"

I leaned forward and struggled to hear David's soft-spoken answer, "My photographs say it all."

Gerald nudged him in the ribs. "Your photos hardly tell the whole story." Gerald's laugh, which sounded as if he were gargling, broke the room's silence. Ruth gave him a second withering look; order returned.

"Moving on, I introduce the notorious author, Dr. Gerald Strupp. He can, on occasion, wield a wicked pen. But he assures me that if I choose him to write Max's biography, he'll write a balanced one that will enshrine Armadillo in the hearts of readers."

Gerald's smile wasn't reassuring. "Thank you, Ruth. The world knows about Max's fifteen minutes of fame with *Maya*

Magic. But that's a misleading understanding of him. The public deserves to know the man behind the myth—a mortal with both character strengths and fatal flaws. I'll cooperate with everyone to ensure readers grasp the essence of the man." I listened to the fawning and ingratiating words of a man whose books had transformed archaeologists from famous to infamous.

Next, Ruth introduced Roland. "After nearly fifty years, Armadillo requires architectural restoration. I met dear Roland Westby, a renowned authority on the topic, several years ago, when he visited for the first time. Roland, I trust all aspects of this stay are exceeding your expectations. I'm doing my best to satisfy your every need." Roland's puckered face morphed into a giant red strawberry, and he lost his ability to respond.

Ruth surveyed the group and spotted Father Lester. "Max's deep Catholic faith inspired my choice for our next board member. I first met Father Lester Sheehan late yesterday afternoon when he arrived. I instantly recognized him as an impressive scholar who might access funding through the Church." She winked at him and added, "I hope I'm not responsible for corrupting your faith."

Father Lester gave a gracious smile. "Have no fear, Ruth. The only thing I can't resist at Armadillo is seconds of Doña María's mango pudding." Everyone smiled but Ruth.

"Next, we have Dr. Harriet Galveston. I invited Harriet to join us because she has impeccable credentials and has written extensively about the extraterrestrial beings that picked Max to help them write *Maya Magic*."

Harriet bowed gracefully. "I welcome the opportunity to contribute as a board member, knowing too many in the younger generation dismiss *Maya Magic* because they fail to appreciate its overpowering implications." She spread her arms. "While I'm here, I hope to educate everyone about the true meaning of *Maya Magic*."

Under his breath, Gerald said, "Crazy old bat."

"I heard that, Gerald," Harriet said, "but rest assured, I'll convert you from a snooty skeptic to a believer."

"That will be the day that I die," Gerald said.

I looked at him incredulously. *Careful what you wish for Gerald.*

"Boards need influential people," Ruth said. "Our board is no exception. The late William Farrell was a mover and shaker in the world of Mexican art. Before his passing, he'd consented to join us. In remembrance of him, I had David unearth a recent photo." Ruth motioned to Doña María, who'd been standing in the doorway. "Please bring it in."

To one side of Ruth's chair, Doña María placed an easel holding a rectangular object draped in black fabric. Ruth jerked the cloth away. "Behold, William Farrell." The man in the photograph wore a tropical-patterned shirt, opened down to reveal gray chest hair. His white linen sports coat and slacks presented a stark contrast to the shirt. His stomach looked as if he'd just sucked it in, while his leering eyes and nasty smirk sent a clear message to women: In my presence, you're not safe.

Harriet stood and rushed to the easel, drew back her arm, and drove her fist into William's face. She seized the damaged photo and tore it to pieces. "Any questions?" she asked. If strangers had suddenly walked into the dining room, they'd have thought they'd entered the ward of an asylum that housed catatonic patients. Harriet nodded her thanks to Doña María. *Father Lester was right—Harriet is impulsive.*

Ruth recovered first. "Doña María, please remove the easel and photo."

"Nobody told me he died," Roland said. "Was it a heart attack?"

Ruth, her voice lacking emotion, answered, "Yes, in the sense that his heart was attacked. He was murdered last night. Paul spotted his body on David's tour this morning. William must have defiled Max's memory because someone killed him in the manner of a Maya sacrifice."

Roland snatched up a napkin and held it in front of his mouth.

Gerald scowled at me because I'd withheld from him the details of William's death. I was pleased I had.

The room was silent, but I sensed the specter of death moving among us.

"Wait, I was on David's tour this morning," Roland blurted out. "Why didn't I see his body?"

"Because you left the group early," David said.

"So why was I the last to be told?"

Once again, Ruth tapped her champagne glass. "Roland, I was thinking of you. Men often find it more difficult to rise to the occasion if they're preoccupied."

I looked over at Sandy, who had pursed her lips to avoid laughing aloud. I felt peeved. While Ruth's sexual advances had bothered me, I was distraught that she considered both Roland and me to be equally desirable, even with my birthmark. If she was attracted to Roland, she possessed absolutely no taste.

I roused from my reflections to hear Ruth say, "Because we have no law enforcement in La Ruta, Paul has accepted my invitation to investigate William's death. Please cooperate with him."

I glanced around the table and saw all eyes on me. I thought fast. "As far as I'm aware, William was despised, hated, and feared. You may legitimately ask, why investigate his death? Why try to solve a murder that seems almost justified?"

"Good point," Gerald said. "I agree."

"Because murder is wrong, regardless of who the victim is. Taking a life tears apart a community by destroying trust. If killing a hated person becomes acceptable, then no one is safe because everyone will be hated by someone at some point in life."

Sandy clapped; Harriet and David joined in. The others waited for me to continue.

"Over the next twenty-four hours, I'll interview those of you staying at Armadillo. Any questions?"

"Was it a real Maya sacrifice?" Harriet blurted out.

"Most authentic. William was lying on his back, stretched out on the sacrificial stone. His nude body was painted blue—

his wrists and ankles bound with ropes. His lower chest was cut open. A ceremonial bowl contained his heart."

"Any scorched ground near the stone to indicate a spacecraft may have landed?" Harriet asked.

"Excuse me, Harriet," Gerald said. "I have an important question for Mr. Sherlock Holmes. Found any important clues?" Gerald's expression was smug.

What a royal pain in the ass. "I found some, but for now, I'm not saying what they were."

"Are you assuming the murderer is one of us?" David asked.

"Yes, everyone at Armadillo is a suspect. No one is to leave during the next twenty-four hours."

"That's not possible, anyway," David added. "Before dinner, I was on the phone with a friend in San Cristóbal. He said heavier rains are on the way. During our conversation, the line went dead."

Ruth motioned to Doña María. "You may serve dinner now."

We were served fresh, natural food cooked to perfection. But one thought spoiled the occasion: the image in our minds of an unknown killer who had ripped out the heart of a man in isolated Armadillo. At the meal's conclusion, I surveyed the table. Ample portions of Doña María's scrumptious food remained.

Once again, Ruth tapped her champagne coupe. "Tonight, we have a unique program. As you are aware, Dr. Paul Seawright is a famous author. I've asked him to give a brief reading from his bestseller, *Freud.*"

A voice that sounded like a petulant child snapped, "Why didn't you ask me? I've written more books than he has."

While looking up at the ornate chandelier brimming with flickering candles, Ruth said, "You're right, Gerald." She motioned for me to begin.

As I stood to speak, I reflected on this opening dinner. Those present had barely talked to each other, and when they did, the conversations were stilted. The infrequent smiles conveyed no warmth. That afternoon, I'd chosen some passages that now seemed inappropriately upbeat—as if Freud's writings induced hopefulness. Aware of the group's somber mood, I flipped through my book and picked passages that emphasized the importance of the unconscious mind.

When I finished reading, Gerald raised his hand. "Thanks for sharing Freud's bizarre mythology. You could as easily have read excerpts from *Grimms' Fairy Tales* to illustrate how evil lurks in the hearts of man—or, ladies, should I say humankind? When are you going to face the fact that nobody cares if William is dead?"

I readied a harsh response, but once again, I heard tapping on a champagne glass. Ruth flashed Gerald a disdainful smile. "We'll convene in the library at ten o'clock tomorrow morning. As usual, breakfast is available between seven and nine-thirty. And because Paul's remarks provide us with much food for thought, please give him a round of applause." Sandy clapped, but the others, having their fill of Gerald—and perhaps me—had begun hurrying to their rooms.

"I've attended eccentric dinner parties," Sandy said as we stood in the corridor, "but this one tops them all."

"Thanks for your applause."

"When dealing with Gerald, people need all the support they can get. I have a suggestion for your talk. Given there's a killer on the loose, next time pick someone a bit cheerier than Freud."

"It's the only book I've written. Any plans for the rest of the evening?" I wanted her to say she didn't have plans.

"Yeah, but sorry, not with you," she said. "I'm heading to the library to look at Max's collection of books."

"I can make you a better offer."

"I'm sure you could, but I don't want to join you searching for William's killer. I'm looking for clues to where Max hid the source material for *Maya Magic*."

"I'm sure Ruth has already ransacked Armadillo looking for his papers." I surprised myself when my reply sounded irritated. Why had I said that to her? I knew both *Maya Magic* and *Memoirs* dropped all sorts of hints about understanding the Maya. Sandy had chosen to look for Max's source material over being with me. *Calm down, Paul.*

She gave me a fleeting kiss. "Today was lots of fun. See you at breakfast tomorrow."

"I'll walk you to the library."

"I'm a big girl now. Besides, I'm trained in Kung Fu to strike with lightning speed."

"Should I be wary in your presence?"

"Not if you're half as sharp as I think you are."

Sandy had a way of vacillating between encouraging and discouraging me. When I was with her, I often felt disoriented. It reminded me of the Silly Silo ride at Adventureland in Des Moines five years ago. I'd walked inside and stood against the cylindrical wall. The whole contraption spun around faster and faster until it reached high speed, and the floor fell away from my feet. But instead of dropping into an abyss, centrifugal force pinned me to the wall, even as my stomach went into free fall, and my brain felt scrambled. After what seemed like a lifetime, the floor returned, and the Silly Silo slowed to a stop. I felt dizzy as I stumbled out. The difference is that the Sandy ride I'm on right now isn't slowing down, and I can't feel anything substantial beneath my feet.

CHAPTER 16

A Limerick

On the way to my room, I caught up with Roland. "I'm investigating William's death. Got time for a few questions?"

"Sure, anything to get that bizarre dinner out of my mind."

"How well did you know William?"

"I arrived early yesterday afternoon and never met him. He wasn't at last night's meal."

"Where were you after dinner?"

"After a fatiguing two days of travel, I was in my room and asleep by nine."

"Any thoughts about who might have murdered him?"

"That's the frightening part. Armadillo is in the middle of nowhere, so I assume his killer is someone staying here. I'm bolting my door tonight."

"Did you hear any unusual noises last night?

"Not me. I have trouble sleeping, so I always take a sleeping pill and wear earplugs."

I thanked him for his time. I took a different route to my room and wandered down a long corridor. Six of David's photos that I'd never seen lined one wall. Because heat, humidity, and bugs had defaced the frames, I expected dust and grime to cover the glass. In the faint light, I saw I was wrong. I could see vivid details through the spot-free glass. David, or perhaps Doña María, wanted visitors to appreciate the photos, and someone had made sure that people could see them.

The photos captured the defining features of Casa Armadillo. In each, David captured Max's personal stamp on Armadillo's foreboding architecture. He also caught the influence of complex Maya elements as they cast ominous shadows. When I stepped back, I saw how the photos alternated with rusted wrought iron roof crosses, which also hung on the walls. Death lingered at Armadillo.

I continued to wander down the corridors, pleasurable fantasies with Sandy occupying my mind. Lost in reverie, I found myself standing outside Ruth's door, taking a second look at David's erotic photo. Quietly stepping forward to see it more closely, I heard voices from inside.

"Dazzling jewelry you wore this evening." I recognized Gerald's ingratiating style. "The stones match the intensity of your eyes."

Staying in shadows, I moved closer to an open window.

"Balderdash!" Ruth said. "If you'd been the snake in the Garden of Eden, Eve wouldn't have eaten just one apple; she'd have ordered a bushel."

"Ah, but if Eve possessed your body, within days, Adam would have died of exhaustion."

"You're extremely clever with words, but the most you'll ever know about my body is that it's unattainable."

He gave a harsh laugh. "Those Hollywood casting directors in the early thirties recognized you as a real beauty."

I struggled between laughing and gagging. Ruth was correct; he possessed the gift of gab.

"But Ruth, I know more about your body than you suspect."

I kept in the shadows as I peered into the room. I couldn't see Gerald's face, but I occasionally caught glimpses of her face with its heavy makeup. Given Gerald's confrontation, she couldn't help but be livid.

"How did—"

"How do I know? As a methodical scholar, I've searched for the untold story about Max and the people around him. I asked myself: Who might shed light on how a young woman from a grease spot on a Kansas map arrived in Hollywood and succeeded in winning the heart of its most eligible bachelor? My persistence paid off. I located Ernie Bowben, a former casting director. Remember him? No? Well, he remembered you. Alas, Ernie was living out his final days in a Beverly Hills rest home. Bored out of his mind, he seemed eager to reminisce.

"I told him I was writing a book on actresses of the thirties —not the most famous ones, but ones who were memorable. I asked if he remembered the actress Ruth Kelly.

"For a long time, he sat there without responding. I thought Ernie had died. Then he suddenly said, 'You mean Lollipop?' He saw my puzzled look and added, 'That was a running joke among the fellows who ran the studio. Lollipop was short for an all-day sucker. Get it?'

"I laughed for his sake, but I still hadn't caught his meaning. Then Ernie said that a witty fellow composed a limerick about you and asked if I'd like to hear it. Of course, I agreed.

'There once was a woman named Ruth,
Who set up a faux kissing booth.
Her hot oral action
Gave men satisfaction,
'cept Dick, who got snagged on her tooth.'"

"You scumbag!" My head jerked back as Ruth's piercing words echoed down the corridor.

"Relax, Ruth. It's an ode to your sexual prowess. Old Ernie started laughing and slapping his thighs, and then he started coughing and gasping for breath. An attendant poked her head into the room and wagged a finger at me, 'Don't you go getting Ernie too excited, or we'll have a dead man on our hands.'

"Between gales of laughter, Ernie said, 'Yep! I'll be checking out with a smile—and a stiffy.'"

Ruth screamed, "You're a pervert!"

I half expected that a lamp or an ashtray might fly and crash into one of her many photos hung on the walls.

"But I digress," Gerald said, "Oral history is one thing—excuse my lame joke—but I'm a historian, I seek evidence to verify people's words. After Ernie stepped back from death's door, he astonished me with another revelation.

"'Reciting that limerick reminds me, there's a drawing of Lollipop in that trunk over there.' He maneuvered his wheelchair to the trunk. After an eternity of rummaging, he cried out like a prospector striking gold, 'It's here! Hope you aren't a prude, but I'm guessing you're not.'

"He handed me a drawing in an Art Deco-style. As to its artistic value, the late William Farrell would have been a better judge. The drawing showed a nude woman performing a sexual act as she kneels in front of a fully aroused man. The artist discretely conceals the couple's identity: the woman's hair sweeps across her face, and he turns away."

"Thanks for the bawdy story, Gerald, but a drawing proves nothing. Now pack your bags and slither home. And forget about writing Max's biography."

"You want proof? Perhaps you've forgotten your message on the drawing, which is in your authenticated handwriting. You wrote, 'Ernie, saying I love you is orally satisfying. Ruth W.'"

"You stole a drawing from a dying man?"

"I said, 'Ernie, that drawing says a great deal about the golden era of Hollywood. May I buy it.' Now get this, he said, 'You take it because it doesn't do anything for me anymore. After I'm dead, my granddaughter will think it's one of grandpa's filthy pictures, and she'll pitch it. It's yours.' I remember thinking that his offer was hard to refuse, sort of like a Lollipop."

As Gerald and Ruth talked, I occasionally saw her pace back and forth in front of the window. I could clearly understand them because their words were loud and distinct.

"Want to hear my second piece of evidence? Gerald asked. "Probably not, but I'm telling you, so you'll know I mean business. Last year, I talked a lot with David. Please be assured, he idolized you and didn't betray you—intentionally. I asked if he'd show me your photos. He proved to be a kind man if one can call him a man."

"What's your point, blackmailer?"

"Patience, patience. David's shot thousands of pictures of you. He proudly showed the ones that made you famous and the ones that the public has never seen. I spent hours digging through photos looking for clues to your identity. Finally, I found the smoking gun. In one photo, you've struck a pose by leaning forward and touching a Maya stone stela. You balance on one leg, and your other leg is stretched back, exposing your lower calf, which your long, signature skirt no longer covers. I observed a shaded area. At first, I thought it a small birthmark—not like that hideous one covering half of Paul's face."

Hearing Gerald's words, I felt the same icy anger that some murderers must experience. I slowed my breath until I felt my body begin to relax.

"Upon closer inspection," Gerald said, "the birthmark appeared to be a tattoo, but its image was still indistinct. I caught up with David later. 'Do you still have the negatives of the photos you showed me?' He told me they were filed by year and then by location.

"To disguise my intent, I said I'd like to see enlargements of several photographs featuring stelae. The next day, he gave me 8x10s of all the photos I'd requested. Using his powerful magnifying glass, I studied them and discovered an intriguing tattoo."

"Pure fabrication."

"I discovered what you deliberately cover up every day when you get dressed: a four-inch tattoo on your calf of a nude woman drawn in an Art Deco-style. She's kneeling, her back is arched, and her mouth is open. The tattoo leaves out the man, but it's a perfect match for Ernie's drawing. You're the woman in the drawing, and your tattoo is a delightful likeness of your Hollywood body."

"You deranged extortionist! The words coming out of your mouth are pure filth."

I inched closer to the window.

"Don't worry about what's coming out of my mouth. Worry about what went into yours. But I can be persuaded not to include the drawing and photo in my book. While my biography of Max might be less than flattering, I want your approval because your endorsement will ensure better sales."

"You're an egotistical swine! You'll die for this!"

"Ruth, you'll cooperate because you have no choice."

While Ruth let out a stream of vindictiveness, I heard footsteps approach the door. I ducked down behind a large earthenware pot. Gerald was so absorbed in whistling the Rolling Stones' song "Sympathy for the Devil" that he didn't spot me. I waited a minute before standing up. I figured Ruth would kill Gerald, or he'd kill her. Who would be the killer, and who the victim? In my mind, it was a toss-up.

I mulled my options. Did I want to write about Max if it meant warfare with Gerald, a heartless competitor? But to honor Neumann's wishes and protect Max's reputation, I was the one compelled to write it, come hell or Gerald Strupp. I laughed. The two options were the same.

CHAPTER 17

A Nightmare Of A Nightmare

I bolted upright, struggling to breathe. The room's blackness provided no relief from a nightmare that left me in a cold sweat, exhausted. I switched on the nightstand lamp and saw it was only three o'clock. I struggled to ground myself by placing my feet on the tile floor—a bad idea. Now I suffered from exhaustion, cold sweat, and frozen feet. I turned on the bathroom faucet and prayed that it would soon release hot water to wash my face. After a long minute, I conceded defeat.

Three hours later, the sounds of the Maya jungle coming to life awakened me far too early. Back in Iowa City, I ritualistically start each day by bounding out of bed and doing my exercises. While my recent experience with the cold tiles helped center me and diminish the impact of a nightmare, the thought of getting down on the tiles in the half-light of the early morning to do push-ups and sit-ups chilled me to the bone.

I dressed and followed my flashlight beam along the sheltered corridor to the back courtyard. The thick door reassured me that no killer would enter Armadillo unless the killer were already inside. I slid the bar aside and started down the narrow footpath that we'd taken to visit Max's grave. Trees wrapped with thick vines seemed to reach toward me. The path would have been frightening even at night, but I told myself that dawn had broken. Yet, dense vegetation blocked the sunrise. At the fork, I veered right.

I sat on the wooden bench near Max's grave and wondered why I was at Armadillo. I'd come to write a biography, but now I was investigating a murder. So far, I hadn't learned much about Max. *Strike one.*

I had met Sandy, a woman I enjoyed a lot, but some of the others, except Father Lester, were a strange lot. And like the people in Iowa City, they stared at me. In Ruth and Gerald's presence, my guard went up as if they were paid assassins on my trail. *Strike two.*

Armadillo added William's Maya-style sacrifice to the mix, and I was the one who cared about who murdered him. *Strike three. So what in the hell was I doing at Armadillo?* From Max's grave, I heard dead silence.

I stood in the corridor and waited for the dining room to open. While I was hungry for Doña María's breakfast, if I pressed myself for an honest answer, I was eager to see Sandy. When a helper opened the dining room, I took a chair, and the food began to arrive. Two women in their thirties served me a tall glass of fresh guava juice and a steaming cup of *café con leche,* followed by a plate piled high with huevos rancheros and mounds of black beans. Despite lingering unease about last night's nightmare, I ate heartily.

When Sandy arrived, we beamed at each other as though beaming was the latest craze. She scrutinized me. "I hate to say this, but you look like you have a hangover. A few too many nightcaps after I left you?"

"Not nightcaps. A nightmare. I was awake at three, and at that hour, it's bitter cold. Only glowing embers remained in the fireplace."

"Same in my room. I was freezing, but I didn't want to walk across the cold floor to get another blanket. I'll ask Doña María if she can find a larger rug for my room."

I cleared my throat as if to make an announcement. "There must be a better solution than building a gigantic fire at bedtime."

"I'm sure we'll think of one." The way she spoke those words sounded promising.

"By the way, Sandy, I never commented on your skills as an escape artist. Yesterday afternoon you slipped into your room to evade Gerald as if he carried the plague."

"If you've read his books, you'd understand."

"I read one and skimmed the other. Both were bloody hatchet jobs on two revered archaeologists."

She winced. "When you write Max's biography, you're not going to trash his life, are you?"

"Perhaps if it would sell more books." A scowl crossed her face. I quickly added, "Just kidding!"

Ruth sat at the other end of our table. We both noticed she was smiling at me. "If I'm not mistaken," Sandy whispered, "Ruth has bedroom eyes for you."

"You mean the woman wearing a blouse only half-buttoned and exposing a black, lace bra?"

"Congratulations, your eyes are finally open." She laughed.

"Yesterday, before lunch," I said, "I briefly met Harriet Galveston, the woman to Ruth's right. Have you talked to her yet?"

"I'm not sure why, but since I arrived, she's given me the cold shoulder." Sandy placed her hand on mine. "She seems a bit eccentric."

I leaned closer and whispered, "Of the other women in this room, not one holds a candle to you."

"You're just saying that...but keep it up."

The servers continued delivering plates laden with savory food. I noticed Harriet ate half her breakfast, while Ruth slowly picked at hers. Gerald hadn't yet appeared.

"Willing to listen to my nightmare from last night?" I asked. Sandy didn't seem too eager, but I needed to tell someone. "Images from last night's dream—and yes, they were of Gerald— keep flashing in my mind, and I couldn't stop them. I felt rage, followed by a sense of powerlessness to shield myself from his deadly attacks."

Sandy grinned. "Perhaps the dream is your unconscious saying that your new-found friend is an evil man."

Impulsively, I shouted, "Gerald's not my friend!" Ruth and Harriet looked up. "Sorry, a bit of a misunderstanding." I turned back to Sandy, who sat wide-eyed. "The nightmare has me spooked. But you're right; there's a message there."

"Tell me the dream so we can move on."

"Thanks," I said, keeping my voice low. "I was Gerald's therapist—which was bad enough. He was a vengeful, sadistic client, intent on destroying me. I was at the top of my game, yet he met my therapeutic moves with brilliant counterthrusts. At one point, I diagnosed him as a heartless personality—a diagnostic category I invented."

"That's also an apt label for William."

I laughed. I could relate to Sandy's sense of humor. "Then Gerald wrote a biography entitled, *Paul Seawright: Psychological Pervert.* His book rose to the top of the bestseller lists, even as *Freud* sank. Gerald's lies persuaded my straight male clients that I was trying to seduce them and my gay clients that I was rabidly homophobic. He convinced my female clients that I sexually assaulted women, and it was a matter of time before they were my next victims. Ultimately, he convinced the parents of the children I saw in my practice that I showed their kids pornographic photos and exposed myself. By the time I woke up, Gerald had shattered my reputation, and I faced life imprisonment."

Sandy reached under the table and took my hand. We finished breakfast in silence. I tried to relax using a simple breathing exercise. The best relief I received was Gerald not showing up.

While a server poured my last cup of coffee, I asked her, "Is Doña María here this morning?"

"She's in the kitchen, señor."

"Sandy, I want to talk to her about Max. She's known him forever. But first, I'll walk back with you to pick up my pen and notebook."

As we neared our rooms, I heard Gerald call my name. I'd be seeing enough of him at the board meeting in several hours; I kept walking. Gerald finally caught up.

"See you soon," Sandy said and walked away. Over her shoulder, she added, "I'll be snooping around for clues. If I discover insights into our mystery man, I'll let you know."

Gerald reached for my arm, but I stepped to the side, and he grabbed air. "As a close observer of human behavior," he said, "you're going to enjoy seeing a superb display of psychological warfare at our board meeting."

"Perhaps I shouldn't go. Might be too bloody for me, metaphorically speaking." My sarcasm was tart, but he missed it. How could he have no sense of humor? I retrieved my pen and notebook and headed to the kitchen. According to Max's *Memoirs*, Doña María held the keys to understanding this place. If anyone, she could shed light on his life. I felt the warmth of the morning sun, but the image in my mind of the naked, blue-painted body made me shiver.

CHAPTER 18

An Excerpt From Max Eicher's Memoirs:
María And Casa Armadillo

*I*n 1925, I received my doctorate in archaeology. But feeling exhausted after I graduated, I drifted into a life-draining job selling State Farm insurance for my dad's company in Dubuque. On June 28, 1927, a drunk driver killed my parents when he ran their Pontiac Coupe off a narrow road and down a steep embankment. My parents died on impact. After that accident, I never touched a drop of alcohol.

Dad practiced what he preached: always have more life insurance than you'll ever think you need. Their $100,000 policy named me the sole beneficiary. I requested the compensation be paid in two ways: some in cash, and the bulk of the settlement in gold bullion bars. True to my propensity for secrecy and hiding, which incidentally are essential magician's skills, I buried the bars in four locations near the family home.

With no plan in mind, I quit my job in Dubuque and drifted south, eventually arriving at the Maya ruins of Palenque. Despite my sterling credentials, the archaeology community—exclusively from Tulane University—was deeply suspicious of a Yale man. I soon grew weary of Palenque's archaeologists, but not of Maya ruins. I wandered farther into the vast tree-covered countryside. I needed time to figure out what to do with the rest of my life—as though life acquiesces to our plans.

Far off the beaten track, I chanced upon the small village of La

Ruta, the route. It was located on dirt roads a considerable distance from both Palenque and San Cristóbal de las Casas. Little did I foresee that I would soon meet the first of four women destined to be my loves, albeit in very different ways, and who would powerfully influence my life. Had I known then, ah, but hindsight is always exceedingly accurate.

As I explored La Ruta, looking for a place to stay, I quickly found that the current inhabitants, descendants of the Maya, spoke little Spanish. To make myself understood, I drew pictures and offered money. My stick-figure drawings conveyed my need for a place to eat and sleep; however, I credit my offer of Mexican pesos with clinching the deal.

One family offered me room and board; we ate our meals together. They were generous and accepted me. Time slowed. I settled into a routine of reading those books I had neglected during my formal schooling and immersing myself for hours in the ancestral languages of the Maya.

My new family consisted of a father, a mother, and María, their eleven-year-old daughter. She crowned her round chocolate face with braided, black hair and carried herself with dignity. During my years at Yale, I had never encountered a face that radiated such intelligence and curiosity. Often in her presence, I felt dull-witted. Her station in life assigned her to grind the family's corn by hand, make tortillas, and keep the house clean. To amuse herself, she talked with me for hours on end.

I listened and repeated the phrases of the Maya dialect that I was determined to learn. After a year, my ability to converse with the locals had gained me a measure of respect. While I possessed an ear for language, María was also a quick study. She learned English, much faster than I learned La Ruta's vernacular, and yet she was the most patient human being I had ever met. She stood at my side as I bargained with the market women, talked with La Ruta's men, and fell in love with being where I was.

A year after I arrived in La Ruta, María and I were shopping in the market. She picked up a small gold pendant shaped like an armadillo. Her eyes and smile told me that she loved it. Practicing my new fluency, I bargained, bought it, and gave it to her in gratitude for all she had taught me. She thanked me profusely and told me the armadillo was her favorite animal because it protected her. When I asked her to explain, she motioned me to follow.

We walked past garden plots where plants clawed their way upward around stones and clumps of sod in their search for light. She led me to the northern edge of La Ruta, where signs of human activity tapered out, and the jungle reigned. Approximately a quarter-mile beyond the last house, she stopped and pointed ahead. I saw nothing but ever-encroaching flora. "This way," she said. Fifty feet more and I ran into a twelve-foot slab of vegetation that rose from the decaying leaves carpeting the jungle floor. As I fell, I cried out, "What the hell?"

By now, María knew enough English to utter an embarrassed laugh. She picked at the moss and vines covering the slab. "Here, use my knife," I said. In a couple of minutes, she reached a stone surface. María ran back home to get another knife. We spend a half-hour removing several square inches of moss and vines. Staring back at us was a Maya glyph of a magnificently carved face. An hour later, we had uncovered two more glyphs. Never in my training as an archaeologist had I been more awestruck.

My discovery—no, that's not right—María's gift marked a momentous milestone in my life. It took us two weeks to remove all the vegetation from the stone that I'd recognized as a Maya stela. Standing in front of us was my contribution to archaeology. María saw I was ecstatic. After I spent two months deciphering the glyphs, I realize that her gift promised to revolutionize archaeology's understanding of the Maya.

One afternoon when the earth was still moist from the midday rains, we walked silently to the stela. "You gave me the English language as a present," she said, "and now I want to repay you with another gift." I protested that she had already given me a majestic stela.

She pointed to an earthen mound in front of us, stretching in both directions. I confess I had been so focused on the stela that I hadn't noticed the obvious. "In the ground below our feet is a big building," she said. "Dig in the earth to receive your present."

I heard her words, but they didn't make sense. All I saw was the *undergrowth covering everything. Recognizing my puzzled look, she said, "Okay. Now I will draw you a picture." She knelt and used twigs to make two stick figures—the smaller one represented her, and a larger one represented me. "Watch me." She placed a long stick under the feet of the figures. With more twigs, she constructed a sizable inverted isosceles triangle beneath the stick people, who stood on its base. I squatted and stared at her drawing. She repeated her words, "Dig in the earth to receive my present."*

"María, it looks like a Maya temple, but it's upside down and underground."

She took a deep breath, grabbed my hand, and pulled me toward the mound. We stopped at a point where the vegetation gripped a four-foot-high wall. I saw now that we were looking at the sides of a squat butte with a flat summit. Still holding my hand, she led me along the base of a wall until it turned at a right angle. We followed the wall, and she steered me about 150 feet. Twice more we made right-angled turns, at which point we were back at the stela.

"I can't believe it!" I said. "It's the base of a Maya temple. Did the Maya or later generations take away the top?"

María was frustrated beyond belief, but she persisted. "Señor Max, you're not paying attention." She picked up a stick and knelt beside the triangle she had drawn earlier. She dug a small hole at its apex, the farthest point from the stick people, placed her armadillo pendant into the hole, and covered it with dirt. Then she spoke words that were to change my life. She pointed at the covered-up hole and said, "The church of the Armadillo."

With those words, she quite literally turned upside down the Maya world I knew. She was showing me the site of a Maya temple dedicated to the armadillo. However, this one was inverted and burrowed deep into the ground in contrast to all other known temples. Our walk had taken us around the perimeter of the foundation. There was no above-ground part except those stones, which formed the walls. If there were archaeological treasures, they were buried at some depth.

"Now, I understand. You have given me a secret Maya temple where they worshiped the armadillo."

"It is not a temple. It is the tomb of a great Maya king who wor-

shipped the armadillo. Because I want to thank you, his tomb is a present for you, my teacher. This secret is for you." María sternly said, "Tell no one, or I will cut out your heart."

I leaped back, and she laughed. "I was joking about cutting out your heart."

"I promise I will tell no one."

"My father and his father and his father and his father have told the story of a gold armadillo in the ground. Now you know the story."

I looked again at the vegetation-encrusted stones. They covered more than 20,000 square feet. What did I know about armadillos? Only that they were scaly, nocturnal, burrowing animals. Was there any truth to María's story? Was I about to go on a wild goose chase after an archaeological Holy Grail based on the story of a young girl for whom I had bought a gold pendant? Could a Maya temple house a tomb head down rather than up?

Then I knew. María, an intelligent and thoughtful young girl, was repaying me with a gift she thought I would love. "Now, I get it. You want me to dig here."

Her smile was a mixture of warmth from her heart for a friend and a slight smirk of exasperation at how dense her friend could be.

Long into that night, I stayed awake. Even as I experienced absolute ecstasy at the possible discovery, panic gripped me that others would deprive me of María's gift. The archaeologist Frans Blom and his colleagues who were systematically exploring the Chiapas region might happen upon my site before I had completed my excavations and made my discoveries. I must prevent others from finding it.

I drifted into dreams filled with tunnels burrowing through stones of maze-like complexity. In one dream, I build a wooden room that rested on the flat-topped butte. When I entered the room, I dug to find the entrance to the inverted pyramid. That dream gave me the answer.

As the dream instructed me, I built a wooden stairway to the top of the stone platform. There I constructed a sizable but lightweight room on a base of balsa wood beams. The shop was so flimsy I could drag it from one area to another with the help of a mule. The resi-

dents of La Ruta saw my little room and thought I was nuts. They soon quit dropping by.

During the following weeks, I relied on the dense jungle to temporarily hide the stela from rival archaeologists' prying eyes.

I systematically explored for possible foundation openings to the burial chamber. Two weeks into my digging, I located an entrance. It was the first, but far from the last, of maddening false starts. Daily, I prayed I might unearth an opening to a burial chamber. Day after day and week after week, the tomb concealed its entryway. A month from the start of digging, I had inspected half of the stone foundation and unearthed four entrances—all dead ends. Was I discouraged? Yes. Days passed slowly. My prayers sounded like curses.

My dream on the thirty-ninth night was no longer of tunnels. Instead, I dreamed about a Maya shaman who conducted a sacred ceremony connecting the heavens, earth, man, and the underworld. The shaman pointed to the foundation and asked, "How do you hide something in plain sight?"

I replied, "You make it appear, like my room, to be something else— the room of a crazy man."

"You have learned well," the shaman answered. "And when is an inverted tomb's foundation not an inverted tomb's foundation?"

In my dream, I immediately answered, "When it is the foundation of my home that I will call Armadillo."

"Armadillo?" he asked, a puzzling look on his face. "A curious choice."

"The Maya built many temples," I said, "but the ones we see soar toward the sky. The tomb I seek is deep in the earth. Why do the descendants of the Maya sell gold armadillo pendants in the market? Because the armadillo is a part of their cosmology, associated with earth, fertility, and sacrifice. In homage to the armadillo, the Maya built this tomb into the ground. I will call my home Armadillo in homage to the ancient Maya. My home will be an outward and visible sign of an inward and spiritual place."

The shaman of my dream moved his hands over my head as if conferring a blessing. "You are not of the Maya, but you do us great honor. You will find what you seek. Build and live in Armadillo."

The next morning, the fortieth day of searching, I found what I sought—the tomb's entrance. The reader of my memories may think me mad, but before exploring the tomb, I took the time to build Casa de Armadillo.

CHAPTER 19

A Penny Jar

From the kitchen doorway, I watched Doña María prepare lunch. Her dark brown eyes, high cheekbones, and a large nose with a pronounced beak gave her the appearance of having stepped forth from a ninth-century Maya community. Gripping a heavy knife, she methodically raised her arm slowly, and then swiftly brought it down. She repeated this until she'd reduced the scrawny chicken to pieces.

I greeted her, and she rested the knife on the counter. "Doña María, the meals you prepare are delicious." I glanced around to see if any organ meat—like a human heart—was being prepared.

She offered me a faint smile.

"I'm writing a book about Max. Would you answer some of my questions?"

The sparkle in her eyes vanished. *Have I inadvertently released evil spirits in her presence?* Doña María squinted at me. "Dr. Gerald wanted me to talk about Max. I told him nothing because I do not trust him. Why should I trust you?"

She had a point. "I recently met Mr. Theodore Neumann. He writes scripts for Hollywood movies. He told me to come here, and to keep the memory of Max safe."

She crossed herself and murmured, "May Max rest in peace."

"He gave me a signed copy of Max's *Maya Magic*, but more importantly, he gave me a manuscript that Max wrote about himself. In the manuscript, he told stories about Armadillo and the people here."

"Movies tell many lies. Maybe Mr. Neumann also does."

"Please, may we talk?"

She placed her finger to her lips, then turned to a woman helping her. "Flora," she said, "Hasta pronto."

I followed Doña María down a back corridor, and into the third courtyard near Armadillo's back door. She led me to a narrow wooden bench hidden behind bedsheets drying in the sun. She placed her gnarled hands in her lap, looked intently at me, and waited.

"Mr. Neumann told me Max was his lifelong friend. He said Max gave him a manuscript called *Max Eicher's Memoirs*. I read it." I paused and decided to take a chance. "Maybe Max didn't die from drinking too much."

Her face remained stoic. "You think you know about Armadillo," she said. "I'll ask two questions. If you can't answer them, I'll tell you nothing."

Feeling like a doctoral student at the final oral exam, I held my breath. "Okay, I'm ready."

She gave a mischievous grin. "How many pennies did Max put in a jar the first year he was married?"

I smiled affectionately at Doña María as I remembered Max's account of his marriage to Ruth. "Max and Ruth had no sex—the kind that makes babies—during their first year of marriage. The answer is zero pennies."

She nodded at my correct answer but offered no congratulations. Her eyes glazed over as though deep in thought, but suddenly they twinkled. "What did Max give me when I was a young girl?"

"As a way of thanking you for all your help, he gave you a small gold pendant shaped like an armadillo." She kept a straight face and held my gaze. "Now, Doña María, it's my turn to ask you a question. What did you give Max when you were a young girl?"

She stared at me but said nothing.

"Permit me to answer my question. You gave Max a Maya tomb." Her eyes narrowed to slits.

"I have a second question. Why are all the plants within the walls of Casa de Armadillo grown in pots?"

She sat motionlessly.

"Again, I'll answer. There are stones under our feet." I stomped my foot. "The ancient Maya used many stones to build their temples. Archaeologists have discovered those temples pointing to the clouds because, despite being covered with trees and vegetation, they can be seen. But you led Max to a tomb that the Maya dug into the earth. They built it for a Maya king who paid homage to the armadillo, which lived below them. Eventually, the Maya stopped coming to the Tomb of the Armadillo. Thick vegetation covered the foundation and hid it. But as a descendant of those ancient people, you heard the extraordinary stories passed down from generation to generation."

As Doña María listened impassively, I told of how she'd led Max to discover the Tomb of the Armadillo, but Max feared others might find it. To disguise it, he built the thick outer walls of Armadillo using the perimeter stones as its foundation.

A faint smile flickered across Doña María's face. "Like Max, you're a smart man. I was wrong. You know many things."

"I know you were Max's closest friend. I know that nobody here knows that they're walking above a Maya tomb. I also know many stories, such as how Max fell in love with Maurine Madanes, who'd flown to Armadillo to visit him. But Armadillo is still mysterious and refuses to give up its secrets easily."

Doña María unfolded and folded her hands, stared down at the stones, and spoke softly. "The animal called armadillo is very hard on the top, but it has a soft underbelly. I think Casa Armadillo is like an armadillo. You'll discover what I mean." She looked up and gazed into my eyes. "Once a visitor said to me, 'Ask me no questions, I tell you no lies.' I say these words to you."

"If I'm correct, will you tell me?"

"Dr. Paul, you are, as an English visitor once said, cheeky, but I like you. If you're right, I'll tell you."

Over the next few minutes, I shared enough to demonstrate I knew a few things about the people gathered at Armadillo. While I spoke, she occasionally smiled. When I finished, her eyes were damp. She clasped my hands in hers. "Max was a good man. He was my best friend. Every day I miss him."

I decided to plunge ahead. "In *Memoirs,* Max said he drank hard after Maurine Madanes left. He believed alcohol would kill him. Would you help me learn more?"

"How do you think he died?"

I was amused at how she turned my question around. She'd make a good interviewer. "That's a difficult question. As far as I can determine, he stopped writing *Memoirs* a month before he died. There are numerous stories about the death of Max. The first is a tragic romance: Max died of a broken heart when Maurine Madanes, a woman he adored, flew out of his life and died when her plane crashed in the Gulf of Mexico.

"On yesterday's tour, David shared a second account, which he presented as the official one: Max drank himself to death. But his friend Mr. Neumann contradicted what Max wrote in *Memoirs.* He believes Max would never have done that."

Doña María shook her head. "I agree with Mr. Neumann. Max didn't drink. He hated alcohol. Even a little sip and his face turned red, his skin looked bad. Then he'd throw up and become violently ill. He stayed away from all alcohol."

"But in *Memoirs,* Max implied he drank a lot."

"Words are words," she said. "I knew that if Max drank alcohol, it made him sick."

"The third account. Some claim that in despair over Maurine's death and the failure of his marriage, he committed suicide. But there's no proof. In his memoirs, Max ruled out suicide because, as a good Catholic, he risked everlasting damnation."

"Max wasn't a good Catholic!"

"What? Everyone says he was."

"Max wasn't a good Catholic. He was a *great* Catholic. He'd

113

never kill himself."

Stunned, I sat back on the bench. In *Memoirs*, Max described Doña María as a faithful friend, but she was much more. Almost thirty years after his death, she still tenaciously defended his honor.

I offered my final account of what happened to Max. "I have no evidence, but it makes some sense that Max was murdered. Perhaps Ruth decided that Armadillo was hers and hers alone. Maybe she hastened his death. The easiest way to find out would be to dig up his body and perform an autopsy. Poison would be my best guess."

Doña María closed her eyes and whispered, "Paul, you're a wise man. But please, let Max rest in peace. He suffered in life. Don't make him suffer in death."

"What do you know about his last days?"

Her eyes still closed, she settled back on the bench. "Max didn't write the truth in *Memoirs*. Max didn't die because he drank too much. If I tell you what I know, you must not tell anyone, especially Dr. Gerald. Promise me."

I promised, and for good measure, I crossed my heart with my fingers. Doña María motioned me to follow her. We walked out the back door and down an overgrown path, the same route I'd taken yesterday on David's tour and very early this morning. For a third time, I was back in the small clearing with the headstone and bench.

Again, we sat beside each other. Doña María said she'd never seen Max as happy as he was with Maurine Madanes. "But after she left, he was never himself. Many evenings, when I walked by the library, I heard Max playing the piano and singing "Night and Day" in a voice filled with pain. He sang that song of longing so often that I still remember the words."

Doña María said she never felt as much sorrow for anyone else as she did for Max. "He seemed lost. In the past, he raved about my cooking; now, he ate little. But he didn't drink. His face turned thin, and his blue eyes dimmed in their deep sockets like a skull. Ruth told me she thought Max was dying.

"When Max and Ruth dined together, he sometimes screamed profanities at her. He talked about Maurine and said how kind and helpful she was. Ruth stared at him with hatred. She shouted, 'You fool. I'll not let you destroy my Armadillo. Look at you. You're killing yourself. I hope you die. The sooner, the better.' Max answered, "I hope I die soon. Life with you isn't worth living.' It was horrible."

Doña María went on to say that halfway through dinner on All Saints' Day in 1950, Max stomped from the table and went to his room. An hour later, he yelled for Ruth to bring him something to eat. When she didn't come for a long time, he again screamed for food. Finally, she appeared in his doorway, but with no food. Max said, "You never loved me. All you want is Armadillo." He picked up a small wooden Lacandon carving and threw it at her. The carving hit the wall and fell to the floor. Ruth looked at the broken carving. Then she looked at him and said, "Die, just die." She slammed the door and screamed, "Don't worry, I'll get your food."

"I feared what I saw and heard. Secretly, I followed Ruth to the kitchen. From the shadows, I watched her ladle a bowl of soup and then pour something into it. Because her back was to me, I couldn't see what it was. She returned to Max's room. Without saying a word, she placed the bowl on the table beside his bed. Then she left, but she sat on a chair outside his room like Max was a prisoner. I was worried because I couldn't warn him not to eat.

"Later, I couldn't stand the tension anymore. I went to Ruth. I said, Señora, it's too quiet in Max's room. Is he asleep? He's not snoring." We stood at his door and listened. We heard nothing. Ruth made us wait for an eternity. Her face kept changing. Sometimes she was filled with fear and sometimes with hope. Finally, she opened the door. Max's long body lay on the tile floor near the stone fireplace. His hand held an empty glass, and an empty mezcal bottle lay nearby. But I don't know why since he didn't drink. The soup bowl was empty."

As tears formed, Doña María said, "We went to Max, and I

knelt beside him. I listened for a beating heart. I told Ruth, 'I hear nothing.' I lifted Max's arm so she could feel his pulse. Ruth put her fingers on his wrist and said, 'I feel nothing.' Then a strange look came over her face, and it scared me. She said, 'I love Armadillo, and now it's all mine.' I cried, but I never saw her shed one tear."

Doña María planned a proper burial. An hour after they'd discovered Max's body, La Ruta's lay religious leader took one look and declared Max dead. The next morning, David hired a man from La Ruta to build a simple wooden coffin. Doña María persuaded a young man from the village to lift Max's body into it. He finished his task and ran from the room. She nailed on the coffin lid and placed the coffin in a locked room far from the guests.

"That afternoon, we lowered Max's coffin into the grave you see before us. Present were a Catholic priest, Ruth, David, the rest of the Armadillo staff, and me. Ruth wore black for one day and then ordered a grave marker. Every day for a week, we laid flowers on his grave."

I was eager to ask more questions, but Doña María stopped me. "Once a year on the Day of the Dead, I talk to Max. He helps me just like the god of the armadillo helps me. You helped me, and I helped you. I must go back to my kitchen now because I know you like to eat my delicious food." She smiled and left me sitting among the sheets.

I wondered about Doña María's reference to Armadillo's soft underside. Before I'd talked to her, I was apprehensive about the future. But Armadillo was being exposed, and the more I unearthed, the more I was fascinated, perplexed, and frightened. Doña María's story was very moving, but I felt she'd mostly spoken about Armadillo's hard surface and barely addressed its vulnerable underbelly.

CHAPTER 20

An Onyx Armadillo

I entered the library for the board meeting with Doña María's versions of events occupying my thoughts. No others had yet arrived. I sat down at Max's piano and played the scales. There was no question that the next piano tuner faced a protracted and challenging task. I speculated that if Max had wooed Maurine while playing the piano in the same shape it was now, both must have been tone-deaf.

Figuring that Ruth would sit at the head of the table, I chose the chair to her immediate left. That way, she'd have to face my birthmark—a psychologist would label my behavior as passive-aggressive.

Yesterday, when Gerald dragged me here to talk, I hadn't surveyed the place. Nineteenth-century paintings crowded the walls. Saints, Madonnas, and wealthy benefactors struggled for breath beneath layers of darkened varnish. Five-foot tall, dark-stained bookcases, crowned with pottery made by Tzotzil Indian women, bordered the room. The library table held a few examples of local folk art. I remembered David mentioning that Doña María still dusted this room each week. To me, that seemed like tidying up a time capsule.

Over the next few minutes, all was quiet except for the board members' footsteps and chairs scraping across the wooden floor as they pulled them up to the table. Members nodded to one another, but no one spoke. Ruth finally arrived and took her place at the head of the table. "I bring to order Armadillo's first board meeting. I'll run this meeting informally. If there are disputes, I'll be the final judge." She'd wasted no time in letting us know who the boss would be.

"We're gathered to preserve the memory of Max Eicher, one of the greatest archaeologists of the twentieth century. We must restore Armadillo to its former glory as a gathering place for world-famous scientists, celebrities, and the wealthy."

She looked at a bare spot on the table in front of her. "Your time is too valuable to be bored with pages of numbers in a financial report. I'll give but one number—the bottom line. We need to raise two million dollars. Before you arrived, I asked each of you to prepare a proposal on how to accomplish this. Any questions before we begin?"

"When will the financial report be available?" Harriet asked in a quiet voice.

Ruth's face tightened. "I hear an edge in your question, yet I assume you mean well. Even as we meet, my accountant is concocting a complete report." I couldn't conceal my wry smile. Concocting wasn't a word I associated with financial reports, but it was precisely right from Ruth. "He'll deliver it soon enough. For now, we'll move on to your proposals." I wondered if Ruth employed an accountant. I couldn't imagine her trusting a soul to know anything about her finances. Max would have known, but his lips were permanently sealed.

Roland raised his hand. "I have an observation related to your bottom line. I've recently begun my architectural-restoration examination of Casa Armadillo. In walking around, I've found antiquated plumbing, widespread mildew, and crumbling stucco. I fear that without immediate and extensive restoration, Armadillo will quickly become a ruin. Also, present-day travelers won't be willing to risk the long, treacherous road to get here. The landing strip is overgrown and far too short for even the smallest of modern planes. In brief, I've concluded that the proposed goal of two million dollars to restore Armadillo is a huge underestimation of the true costs."

"Thank you, Roland," Ruth said as she turned away from him. "Harriet, would you please present your proposal?" Instantly, Roland, in his desire to present a realistic assessment of Armadillo, lost Ruth's support. *Roland, forget about Ruth doing her best to satisfy your every need.*

Harriet rose and gave a slight bow. "The Board of UMass—Amherst has unanimously supported my proposal to be the official archive of Max Eicher's papers. Notwithstanding today's tight fiscal constraints, the Board authorized two million dollars for the privilege of housing them."

Gerald pounded the table. "Wait a minute, Harriet! Those papers are necessary for Max's biography. I refuse to descend into a musty archive in the basement of the oldest building on your campus to study Max's papers."

During his outburst, Ruth kept her eyes fixed on Harriet. "I'm honored that the UMass Board recognizes the value of Max's oeuvre."

"I'll only feel satisfied," Gerald said, "when they're in my hands. What are you doing, Ruth? I thought you wanted a biography of your loving husband. You're betraying me when you support a wacky scholar that searches for creatures from outer space."

"Gerald, you're a real loser," Harriet said.

Gerald ignored her. "Ruth, those papers are mine."

Harriet's hands shook. "Gerald, you've defiled the subjects of your previous books. I'll not let you dissect Max and present his mutilated body to the public as the truth. I'll battle you all the way to prevent you from destroying his good name."

Gerald spat on his hands, rubbed them together, and held them out toward her. "Want a little hand-to-hand contest?"

As Harriet glared at him, her hand lifted a small onyx sculpture of an armadillo from the table. She cocked back her arm and swung it forward like a baseball pitcher. A split second before she released the deadly projectile, my hand deflected her aim. The onyx sculpture sailed upward and hit the wall to the right of the fireplace. "Why did you stop me, Paul? I was going to knock a little sense into his Neanderthal skull."

Gerald looked shaken but continued his verbal sparring. "While I love a woman who appeals to my head, I love even more one who goes after my heart."

Harriet's eyes blazed with anger. "When I go after you, you'll be as heartless as William. You're no better than he was—both of you treat people with absolute contempt."

"Too bad about your encounter with William." He flashed a chilling smile. "Perhaps he mistook your passivity for consent."

Shouting obscenities, Harriet lunged across the table at Gerald. For a second time, I thwarted her by grabbing her arm. I led her toward the door. She pushed away from me but made no moves to attack him. "There's no way I'm leaving this room while other board members present their proposals."

Ruth appeared unfazed. "I expect all board members to be civil. But I believe this is a good time for a break. Doña María has prepared coffee and tea, and as a special treat, you'll find her *duraznos pasa* in the small wooden containers. She made them with peaches washed with coal ashes and cooked in sugar water."

I loved Doña María's cooking, and my sweet tooth was available at a moment's notice, but I didn't need the taste of coal ash in my mouth. The bitter taste of Gerald's scorn was already present.

After a short break, we reconvened. Gerald straightened his tie. "Ruth, I'd like to present my plan to make you a multi-millionaire."

"Proceed."

Harriet fumed as she stood beside me. "I'm staying to hear this, like it or not."

Gerald stood and puffed out his chest. "Armadillo desperately needs cash. We marvel at the flowers blooming in the hallways, but observe, as Roland suggested, the falling plaster. Only a few of Armadillo's many gardens remain well-tended. Armadillo once attracted the best and brightest minds in the arts and sciences. But I won't belabor my point."

While he talked, I watched Ruth. Most of the time, her face was a mask, but when he uttered flattering words, her eyes sparkled.

"What will restore Armadillo to its former glory? Not the late William's harebrained proposal that baby boomers with credit cards will want to soak up the sun in Club Med—Armadillo. Armadillo is a five-hour drive to white sandy beaches. We must recapture the incredible essence that once defined this sanctuary. We need to celebrate the man who built this place. We need a definitive biography of Max Eicher to lure back the elite.

"But changes must occur. For example, we could rename the Douglas Fairbanks, Jr.'s room for Robert Redford in honor of his occupancy. Today, who's heard of Dorothy Parker? But when Julie Christie and Paul Newman arrive and we name rooms after them, celebrities from the entertainment world will beat a path to our door."

Gerald was on a roll, yet all, excluding Ruth, seemed unmoved. "Armadillo will become a magnet for celebrities who will delight in eating Doña María's mango pudding in other celebrities' company. No unrelenting paparazzi will harass guests and take indiscreet photographs. Appointments with David will produce glamor shots like those which characterized the thirties and forties. And yes, the cost of staying at this secluded retreat will be astronomical."

Pretending that he was talking on a phone, Gerald continued, "Yes, I understand you're Jack Nicholson's agent, but Mr. Nicholson must wait his turn. A suite for him will be available in approximately four months, but we'll need a deposit to hold it. Yes, I believe it may be possible to accommodate him sooner, but you realize it will be considerably more expensive." He paused to take a breath.

Harriet, who'd returned to her chair in the middle of his speech, took the opportunity to say, "Gerald, considering academia is your home, I'm astonished at your naiveté. I predict your definitive biography of Max Eicher will sell but five hundred copies to those who might have heard of him. Academics aren't superstars who will flock to Armadillo and pay out the wazoo to stay in cramped rooms, sleep in single beds, and stop to smell the frangipani."

Gerald again straightened his tie. "I can't count the times I've read *Maya Magic*. I'm not the only one who finds Max's work enthralling. And Harriet, I've read your book, *Maya Magic: The Key to Contacting Extraterrestrial Beings*. I find the incoherent jumble of words coming out of a schizoid's mouth more coherent than the dingbat babbling in your book."

She looked stunned and said nothing, but her face flushed as if she'd keel over with a heart attack.

Gerald took his seat and gave a knowing smile. "Readers of my best-selling biography will also be intrigued by David's photos, which subtly reveal celebrity secrets."

During his monolog, I'd been studying Ruth's face again. Before Gerald's mention of photos, she appeared unruffled, perhaps because his voice's resonance sounded reassuring. Even I acknowledged that Gerald's words were as smooth as Doña María's mango pudding. But his words also lured like the sticky sweet nectar issuing forth from the interior of a Venus flytrap.

Someone needed to stand up to Gerald, but no one stepped up to take him on. *Go for it, Paul.* "Gerald, you're making a mistake. You've assumed Ruth will sanction your biography of Max. But, for all you know, she may select me as its author."

For several seconds, Gerald looked as though I'd given him a sucker punch, but his sneer rapidly returned. "Be serious. *Freud* was a one-hit-wonder. But to demonstrate my generosity, you may assist me in writing Max's bio. I'll give you credit in the footnotes."

"In that case, you'll be much more generous than I'll be with you in my book."

Gerald stood and glared at me. "Listen, Paul, I can—"

"Stop!" David shouted. After grabbing everybody's attention, he continued softly, "Before you continue fighting over Max's legacy, I must inform Dr. Galveston, Dr. Strupp, and Dr. Seawright of one important fact. For practically thirty years, Ruth and I have searched for Max's papers. While we have copies of *Maya Magic,* we haven't located a notebook, journal article, or paper bearing Max's handwriting or typing. Quite simply, we can't find a trace of his other work."

Harriet slowly rose. "Ruth, for two million dollars, UMass was going to be acquiring Max's papers—if you found them?"

"Give it up, woman," Gerald said. "When Max's papers are found, they're mine. Your university can keep its money. Ruth is guaranteed a great deal in royalties from the sale of my book." Pointing his finger at Ruth, he pressed on, "However, Ruth, there's one problem. You failed to tell me they've been lost, misplaced, or stolen—or perhaps never written."

Ruth stood, walked to the library door, then turned and said, "I officially adjourn today's meeting."

The others, eying one another with suspicion and contempt, left the room while I stayed on to think about Max's *Memoirs.* The book was essential to understanding Max, and right now, I wasn't willing to share what I knew. Then it occurred to me that perhaps Armadillo's secrecy was contagious, and I was infected.

I'd been with Gerald for less than an hour this morning, and I felt drained. But more than that, I felt cold anger toward the man. Given his skill in provoking everyone, he provided reasons for each of us to kill him. I winced. Twelve years ago, with the war in Vietnam raging, I'd volunteered for alternative service and served two years. I'd long held the belief that human beings must find viable alternatives to killing each other. Yet here was Gerald, stirring within me a primordial urge to murder.

CHAPTER 21

Numbers One To Four

Anxious to be away from others, but eager to be together, Sandy and I skipped lunch at Armadillo and walked to Diego's Mustache. "You look drained, and I don't mean from this sweltering heat and humidity. What happened at the board meeting?"

For almost two-and-a-half years of college teaching, I've sat through faculty meetings during which I witnessed the seven deadly sins: pride, greed, wrath, envy, lust, gluttony, and sloth. After today's board meeting in remote Armadillo, I was convinced that those seven sins are alive, well, and universal. And while it seemed to me that Armadillo is a decaying monstrosity in the middle of nowhere, and less than a handful of people would think anything of it if it collapsed, that handful cared passionately about its fate. And I feared that given the way tensions were escalating, I might soon discover yet another sliced-open body.

"Gerald believes Ruth will anoint him to be Max's biographer," I said. "He'll stop anyone who gets in his way. That includes Harriet, Ruth, David, and now me. You're safe, for the time being."

Sandy touched my forearm. "Promise me you'll be careful."

"Before I left Iowa, a friend said, 'Keep your friends close and your enemies closer.'"

"Good advice," she said, "as long as you remember that Gerald is your enemy." Given that Neumann and now Sandy had expressed concerns about my safety, I was getting the message.

"May I be blunt?" she asked.

"Yesterday, I'd have hesitated in saying yes, but I'm learning to appreciate your frankness. Go ahead."

"This may sound ridiculous, but if Ruth chooses you to write Max's biography, I think we should join forces to write it. We'd make a great research team—we get along so well together." She winked.

"Interesting."

Sandy immediately rolled her eyes. "Oh, please! Saying something is interesting is a spineless way of saying forget it."

"Hold on," I said, lifting my hands as a shield. "Give me some samples of your writing to help me decide if we'd make a good team."

"That's fair. I've read *Freud,* and that masterpiece convinced me of your talents."

"Thanks."

"Here's another thought. If something should happen to Gerald," she glanced around Diego's Mustache, leaned forward, and whispered, "I can get you a special price on a bucket of blue paint and a wickedly sharp knife."

We broke into loud and nonstop laughter. Heads turned toward us.

"Seriously," she said, "I think there may be buried treasure at Armadillo."

"Say more."

"Why did Max call the home he built Armadillo?"

"You're slipping—you used to ask much harder questions. Perhaps Max was obsessed with armadillos. Nobody can miss that white plaster one in the front courtyard."

"Agreed. That's one hideous piece of art. But that aside, there's something peculiar about this place. Look around. No plants are growing into the ground; they're all in pots. All the big trees are outside the walls. I think Max built Armadillo on a stone foundation. Otherwise, he'd have needed a crew the size of the one that built an Egyptian pyramid to move all those stones. I've walked around its perimeter. Armadillo is a perfect square. But give me time to figure it out." She stopped, slightly out of breath.

What a woman! On her own, she'd almost figured out that Max built Armadillo on the foundation of a Maya tomb. In my mind, her request to become a writing team suddenly made more sense.

"Paul, are you listening to me? What's that in your hand you're playing with?"

I opened it and showed her a gold armadillo pendant and its chain. "It was on William's body."

"May I hold it?"

I laid it in her hand. "It's beautiful," she said. "Given Max's armadillo in the courtyard, I'm sure he didn't make this. May I put it on?"

"Unfortunately, no. It's too morbid. I didn't share one gruesome detail at last night's opening dinner. I pulled on a chain dangling from William's mouth and drew forth this pendant."

"Gross!" she said, "still, it's exquisite. If you find another in less appetite-losing circumstances, I'll accept it as a present." She tossed her hair in a flirty way, and I felt good inside.

"Pendants were important to Max," I said. "He gave one to each of the four women he cared about. Doña María was the first."

"A busy lover."

"Not in the way you think. He loved these women in different ways. Doña María's love appears to have been platonic. She taught Max the local dialect, and he taught her English. She became his most loyal friend."

"You can't tell me that Ruth was also a platonic love."

"No, that was lust on Max's part, which Ruth did her best to encourage—before marriage."

Sandy raised three fingers. "Who was the next contestant for a pendant?"

I thought about Max's account of Kate in *Memoirs*. "The artist

Kate Davis. With her, I suspect it was more like Max getting his rocks off after a long drought with Ruth."

"Men! And number four?"

"Maurine Madanes."

"Was she the woman whose plane vanished in the Gulf of Mexico years ago?"

"The same. When I asked Ruth about her, she gave me a dismissive wave of her hand. She said, 'It was important for Max to have his dalliances, Kate and Maurine, or he'd get too tightly wound up.' I confronted Ruth when I said, 'Kate may have been a dalliance, but people say Maurine would have been a real contender for his affections.'"

"You took a chance saying that."

"Exactly. Ruth turned on me as if I'd stabbed her. She said, 'You can think what you want about that woman, but she ended up in a watery grave as fish food.'"

Sandy's eyes opened wide. "Words like that start fights."

I remember Max's description of a fight in *Memoirs* and decided to use my photographic memory to recreate the scene for Sandy. "In this case, they did. The day before Maurine left Armadillo, Max entered the dining room for breakfast and overheard Ruth ask Maurine, 'Making progress in your conquest of my husband? Give it up! The only way Max will leave our marriage is in a pine box. Better dead than in your bed!'

"Until that moment, Maurine had suffered Ruth's insults in silence. She gazed at Ruth and replied, 'Better my bed than you giving head to every male who visits Armadillo.'

"Ruth recoiled and then charged at Maurine, all the while screaming obscenities. They rolled across the tile floor and knocked over chairs as they hit, bit, and scratched with unchecked ferocity. One of their hands reached up and grabbed hold of the tablecloth, and huevos rancheros and orange juice rained down on them. Their combat continued.

"Maurine spotted an opening and sent a right to Ruth's jaw. David, who'd just entered the room, watched Ruth fall back and hit her head on the tile floor. Max raced to Maurine, and David

127

to Ruth. The two men looked at each other as though the other man was crazy.

"William, who was visiting Armadillo at the time, entered the room during the fight. He stood back from the fray and chuckled.

"Maurine looked down at the unconscious Ruth. 'Don't worry. I'm leaving tomorrow. Max doesn't need a pine box.'"

"Those two women had a way with words!" Sandy said. "Armadillo brings out the passion in people. Ruth's my senior by almost two generations, but she's eyeing you like her next conquest." She reached over and stroked my hand, "She hasn't already succeeded, has she?" I shook my head. "Good, because I want you all for myself."

"You also have a way with words—ones I love hearing."

"But a word of warning," Sandy said as she waved a finger at me. "When a woman like Ruth feels rebuffed, she can be furious. And full of vengeance."

Sandy's room was a mirror image of mine, but she'd added a few touches to make it more inviting. Like draping colorful serapes over chairs, rather than, as in my room, leaving clothes scattered on the floor.

"I'm feeling a damp chill," she said and rubbed her hands together. "Would you mind building a fire?" I knelt on the small Oaxacan rug in front of the fireplace, and soon the room glowed. "We can share my bed," she said. We laughed about David's funny bow ties, Ruth's heavy makeup, and the quirkiness of providing only twin beds.

I flinched as Sandy's hand approached my birthmark. She laid her hand on the smooth purple skin. Instinctively, my head jerked back. But instead of a scorching touch, her hand was like soothing water washing away a top layer of my disfigurement. Sandy wasn't freaking out about my birthmark. She gently kissed my lips. My hands began exploring her body. Searching through my Spanish vocabulary, I said, *"Estoy caliente."*

She giggled. "Keep working on your Spanish, but I like the

meaning."

"Why? What did I say?"

"I think you were trying to say the room is hot, *hace calor*, but you said, 'I'm hot' as in 'I'm horny.' But I like what you just said. *Estoy caliente, tambien.*"

She unbuttoned my shirt, then looked down at her blouse as if to tell me it was my turn. Resting on the bridge of her black bra was a gold armadillo pendant. My mouth flew open. "Isn't that...?"

"Oops, I forgot to give it back to you."

"It looks beautiful on you, but I need it back. It's evidence. Besides, for me, it brings up William's sacrifice."

"Focus on me, and I'll bring up something else."

Speaking in a sultry voice, she said, "Remove my bra...that's right...and cup my breasts...oh, that feels good...and gently kiss them." Her deep-throated sounds increased my arousal and spurred me to satisfy her more deeply. And just like that, I no longer needed her instruction. That afternoon she took me to a place I'd fantasized about, and I learned the intense pleasure of giving and receiving with abandon.

Later, I watched as she dressed, the dying fire silhouetting her body on the wall. A song from a decade ago, "Love the One You're With," played in my head. Back then, I was miserable because it seemed the lyrics were mocking me for what I found unattainable. But with Sandy, I finally appreciated them.

CHAPTER 22

An Excerpt From Max Eicher's Memoirs: *Ruth Eicher*

R uth's hobby was collecting butterflies, and I was the innocent one she momentarily desired. I was captured, placed in a killing jar, and mounted in a display case, so she was free to declare open season on the men who stayed at Armadillo. Over the years, a succession of celebrities and social scientists came to know Ruth intimately. But always on her terms.

One example is all I have the stomach to recount. In the summer of 1936, Professor Patrick W___ and his wife Betty visited Armadillo. During their visit, Ruth inaugurated a routine: she seduced male visitors and treated their spouses and girlfriends with disdain. For my part, I abandoned any hope of a happy marriage.

The morning after Patrick and Betty arrived, I was eating breakfast and lamenting the unavailability of Kellogg's Corn Flakes—a glaring example of self-pity. I looked up to see Ruth parade into the room dragging Patrick by the arm. "Max, I'm taking Pat to visit some archaeological ruins. We'll return by early evening." Her manner conveyed a done deal.

Patrick looked at me, his face flushed with embarrassment. "Mrs. Eicher is kindhearted, but surely she's too busy to take my wife and me to distant ruins."

Ruth raised her right eyebrow and bestowed on him a broad smile. "Pat, you've misunderstood. Just you and I are going. Since your wife arrived, I've watched her suffer from heat and altitude. I'm worried about her health. For our trip, I ordered horses and provisions for two. Please tell your charming wife that this is far too strenuous for her."

Ruth turned to me and added, "By the way, Max, see that Betty is cared for while we're gone."

Alarmed at the sudden turn of events, I attempted to side with the professor, "Perhaps, Patrick, you don't want to leave your wife, especially if she's not feeling well."

Before he could say a word, Ruth tightened her grip on his arm—like a python's death squeeze—and said, "Oh, now I get it, Pat. You're afraid to leave your defenseless wife with my good-looking husband. Goodness knows most men would balk at that. But you're not the jealous type, are you?"

Patrick held his head high. "I trust your husband is a gentleman."

"And I trust you'll be a gentleman as we travel together." Ruth clapped her hands three times. "Then it's settled. We all trust one another. Trust is important among friends. Don't you agree?"

Neither Patrick nor I spoke. My stomach was a knot, and my brain was screaming obscenities at Ruth for her masterful maneuver.

Rather rapidly, Ruth perfected her strategy. Piecing together bits of stories I overheard, it went like this: On the trail with her future conquest, Ruth rode the lead horse. After a while, she would call back, "It's beastly hot." She would undo some buttons on her blouse. The ride continued, and the heat took its toll on those that remained fastened. And naturally, she often turned around for the guy to notice she wasn't wearing a bra. By mid-morning, she had tied her blouse around her waist, and the guest could ogle a half-naked woman. Eventually, they would chance upon a small cottage beside the trail where Ruth served tequila—quite conveniently available—and performed her oral specialty on the man.

Some men, such as Patrick, were initially innocent. Others, based on stories they had heard, came prepared for their adventures with Ruth. From what I ascertained, the wives and girlfriends were altogether ignorant of the sexual experiences their husbands would relish. However, I know for a fact that five marriages failed not long after the couples left Armadillo. The wife of one man killed herself.

CHAPTER 23

Means, Motive, And Opportunity

I knocked on Ruth's door, and she opened it. She wore a colorful huipil, but instead of the traditional round neck opening, this one featured a plunging neckline. She displayed no sense of embarrassment as she glanced down at her breasts. "I love wearing the native clothing of this region." While she may have loved the local women's clothes, she entirely failed to emulate the wearers' modesty.

"Do you have time for some questions?" I asked.

"With you, dear, any time is a good time, if you catch my drift."

In my head, I heard Mae West's famous line: "I used to be Snow White, but I drifted." I couldn't imagine Ruth was ever snow white, but I corralled my amusement. "Is there any truth to the rumor that there's a sizable gold armadillo sculpture located nearby?"

"Use your eyes. Nobody can miss Max's hideous white one in the courtyard. If you'll pay to ship it home, it's yours. But no, the only gold armadillos around here are this small." She mimed a one-inch distance between her thumb and forefinger.

"Those small gold pendants shaped like armadillos?"

"Sweetie, Max handed them out like candy to every woman he thought he loved."

"May I see yours?" *Stupid choice of words.*

"If I can see yours." She punctuated her response with a nerve-racking laugh.

"May I see the pendant Max gave you?"

"When I heard Max gave one to Kate, I stopped wearing mine. It lost its meaning."

"Where's it now?"

"Hidden in my locked keepsake box. The hired help is forever helping themselves to my valuables. Later, I'll try to locate it for you."

"Where were you the night William died?"

She snorted. "Are you suggesting I persuaded a sixty-year-old, beer-bellied man with the charm of a cobra to take off his clothes and lie down on a cold stone so I could rip out his heart? Granted, I exude substantial seductive allure, but nobody possesses that much."

"I'm not suggesting you killed him. I'm looking for means, motive, and opportunity."

"Paul dear, I apologize for burdening you with trying to solve William's murder. You seem quite tense. Come around more often, and I'll help you relax."

"I don't know how strong you are, but stabbing an opponent doesn't look like your specialty."

"You're right, honey, I'd prefer poison—much less messy."

Her smile sent a shiver through me as I remembered that Doña María implied Ruth might have poisoned Max. "You and most of the people staying here had motives to kill William."

She glanced around her room. "If I despised William enough to kill him, I wouldn't have waited this long. Personally, his instantaneous death was wrong. Much better to inflict him with writhing pain so that he yearned for death. But why kill him, when castration would be a worse fate." She laughed in her irritating way. "I'll bet that's the way Harriet hoped he'd die. But Paul, rather than worry about William's murder, why don't you and I explore the countryside. We can unwind at resting areas along the way. Don't stay cooped up here, playing detective."

Shit! I'd calculated that Ruth would eventually stop pursuing me. Wrong! She just turned up the heat.

"But first, scoot over and sit beside me." She patted a spot on the sofa next to her. The prospect of slowing Ruth's advances vanished.

I didn't move. "Why didn't you discuss William's idea of Club Med—Armadillo with the board of directors?"

"Because they're fools. I hope you don't become one before we have some pleasurable fun together. Take Harriet; she foolishly revels in all that Max fiddle-faddle. She's even added flying saucers and space creatures. Given her accusation that William raped her, I don't believe it. I'm convinced she actively participated in William's carnal game but then had serious regrets—as well she should've. Given the women he seduces, there's no telling what diseases he passed on to her." Ruth shuddered.

"Wait a minute, Ruth. I've read William's journal. He said he neither raped nor had consensual sex with Harriet. He doesn't strike me as a man given to false modesty."

"You're right about that. If William had had his way with her, he'd have exaggerated the whole thing and claimed the credit."

"But you seem to think Harriet participated with William and then cried wolf."

"Listen to me, sweet. All men, including you, are just boys with an occasionally stiff toy. Smart women manipulate those toys to get what they want. Brainless women get pregnant and produce children. Shakespeare said it best: 'In their quiet desperation, the mass of humanity needs opium.'"

And Ruth thinks Harriet is wacky! I was glad Ruth wasn't my student. She'd taken snippets of quotes by Thoreau and Karl Marx and put them in a Waring blender. The final concoction didn't make a bit of sense.

"I admire women with brains," Ruth said. "Doña María has brains most of the time, but even she couldn't resist having children. I suspect Harriet has a brain, but like an egg, it's scrambled. Sandy seems to have a brain, but at some point, she'll want your child."

Before Ruth said it, it hadn't occurred to me that Sandy might want to have a child. She'd said she was on the pill, and I'd believed her, but now doubts surfaced. Feeling anxious, I changed the subject. "Who do you think killed William?"

"My best guess? The woman he said he didn't rape—Harriet."

"You think she's capable of killing him?"

"If he'd raped her, she wouldn't be a pathetic victim. She'd thrust a knife through his heart. Ah, sweet revenge!"

"Revenge?"

"If William had ever raped me, I'd seek revenge, and he'd be a dead man. As it was, William and I shared an unwritten agreement not to encroach on each other's territory. But Paul, you can encroach on my territory anytime you want." She looked toward her bedroom, turned back, leered at me, and grabbed my arm. "If any other woman besides Harriet said a man had raped her, I'd take her word for it. But with Harriet, I'd want more evidence. She presents herself as a leftover from the beat generation, but I bet she's starving for sex—any kind she can get."

"So why invite her to be on the board?"

"Money. I need it to keep this place up. Would you like a drink?"

"I'd like a rum and Coke." *Are you an idiot? She's plying you with liquor.* Perhaps the hot, humid air and the parched feeling in my mouth at 7,000 feet caused a brain fart. I didn't even like rum and Coke.

She returned with drinks and sat down on the couch beside me. "I bet that a big strapping guy like you is cramped in that twin bed in your room. I'm most willing to share my large bed with you." When her hand moved up my thigh, I started coughing. "Asthma attack!" I gasped. "I need my inhaler!" Within seconds, Ruth's apartment door was a welcome barrier between us.

CHAPTER 24

An Excerpt From Max Eicher's Memoirs: *Maurine Madanes*

R uth loved the portrait Kate painted of her. Ruth even embraced Kate as a "close" friend. As if Ruth were capable of that. She sorted women into two categories—safe and dangerous. Because most women didn't disturb Ruth's world, they weren't a threat. Ironically, Kate fit the safe category: She had offered me a good time, but she didn't provide me with what Ruth most feared—heartwarming, reciprocal love. Our marriage had one unspoken rule: each of us could have sex with others, but we weren't to fall in love. Then Maurine Madanes descended from the heavens into my arms.

On August 15, 1950, the oppressive heat of the mid-afternoon sun crept down the corridors of Armadillo and drove me from the library to a hammock, purposely hung to capture the shadow of a northern wall. I listened to the droning of insects as I daydreamed about my work on Maya hieroglyphics. Glyphs—drawings that stood for syllables or whole words—danced to the droning rhythms and floated in and out of my awareness. The droning intensified, and a kaleidoscope of glyphs came together. As they did, they sprang to life and spoke their names to me. Finally, I comprehended their meaning!

I was delirious with excitement as I perceived the hidden structure of the Maya written language, which had eluded countless others. The droning grew to a crescendo, and I suddenly realized it wasn't insects but a plane's twin engines. Looking up, I noticed it flying quite *low.*

We weren't anticipating visitors. I swung my feet out of the hammock and started for the small airstrip close to Armadillo. As I entered the clearing, the wheels of a Beech 35 Bonanza were whipping up red dust. The plane taxied to a stop, several hundred feet away, and I arrived at the plane just as the pilot climbed out of the cockpit.

I saw before me the woman who would change my life. Her face was an intriguing mixture of Eastern European and Oriental influences, that spoke of no specific country but synthesized the beauty of them all. Her face radiated a love of life, but her dark brown eyes revealed a touch of melancholy that momentarily alarmed me.

"I sure hope you're Dr. Eicher and this is Casa Armadillo because otherwise, I have no idea where I am."

Basking in the glow of the angelic vision who'd arrived, I answered, "You've found the right place."

She must have sensed our first meeting had started awkwardly, and she attempted to correct it. "You're much more distinguished than I thought you'd be. Oh, I can't believe I said that. I'm sorry. I mean, I'm not sorry you look distinguished." She closed her eyes and lowered her head.

With an open palm, I lifted her chin and looked into her eyes. "Please tell me your name."

"I'm Maurine Madanes. Last week I finished reading Maya Magic. I loved it and decided to visit the author."

"I, the author of Maya Magic, welcome you to Armadillo."

"Thank you, Dr. Eicher. I'm sorry if what I said hurt you."

"No, no, and please call me Max." Then with an audaciousness that surprised me, I added, "I'm delighted you've flown into my life." I offered her my arm.

As we approached Armadillo, Ruth stood in the back doorway, wearing the icy expression she had perfected. I whispered to Maurine, "I'll introduce you to Ruth, my wife. But be prepared—occasionally, she's not overly welcoming." My statement proved prophetic.

While I introduced the women to each other, the expression on Ruth's face didn't change, and I surmised that she already perceived

Maurine as an enemy. Ruth granted Maurine no grace period and drew first blood. "Miss Madanes, you appear to be eyeing my stallion. Don't ever think about riding him."

Although Maurine's face flushed, she displayed a presence of mind. "Mrs. Eicher, I appear to have been misinformed. A friend told me that Armadillo is a home, not a stable."

"Look, sweetie, Max is a one-rider horse, and he'll stay that way."

Maurine refused to blink. "Then I suggest the present rider provide more attention and employ less whip."

"Dear, I'll decide what's good for the stallion without consulting you." She pivoted and walked away.

I wiped the tears from Maurine's eyes—eyes so warm and inviting. "Don't worry; we'll make things right." Her smile was all the affirmation I needed.

As was our custom at dinner, Ruth sat at her end of the long table, and I sat at mine. Halfway down the table, Maurine sat bathed in soft candlelight. Ruth didn't attempt to make Maurine feel welcome. To revive a stalled conversation, I asked, "Maurine, is Armadillo what you expected?"

"Yes, Miss Madanes," Ruth said, "were you expecting a man who lusts after beautiful women?"

Maurine's head jerked in Ruth's direction. She replied gently, "I came hoping to find a home filled with the caring generosity of the people who live in the Chiapas region."

"Sweetie, find what you were hoping for?"

"I've found both more than I expected and less. I believe that Armadillo has unrealized potential for happiness." She looked at me. "Max, you built Armadillo, but it does not belong to you." She turned to Ruth. "You came to Armadillo, but it can never be your true home." She looked straight ahead at the flames of the candles. "This place belongs to the Maya and their descendants who have lived in this region for thousands of years. Despite Armadillo's attraction, it isn't a place for strangers from afar. Both of you should leave this place before it destroys you. I know I won't stay and have Armadillo destroy me." Maurine's searing judgment—so full of truth—came directly from her heart.

Ruth and I sat in silence. Maurine had peered into our souls and grasped who we were. She saw hope, but only if I left Armadillo, the place I had built and loved. I knew I would change if I were around Maurine, more than I ever imagined I could. For the first time in my life, I wanted to be worthy of someone—I wanted to give of myself. At the same time, I felt profoundly undeserving of her.

We finished the meal in silence. By the time I escorted the two women from the room, I knew in the depths of my being that my marriage was dead. I also knew a messenger from God had appeared, and I was experiencing a conversion destined if only briefly, to bring me serenity. Conversely, Ruth acted as if Satan had sent her an archenemy.

I proposed after-dinner drinks in the library. "I'm going to my room," Ruth said. "Don't stop on my account." I wasn't planning to, and I hoped Maurine wouldn't either.

Maurine said she was tired from her long flight, but she would stay for one drink. I poured her a small glass of Kahlúa and myself some iced tea. As I filled our glasses, I noticed my hand was shaking. Despite my forty-nine years, I felt like an adolescent with a new crush. I turned to music, my tranquilizer of choice. From the piano bench, I removed the sheet music to Cole Porter's haunting song, "You'd Be So Nice to Come Home To." Maurine sat beside me, and when I finished playing and singing the song, she said, "Again, please."

This time her voice joined mine. I swear I went crazy thinking maybe a miracle might happen, and she might return the strong affection I felt for her. When the song ended, she said, "Max, I must get some sleep, but let's sing together every night."

"I'd like that very much, Maurine. Very much." Something was happening that seemed destined to change my life forever. I had cared for María, Ruth, and Kate in different ways, but they had not loved me for who I was. María adored me as a teacher and mentor. Ruth saw me as a ticket to an exotic mansion where she could reign. Kate, as a playful diversion.

On another evening, after we had sung together, Maurine said, "My goodness, your eyes are full of sorrow. I hope someday you'll find happiness." Her words reverberated throughout my body and swept me back to childhood and the night of my thirteenth birthday when I stood in the church and looked up at the statue of Mother Mary. I had felt she understood and had compassion for my loneliness. Maurine also understood and had compassion. Tears rolled down my face.

Maurine watched me, then placed her hand on my forearm and said, "Don't worry, we'll make things right." In my heart, I believed her; she had spoken from the depth of her being. I dried my face on my shirtsleeves and stood before her like a complete fool, knowing that judgment was mine, not hers.

By the end of the week, I had fallen deeply in love. In turn, Maurine loved the Max I sincerely aspired to be. By nature, she was tender, giving, and nourishing. She woke in me a sense of vulnerability and strength. Bathed in her unselfish love, I learned to affirm myself. But in awakening me to new facets of myself, she increased my awareness of how loveless my marriage was and how unbearable my life had become.

Schemes of what to do crowded my mind. Maurine and I were in love, and yet I recognized I could never divorce Ruth. Much as I despised my wife, I had made a vow before God that I would marry for life. Catholicism was the one constant in my life; its way dictated my choices. I looked back on my life. Every Sunday from infancy until I left for college, my family sat in the front pews of Dubuque's St. Columbkille Catholic Church, illuminated by the glow of wax candles flickering patterns of dark and light on forms emerging from and vanishing into shadows. Sunday after Sunday, I witnessed the ultimate magic act performed by a priest who transformed bread and wine into Christ's body and blood. Although Holy Communion absorbed me, Easter held the tightest grip on my imagination. I delighted in the Easter drama. I loved the story about how Joseph of Arimathea and Nicodemus wrapped Jesus' body in cloth containing spices and placed Him in the tomb, and then the sacred words told of His coming back to life.

But now I was consumed with despair. If a divorce wasn't an option, neither was murder, although multiple methods presented themselves as fantasies. "Thou shall not kill" was imprinted on my brain from childhood. I felt powerless to act. The thought of suicide occurred briefly, but it was synonymous with murder; therefore, not an option.

One of my choices was to forget Maurine and persist in an intolerable marriage. I had never appreciated the Book of Job before, but suddenly, I identified with Job's bewilderment and torment as his world disintegrated.

Maurine stayed at Armadillo for twelve days. We were always together; Ruth kept her distance. I worried about what she might be planning, but her silence was total, except for barbs directed at Maurine like, "Oh, by the way, has Dr. Eicher told you about his previous fling with Kate?" and "It was a shame Kate left. She and Dr. Eicher got along fabulously together."

Ruth's oscillation between silence and digs exhausted Maurine. My response was to tell Maurine everything, hoping my honesty might be an antidote to Ruth's spiteful nature. To some extent, it worked, but then Maurine would compare herself with Kate, who, in her eyes, possessed beauty, confidence, and spirit. Maurine worried that she would never measure up to Kate. In answer to Maurine's doubts, I told her that I loved her more than any other woman I had ever known. She said, "If that's so, come with me when I leave Armadillo."

At the end of Maurine's stay, I carried her bags to the plane, while she carefully inspected it. When it was time for her to depart, Ruth and David stood about thirty feet away; Maurine and I lingered near the door of the plane. I gave her a short kiss and wished it could have lasted much longer. Maurine said in a voice loud enough for Ruth to hear, "Max, this is your last chance if you want to leave with me."

I staggered and choked out, "Only death will unite us."

Maurine climbed into the cockpit, and I retreated. She started the engine, the propellers spun rapidly, and far too quickly, the plane vanished over the trees. Ruth, David, and I walked back to Armadillo in silence. Late into the night, the plaintive notes of "Begin the Beguine" hung in the still air of the library as I sang about people cursing the chance that they wasted.

After Maurine left, I was miserable. My love for her was more than I could bear. I had ruled out three options: divorcing Ruth, killing Ruth, or killing myself. That left me with nothing. Throughout my marriage, my evening beverage was always a Shirley Temple. But beginning on the day Maurine departed, Ruth never saw me without a bottle of mezcal in my hand. Slowly I changed. At times, I bellowed at her. I lost my concentration: playing the right notes on the piano became increasingly problematic, as did writing this memoir. I was aware that, even in the daylight hours, I was weaving across courtyards and down corridors. Evenings saw me heading to my room with a bottle of mezcal. Every morning when María cleaned, she removed one— sometimes two—empty bottles. I reasoned that I wasn't committing suicide if I died slowly enough.

CHAPTER 25

An Arrogant Bastard

After escaping Ruth's clutches to fetch an inhaler, my coughing spell abruptly ended. No surprise, since I'd never suffered from asthma. I was now free to interview my next suspect—Gerald.

"Glad to see you, old sport," he said. For the second time within minutes, I choked intentionally to avoid laughing at Gerald's pathetic imitation of Jay Gatsby. Adding to my amusement was his failure to notice how corny he sounded.

I asked what he knew about William's murder. Gerald didn't suppress his laughter as he asked, "Is our Maya-murder investigator not finding enough excitement in his own life? Will he now go to great lengths to frame me for William's death?"

"I'm gathering suspects' alibis."

"Why do that? William was a swindler of gullible woman seeking to buy art. Let's face the facts: he prided himself on being a greased zipper. If he had a moral compass, it hadn't been calibrated in ages."

"Alibi."

"You're persistent if nothing else," he said. "It's apparent that last night Harriet channeled an ancient Maya warrior and sacrificed a man on the altar of her woo woo beliefs. But her antenna doesn't pick up all the channels. And because we all know she did it, soon she'll have to sacrifice you, David, Roland, Father Lester, and me, and everyone else to stop us from blabbing the truth."

Asking for an alibi wasn't going anywhere. "You had no reason to kill William?"

"Right. I'd heard much about him, but we just met several days ago. Frankly, I marveled that someone hadn't killed him years ago. You, I, and the late William shared one thing in common: we're students of human nature, but we differed in fundamental ways. William was a predator; I'm not, and I assume you aren't either. He had a dick for a brain; you and I have analytical brains. His goal in life was to have sex with every woman he met. I prefer to observe and analyze as a critic. If I'm not mistaken, you are a one-woman-at-a-time man—given your current infatuation with that woman who calls herself Sandy."

Gerald fascinated and repelled me. *How does he manage to squeeze so many insults into so few sentences?* "Did you kill William and remove his heart?"

"No. I favor typing on my Tandy computer to performing involuntary heart surgery. I am, however, dissecting Armadillo. Future critics will conclude I wrote a masterpiece exposing the sordid lives of Max and his entourage. I guarantee you that I'll win the Pulitzer Prize for General Nonfiction. I'll be immortalized."

What an arrogant bastard! He was shooting for a Pulitzer before obtaining Ruth's permission, locating Max's papers, or writing a bloody word. His audacity dumbfounded me.

"However," Gerald said, "I'm puzzled. How do I write about a weak man and not have readers conclude that they're wasting their time? You must agree Max possessed fatal flaws. He couldn't cut his ties to Ruth. And while his marriage tormented him, he stayed with Ruth despite his love for Maurine Madanes."

"Now, get this—did Max even try to stop Maurine from leaving his life? No. After she left, did he realize his mistake and take off after her? No! Did he do anything? Surprisingly, the answer is yes! Pathetic Max sat around in a drunken stupor tickling the ivories and warbling forlorn love songs! Imagine a tall man hunched over an out-of-tune piano, crying his heart out."

Gerald proceeded to belt out an off-key stanza of "So in Love," which made my ears bleed. "You must admit, Paul, that the word 'delirious' in the song is the precise one. It describes Max, a man trapped in a religion that destroys more people than it helps."

"Your books destroy people's lives."

"Clever, Paul, but there's a big difference. I truthfully report events from the past."

"You shatter the lives and careers of those still living."

"For people who are living lies, I put the truth out where they can see it. The bumper sticker stated, 'The truth will set you free, but first it will make you miserable.' Max surrounded himself with extraordinary people, and I'll write the truth even if it makes those who knew him miserable. His story deserves to reach a wider audience, and I'm the one to disseminate it. William's murder helps create a sleazy and cheap tale—not unlike Max's life. The unwashed masses will eat it up."

An acid feeling burned in my stomach.

"By the way, your new friend is avoiding me."

"Sandy?"

"Don't be sure you know who she is."

"Meaning?"

"You're smart; you figure it out."

As I walked back to my room, I realized how exhausted I felt listening to Gerald. Ensconced in academia, I had my share of teaching to do, but engaging in scholarship meant I could retreat to the library and have time to think through problems. Because there were but few of Freud's contemporaries to interview when writing his biography, I could concentrate on his written words. Much simpler, despite first having to master the German language.

After but four days at Armadillo, my current fatigue was twofold: the stress of a very long trip from Iowa City to Armadillo and an onslaught of people, one of them dead. The mystery of Max Eicher kept getting more baffling, and right now, I wasn't any closer to figuring out who'd killed William Farrell than when I'd peered into his chest cavity.

Like William, Gerald's threatening behavior offered ample reasons for someone to kill him. As a conscientious objector, it hurt to think about where hatred can lead some people. But I wanted to avenge the suffering Gerald had inflicted on others with his spiteful writing and prevent him from hurting others in the future. I began to fantasize that I'd sealed him alive in a Maya tomb.

Paul, this isn't a good use of your time. Rather than fantasize, I needed to think about the questions jostling for my attention: Why should I play detective and try to solve William's murder when everyone believed it was the best thing that ever happened? What did I know and not know about the suspects' motives, opportunities, and means? One fact was indisputable: a small storeroom in the back of Armadillo contained William's body.

My list of suspects held seven names: Ruth, David, Doña María, Harriet, Gerald, Father Lester, and Roland. Eight if I counted Sandy, but she barely knew William. Not one had expressed a bit of grief. On the contrary, several seemed elated. Then I realized that even I hadn't felt sad.

One element of William's case bedeviled me. Without help, how could one person have sacrificed him? Cooperation and coordination seemed essential. Two people must have held the ropes to hold him down. That freed the killer to plunge the knife into his chest. Most of my suspects had motive, ample opportunity, and access to a knife. But none of them seemed prone to cooperate with others. Given my lack of success in solving the murder, one thing was sure: returning to Iowa, I wouldn't quit my university job and open a detective agency.

Sadly, my failure as a detective matched my inability to locate source materials for Max's biography. Except for *Maya Magic* and *Max Eicher's Memoirs,* the former I owned, and the latter I borrowed, I'd uncovered nothing. No journal articles, academic papers, working notes, or correspondence. Without additional material, I was stymied. I was at Armadillo look-ing for a killer no one cared about and wondering where Max's hidden papers were. I reached my room and determined to put everything out of my mind; I lay down for a short nap.

In my dream, a knife kept plunging into William's chest. Each blow to his rib cage was a loud bang. Blow followed blow until I realized someone was pounding on my door. "Come in," I man-aged to say in my groggy state.

"Oh, did I wake you?" David asked. "I thought I'd drop by to see how you're coming with your investigation."

I scrambled to think of what to ask him. I settled on asking about Doña María's routine of locking the two doors every even-ing. He confirmed it was one of her duties. "She's the most trust-worthy and reliable person at Armadillo. And I venture to add, the most responsible. If we need something done around here, we turn to her."

"Who do you think killed William?"

"That's a hard question. Harriet insists that William raped her. That provides her with a strong motive. Ruth tolerated him because he promised to bring in needed money. I can't see her killing him. Besides," he paused for dramatic effect, "Ruth would have used poison."

Poison. For once, two people agreed. "Could Harriet and two others have worked together?"

"Possibly, but Harriet's a loner. If she'd had any assistance, it would have been with her extraterrestrial beings. Sorry, I jest."

"Any other suspects I should be aware of?"

"Perhaps a woman from William's past. Most women who fell for him ended up hating his guts. Or maybe it was some guy who hated William for messing around with his woman. If that's the case, we're talking about a lot of men."

It was time to hit hard. "Like you, if William was messing with Ruth?"

"If William were messing with Ruth, she'd have handled it herself—"

"By killing him?"

"Sure, but if she killed him, we wouldn't have found his body. I suspect William would have vanished like Maurine Madanes."

"Any chance Ruth sabotaged Maurine's plane?"

David thought for a moment. "No, not a chance. Ruth can't even screw in a lightbulb. And except for Ruth, everyone loved Maurine. She was right for Max, but he let her go, and that hastened his descent into alcoholism. I wish he'd been stronger and left with her. He didn't, and he soon wasted away."

"That doesn't leave many suspects. Where were you—?"

"Lest you forget, I met you and checked you in the night you arrived. Later, I was in the same place as everyone else that night, in bed—but not with anyone else. Beyond Armadillo's walls at night, it's a graveyard. Few guests venture out. Since William's body lay on the sacrificial stone overnight, it's a wonder that a stalking jaguar didn't gnaw his body to pieces." *Thanks, David, you've added one more image to my gruesome image collection.*

As I was saying goodbye to David, Father Lester called out to us. "If you have some time now, please join us at a burial service for William Farrell. The three of us followed the path to the sacrificial altar, and in twenty minutes, the service was over. As we walked away, a workman from La Ruta threw shovelfuls of dirt onto the wooden coffin.

CHAPTER 26

Holy Spirits

At the head of the dinner table, Ruth regally presided over her court. I suspected she'd have preferred her subjects to bow low upon seeing her, avoid eye contact, and back out of the room when leaving her august presence.

I concentrated on the food. After one spoonful of Doña María's *sopa de tortilla,* I flagged her down to tell her how delectable it was. Sandy seconded the motion. While the soup was a highlight of our gathering, Gerald's absence was the second. And while Ruth's presence was somewhat intimidating, the overall atmosphere was upbeat and appreciative.

After dinner, Sandy and I stood in the corridor outside the dining room. She told me she was heading to the library to look at Max's collection of books.

"That's two nights in a row you've worked late. Hot on the trail of something?"

"I am. Talking with you about Max's armadillo sculpture jogged my memory. I hypothesize that Max built this place on the stone foundation of a Maya temple in homage to the armadillo, but—and get this—it goes into the ground. Somewhere in Armadillo is a secret passage leading to a master chamber that's possibly teeming with gold, priceless Maya murals, and perhaps even codices!"

"I wish you luck and keep me posted," I said as casually as I could. I longed to tell Sandy what I knew about the Maya tomb and how she was spot on, but I hesitated. Would she discover Max's secret study before I did? Would it be her discovery? I felt guilty, but a part of me didn't want to share what I knew.

She leaned in and said in a hushed voice, "My hunch is I might find clues in some of the library books about where Max's papers are."

"Sandy, please help me find William's killer."

"On that topic, it's you against the rest of us. Don't waste your time looking for someone who did us a favor. Help me learn more about Max, and then we can co-author his biography."

This was an argument I wasn't about to win. While I thought William was a sleaze and the bane of women's lives, nobody should die the way he did—though I could understand why some people might think that. With Sandy, I needed to be careful. If I didn't show more interest in finding out about Max, she might conclude I wasn't serious about writing his biography. *Tread carefully.* "I'll be in my room if you want to stop by."

I was eager to experience the barely perceptible moment at Armadillo when the day's muggy heat changes to the cool of the evening. Instead, as I wandered down the corridor, the image of William's blue-painted, nude body chilled me more than the dropping temperature.

I was taking a shower and thinking about Sandy when I heard loud knocking. I called out and said I was coming. By the time I opened the door, the corridor was empty. A piece of paper with hurried handwriting lay at my feet: *Paul, meet me in the chapel at ten tonight. I have revealing photos to show you. Gerald.* I'd stomached enough of him for one day, but then my curiosity kicked in. When I overheard him talking to Ruth last night, he made it clear he possessed incriminating photographs. And this morning at the board meeting, he alluded to photos of Kate. Why did Gerald want to show me those photos? Instantly, I knew the insulting answer—he honestly thought of me as his lowly graduate assistant who was unworthy of his attention except as an audience to hear his grandiose opinions of himself.

I saw I had an hour before our meeting when I heard more knocking on my door. *Please, let it not be Gerald.* Sandy stood before me, looking as breathtaking as ever. She said the library was damp and chilly, and she wondered if she'd left her sweater in my room.

I looked around my room. "No sweater here." I handed her Gerald's note. She read it and frowned, which prompted me to say, "I'm going to meet him at ten. If I'm not back by ten-thirty, send out a search party."

She gripped my arm. "Stop scaring me. I hope Gerald isn't the killer, and you're not his next victim."

"Now you're scaring me."

She kissed me goodbye.

Lots of time left before my meeting. With any luck, Gerald-filled nightmares wouldn't produce another night of fragmented sleep. Suddenly, I realized I hadn't interviewed Harriet about William's murder or told her what William had said about her in his journal. I grabbed my flashlight.

From the darkness near her room, a raspy voice asked, "Care to share some holy spirits?" In the faint light, I saw the glow of a cigarette. The air held a whiff of cloves. Harriet sat on a chair she'd dragged from her room. A Chiapas shawl shielded her from the crisp night air. "My friendly spirits come from a bottle of tequila."

One drink might help calm my nerves. "Sure, I've got time before I meet Gerald. He's promised some new information."

A look of fright streaked across her face, followed by a deep-throated laugh. "I can't offer enough spirits to make that meeting any easier. But, here, have a shot." She poured my drink into an empty glass. Had she been expecting a visitor?

I surprised myself by how fast I downed it.

"You can count me one of the lucky ones," she said. "I haven't seen Gerald since the board meeting."

"I wish I had your luck."

"Incidentally, if you're planning on sacrificing him, I'll help you paint him blue." We laughed it off, but she disturbed me since she was the second person to suggest killing Gerald.

"You're making an offer that seems impossible to refuse. But, since I'm Armadillo's "official" detective, I'll have to recuse myself."

"William's murder isn't solved? What's taking you so long?"

"Dealing with people who think it's not worth solving. But I must apologize because earlier I forgot to tell you what I found in William's journal. He bragged about drugging you, but he also wrote that he didn't rape you. His exact words were, 'I was set to have my way with her, but I lost interest. She didn't have an ounce of fat on her, and that turned me off.'"

"Oh, my gosh! My diet has finally paid off. But don't get me wrong; I'm not letting that loathsome womanizer off the hook. But what if he lied in that journal entry."

"Do you think he wouldn't take all the credit if he raped you?"

She thought for a moment. "You're right. But on to the next topic. I want you to know, Paul, I think you're the most qualified person to write Max's biography." *She doesn't sound like she's mocking me.* "Besides, if you're as evenhanded as you were with Freud, I've no problem championing you. But there's a huge problem. We have *Maya Magic,* and that's it. Where is anything else that Max wrote?"

Since our encounter before lunch yesterday, I'd continued to be wary of Harriet. Initially, she'd reacted negatively to my birthmark, and we'd both maintained our distance. Tonight, she was quite friendly. "I apologize for my antagonistic attitude when we met," I said. "Discovering William with his heart removed unnerved me."

"I could make it easier for you if I confessed to killing William." She paused, and I waited. "But I won't because I didn't."

"Where were you when he was killed?"

"I was in bed just like everyone else, except William and his killer."

"Both William and Gerald are cruel," I said, "but Gerald's

cruelty is larger in scope, not focused solely on women."

"You're right! He's the epitome of evil." She looked in my direction for a short eternity. "Next, you should ask me about a possible motive. And yes, I had one. Our dead man provoked, disparaged, ripped off, and raped—literally and figuratively— any woman he could. But if I'm to believe what you told me from his journal, I was only figuratively raped."

I tapped the arm of my chair. "Harriet, I'm just trying to find the one who killed him."

"In my opinion, I don't think this is a problem to be solved. The solution has already occurred. William's dead; the case is closed. Sorry, I'm not usually this cynical."

"I have a critical piece of evidence. When I found William's body, several links of a chain hung from his mouth. I pried open his jaw and pulled on the chain. Attached to it was a gold armadillo pendant." In the dim light, I could barely make out the expression on her face.

"I'll look at it later. It's time for your meeting with Gerald. If I'm still here after you talk to him, I'll share more holy spirits with you."

"I'll take you up on that."

"By the way, you may think that you and Gerald are in a pissing contest—a male ego thing. Not so! You and he are at war. Be very careful, Paul."

CHAPTER 27

The Emperor's New Clothes

A single fifteen-watt light bulb lit the corridor outside the chapel. I watched my footing on the uneven cobblestones. The faint light convinced me that Ruth truly needed to raise money for Armadillo. If the money started pouring in, I'd suggest she spend the first hundred dollars on higher watt bulbs.

On yesterday's tour, Father Lester waxed enthusiastic about how the white paint gave the chapel an airy feel. But this evening, when I opened the door and peered in, the chapel's pitch blackness struck me as ominous. I remembered a light switch to the left of the door, but nothing happened when I flicked it. *Paul, if this were a horror movie, you shouldn't venture inside because bad things will happen to you.* I turned on my flashlight, and I reassured myself that I was safe. Its flashlight beam caught the glint of the gold cross at the other end of the room. I repeatedly called out, "Gerald." I heard only the echo of my words and the shuffling of my shoes on the stone floor.

I cast the fading beam around the chapel and berated myself for buying cheap batteries. A chilling thought raced through my mind. Perhaps I might find another body just beyond the range of the flashlight. I took measured steps forward, scanning with the feeble light. The chapel held several rows of wooden pews facing the chancel. On the altar rested an ornate two-foot-high cross, a real collector's item. Where was the security? Inching forward, I flicked the light to the right and left as I continued saying Gerald's name. Silence. I circled the altar and walked back toward the confession box at the back of the chapel. My breathing disturbed the silence. I pulled on the box's nob—that was the last thing I remembered.

I awoke. An icy numbness permeated my naked body. I felt like I was freezing to death in an Iowa blizzard. Someplace deep in my gray cells, the line from "Snake" by Emily Dickinson kept repeating: "zero at the bone." But my face wasn't numb—it throbbed. Someone kept slapping me. Using all the willpower I could muster, I opened my eyes, but they closed just as fast.

At last, Sandy's face came into focus. In my peripheral vision, I saw a blur and felt another jolting slap. "Stop!" I said, but I wasn't sure Sandy could hear my words.

"Oh, Paul, thank goodness you're alive. We've got to get help. Harriet, find David quickly. Paul, I'm staying here with you. Don't move." *That's silly. I couldn't move if I tried.*

Occasionally, the beam of a flashlight blinded me. My head howling with pain, I swore to myself I'd kill Gerald.

At some point, I became aware of a damp sponge wiping my forehead. This time it was easier to open my eyes. I saw Sandy's silhouette, her hair backlit by a crackling blaze in my fireplace. I struggled to make sense of her words, but her soothing tone reassured me. She sponged my body with warm water and patted me dry with a towel. "What are you doing?" I asked.

She laughed but added, "What happened?" While her voice sounded urgent, her words sounded strange and far away.

I tried to express my thoughts, but scraps of memory, which kept tumbling around in my brain like numbered balls in a lottery cage, delayed them. Words came out in fragments and with no order.

Sandy continued to sponge and dry my body.

I raised my hands as if I could make myself understood with gestures. That's when I saw my arms. "I'm blue."

"I agree, not your best color," she said.

I struggled to lift my head. "Why am I blue?"

"Someone painted you that color."

"I don't understand."

"I found you naked behind the altar. Your whole body was painted blue."

"I don't understand." Repeating myself didn't make things any clearer.

"We don't either, but you were seconds away from becoming Armadillo's next sacrifice." Her words terrified me. "What's the last thing you remember?" she asked.

"I was looking into the dark confession box." My head felt bloated. I looked at Sandy with a puzzled expression. "Why are you here?"

"You told me you were meeting Gerald in the chapel, and I was to look for you if you weren't back in thirty minutes. The atrocious lighting in the library was hurting my eyes. I dozed off while waiting for you. I woke disoriented and remembered a murderer was running loose. My last words to you were, 'I hope you aren't the killer's next victim.' I felt guilty as hell, but mostly, I felt panic."

"You're so nice," I said in a singsong voice as I tried my best to follow what she was saying.

"I went to the chapel looking for you, Paul, but it was dark as a moonless night. I saw a beam of light moving behind the altar. I got scared and called out, 'Paul?' A muffled voice said, 'Come over here.' The voice wasn't yours. I stood petrified. Then I heard running steps and a door slam near the altar.

"My keychain had a tiny flashlight. I freaked out when I swept the light around the chapel, and it illuminated something next to the altar—It looked like the top of your head. I was afraid you might be dead. I was scared, but then I raced to you and found you unconscious. I was leaning over you when I heard Harriet calling out your name. I screamed for her to get help because someone had attacked you. Your naked body was painted blue. I kept slapping your face to wake you up. It took several minutes for you to regain consciousness."

"After Harriet found me, we ran to the chapel," someone said. It sounded like David. "The three of us carried you to your room. Lucky for you, it's latex paint. Sandy's been doing her best to remove it."

I knew I wasn't thinking clearly, but I asked, "Did you find a knife?"

Seeing the looks on their faces, I knew the answer before David said, "Yes, a large kitchen knife with a towel wrapped around its handle. I checked with Doña María. She confirmed it came from her kitchen."

"Oh, Paul," Sandy said as she held my face in her hands. "You were almost killed." Her tears flowed. I wanted to comfort her by telling her that I was okay, but the pain in my head was intense, and I felt confused.

I opened my eyes. Sandy, her face looking haggard, was asleep in the chair beside my bed. I felt reassured knowing she was there. I turned on my side and was aware of bedsheets touching most of my skin. "Look at me! I'm wearing the Emperor's new clothes."

Sandy opened her eyes and managed a smile. "True, but only because we refused to let you wear that hideous blue outfit."

Every inch of my body itched. My head hurt something fierce. "I'm freezing to death."

"That's nothing compared to your close call with death by open-heart surgery." She leaned over and kissed me on the forehead.

From across the room, David added, "All we know is whoever tried to kill you wasn't a Rembrandt."

His words were peculiar. "What do you mean?"

He dragged his chair over next to Sandy's. "Your would-be killer slopped paint all over, leaving half of it on the floor behind the altar. More like an amateur house painter than an artist."

"Thank you, David, you just helped me piece together a part of the puzzle. William's killer was a Rembrandt who painted precisely. If William and I were paintings, he'd be a masterpiece, and I'd be paint-by-numbers schlock."

Sandy leaned in and whispered in my ear, "Quit babbling, Paul, and go to sleep."

But I was on a roll, despite pain shooting through my body with every word I spoke. "We're not looking for one killer; we're looking for two. One is a Rembrandt who killed William. The person who came close to killing me is a third-rate imitator. Their differing talents as artists don't mean they aren't equally dangerous, but now we know we're looking for two killers."

"Great!" Sandy said. "Now, we can be twice as scared."

"Or twice as likely to solve one murder."

Sandy poked me in the side with her forefinger. "I admire how you can reframe situations, but get some sleep."

"Our next job is finding them."

David frowned at me. "I don't mean to be argumentative, but there's a problem with your reasoning. Maybe a lone killer didn't have enough time to paint the next masterpiece using your body as a canvas. Hearing Sandy in the chapel, the killer dropped the knife and left by the side door near the altar."

"David's right," Sandy said.

"And what's more," David continued, "the Rembrandt killer painted William before removing his heart. Luckily for you, this killer hadn't yet finished the body painting."

My head continued to throb. "So, we don't know if it's one or more killers we're after."

"I know one thing," Sandy said, "Go to sleep—now!"

"But—"

She grinned. "Looking for a second bump on your head?"

"Goodnight, Sandy."

"Goodnight, Paul. And this time, I hope you have sweet dreams."

I closed my eyes but stayed awake. After a while, I heard footsteps, the door to my room opened, and Sandy and David left. I thought how reckless I'd been to enter a dark chapel with a killer on the loose. Then I remembered how lucky I was that

Sandy had found me in time.

Drifting off to sleep, I thought of Max sitting at his piano in the still of the night. He waited for Maurine, but he died before learning of her tragic fate. Like Max, I too had paused in the still of the night, but unlike him, I'd been lucky. Sandy found me before I became the killer's next victim. I felt relieved but also scared. Luck saved me this time, but I knew that luck always runs out eventually.

I slowly opened my eyes and saw sunlight bathing the Chiapas floor rug. Sandy was asleep in the other bed. The sliding bar on the door securely locked the room. She'd returned, realistically fearing the person who'd tried to kill me might try again. I whispered, "Thank you, Sandy." She made a soft, throaty sound, rolled over, and faced the wall.

Despite my throbbing head, I forced myself to think. I remembered entering the chapel and being there a minute before someone knocked me out. Sandy found me no more than thirty minutes later. That didn't give my would-be killer—undoubtedly, it was Gerald—much time. He knocked me out when I opened the confession box, dragged me across the chapel floor and deposited me behind the altar, stripped off my clothes, and painted my body blue. But he dropped the knife and left when he heard someone enter the chapel. On the other hand, I suspected Gerald would have preferred to enlighten me with his supposed brilliance, not recreate a Maya sacrifice.

Another possibility was a team of killers working together: Gerald and an accomplice, perhaps Ruth. *What am I thinking!* She wouldn't have cooperated with him under any circumstances. While he painted my body blue, she'd have driven the knife into his back, claimed the credit for stopping him in time, and approved me to write Max's biography.

But Gerald would have needed an accomplice. Perhaps he and Doña María had worked together. Those two working together? Again, no way. Doña María assuredly knew about Maya sacrifices, but so did about everyone else staying at Armadillo. As far as I could tell, Doña María seemed, like everyone else, to have avoided William and Gerald.

Was Ruth acting alone to kill me? I didn't know. But I was sure she needed me alive to extract the best deal from Gerald if she were to choose him. Perhaps she enlisted faithful David to assist. I ruled out David because Harriet found him in his room. Too late now to check for blue paint on his hands or clothing. But the bottom line was that David would never use a knife. He'd shoot his victims with a 35 mm camera. I started to laugh at my humor, but the throbbing in my head increased.

Harriet? Perhaps she put knockout drops in my Tequila, yet how did she happen to be sitting there waiting for me with a powerful sedative? Furthermore, how could Harriet have hidden in the chapel when I'd started ahead of her? Perhaps she used the side door near the altar that David had mentioned.

Sandy stirred. I said, "Thanks for all your help last night."

She didn't turn over, but said, "I'm thankful you're alive."

"Me, too. I've been lying here trying to sort out what happened. By the way, should I rule you out as a suspect?"

She rolled over and faced me. "Excuse the pun, Dr. Seawright, but I'll take a stab at your question." She still sounded groggy with sleep. "Let's assume I'm lurking in the unlit chapel. I'm lying in wait with a razor-sharp knife, and I've hardened my heart to kill. In the dark, I believe I've knocked out Gerald. I pull my victim behind the altar, strip off his clothes, and apply paint from his head to foot. Finally, I shine my flashlight on my victim's face and realize I've nearly killed my lover, not a man I despise."

I marveled at her impeccable logic. "You can stop. I get your point."

"There was another way for me to realize I'd made a ghastly mistake. I start to take off my victim's clothes, but I feel a muscular torso. Luckily, I've embraced yours, and I realized my mistake. Besides, no woman with half a brain would ever confuse your hard body with Gerald's soft one."

"Thanks for the compliment."

160

"May I, now that I'm no longer your number one suspect, approach the bed, climb under the covers, and caress an awe-inspiring—made by Royal Canadian exercises—body?"

"The pleasure is ours."

CHAPTER 28

A Passport

I turned on the faucet and splashed cold water on my face. I called out to Sandy, "Trying to kill me was Gerald's worst idea. Want to come along and watch me confront him?" I conveyed more bravado than I felt.

"Seeing that horrible man is the last thing I want."

I stood in front of Gerald's door and reached up and felt the large, tender lump on my head. That re-energized my anger. *Time to take him on.* When I was growing up, if my adoptive mom caught me misbehaving, she'd say, "Remember that we raised you right." Ignoring her admonishment, I barged into Gerald's room without warning or a plan other than I'd beat anyone else to the punch by hurting him. But from the moment I entered, second thoughts assailed me—as did Gerald's angry-sounding voice.

"Hey! Don't go charging into my room!" Despite his tone, he lounged in a rocker as though he hadn't a care in the world. "Oh, my. Paul looks mad, and when he's mad, his birthmark gets all red and scary."

I looked around for something with which to hurt him. "You're a fool to think you can sacrifice me like William."

"What are you talking about?"

"I'm talking about your note at my door inviting me to meet you in the chapel last night to see photos. I'm talking about your knocking me out and painting my body blue and just about plunging a knife into me."

His smile widened. "You can believe that if you want, but you're wrong. I think of you as a colleague. If I'd wanted to kill someone, I'd have picked that low-life woman you hang out with—the one with the alias."

I clenched my hands and stepped forward.

"Before you get carried away, Paul, you need to know that I finally figured out who Sandy is. She isn't who she claims to be. She's playing you for a sucker."

My rage had been building. I took another step and heard a click and saw a glint of light. He pointed a switchblade at my face and flashed an abrasive smile. He waved the blade back and forth like a downtempo metronome. "Time to leave, buddy. If you stay, I'll do you a favor and remove that blotch on your face." He paused and added, "Or you could calm down, and we could have a civil conversation."

"I'm serious. You tried to kill me."

"And I'm equally serious when I say you're out of your mind. Check my alibi."

I said nothing.

"After last night's dinner—the one during which Ruth told that silly story about champagne coupes—I met with David to go over his memories about Max. Unfortunately, he rattled off the most whitewashed version of Max's life I'd ever heard. As for an alibi, I didn't leave David's place until about ten. Check it out."

I looked at him for a long time. Did his alibi make sense? Maybe it did. David hadn't said he'd met with Gerald, but that was easy to check. Still, he had an alibi for the time someone delivered the note inviting me to the chapel. I backed toward the door.

As I left, he added, "You know, Dr. Birthmark, it's polite to knock before entering a room. I'll accept your apology—once you give it."

Standing in the corridor, I heard him bellow, "I'll give you a second chance, but knock this time. I have some juicy information—about photos, no less—to share with you, my amusing but volatile associate."

I stood outside for a bit before swallowing my pride. "I'm sorry."

"Come in, dear colleague. Make yourself comfortable."

Gerald continued sitting and playing with his switchblade. "Last year, when I visited Armadillo, I entered the darkroom once shared by Max and David. Bottles of chemicals, shelves storing vintage cameras, and numerous small drawers filled the room—a photographer's joy. Being compulsively curious, I searched for signs of Max's presence. Eureka! I found a short strip of film containing two photographic negatives that people would kill to possess. They'd slipped down and lodged between abutting tabletops. Remember in the early sixties, when *Eros* featured drawings of Maya in various sexual positions? Their source was unidentified."

"Yeah, I saw the issue."

"I bet you did."

I bit my tongue and kept quiet.

"Read this." He pulled a magazine from a stack of papers on his desk and handed it to me. "Turn to page twenty-eight for Dr. Richard Scrivener's concise introduction to the article featuring Maya drawings. He's a distinguished professor at Indiana University's Institute for Sex Research.

Three of the twelve poses do not appear in our extensive collection of Asian and Western erotic archival material, including sex manuals and art considered pornographic. Even if experts never verify the poses as having their origins in the Maya culture, they represent the expression of a fertile imagination unconstrained by repressive societal forces. Peruse the drawings, and if inclined, enjoy practicing and mastering these poses. Variety indeed is the spice of life. *Bon appétit.*

Gerald wiped his hand across his mouth. "Look at the drawings and tell me, are they real or forged?"

I shrugged.

"I don't know for certain. But I have two photo negatives showing a couple performing two inconceivable positions. Both are poses shown in the Maya article, but at least a decade before it was published. The negatives help me understand considerably more about Dr. Max Eicher and—insert drum roll here—his young "friend" at the time, none other than the lovely Kate Davis. They wore masks to disguise their identities."

I continued to stare at him.

"Frankly, I was astonished at how two humans could assume those particular poses and not shriek with pain. Either love conquerors all, or those positions are a powerful analgesic drug."

Listening to Gerald, I remembered the maxim: Sarcasm has no place in a helping relationship. But I wasn't in a helping relationship with him. "I applaud your attention to details. You've carved yet another notch on your scholarly six-shooter."

Gerald glanced at me as if I were his secretary chiding him for a misplaced comma. "But you're diverting me from what I want to tell you. I can't yet divulge details, but Ruth will select me as Max's biographer. I've discovered a most beguiling photo from her Hollywood days."

I kept a neutral look on my face. The night before last, I'd overheard him blackmailing her. Because he still held the switchblade, I restrained the impulse to punch him in the face.

"When I told her what I'd discovered, she became testy, but she'll become much more cooperative. The capacity of our species to sacrifice other humans is truly phenomenal. Incidentally, who are you willing to sacrifice? Perhaps Sandy?"

That was it. I cared a lot about Sandy, and Gerald was attacking her. I felt a black rage. I experienced the impulse to murder him, and it scared me. Historically, to ensure their community would survive and flourish, the ancient Maya sacrificed others. And while a killer's rage had perhaps driven William's murder, his death allowed the community to survive and flourish. I recognized that my urge to kill Gerald arose from the same two motivations—a killer's blinding rage and sheer altruism.

"You've torn out people's hearts with your writing. Perhaps someone will tear out yours—literally."

Gerald's perpetual smirk broadened. "My! Am I witnessing your inner anger looking for an opportunity to escape? I do regret you're not a famous archaeologist because I'd love to dissect your life."

I turned to leave.

"Before you go, I've learned you've teamed up with one of my adversaries. None other than a woman who tried to defame my character."

"If you're talking about Sandy Martin, you're crazy."

"Not at all. I finally remembered where I'd met Sandy before. Want to know the truth? Check out the photocopy of her passport in the office. She's here to sabotage my work."

If Gerald was right and Sandy wasn't who she appeared to be, then who was she?

"I study my enemies," Gerald said. "I hope you'll give her up and remain my faithful sidekick. You're too much of a lightweight to be an adversary. It's your call: cooperate with me or suffer the same fate as the alias Sandy Martin. Incidentally, ask her if she still likes Bob Marley."

I left. Where could I find a knife sharp enough to cut out Gerald's heart? Assuming he had one.

Gerald's comments about Sandy were ominous. Still tense from my close call with death and now getting no response to my knocking on her door, I opened it and called out. I glanced around the room and saw her purse on the nightstand. Gerald was lying, but no harm in peeking to see how old she was.

Her driver's license showed a slightly younger Sandy. She was even more beautiful now. Born May 9, 1947. I smiled. Yesterday, this woman, three years older than me, functioned as my guru in the art of making love. I scanned the rest of the information. Sharon Silverthorne. *Oh, shit!* Only two days ago in the library, Gerald bragged about destroying S. Silverthorne's career. Why was Silverthorne now calling herself Sandy Martin? Why lie to me about who she was? One thing was sure: Gerald played hardball with everyone.

When I opened my room door, I saw Sandy going through my suitcase. She looked up startled but then asked teasingly, "Tell me, does Gerald now have his first friend?"

"What are you doing?" My tone was firm, but my hands shook.

"I've got a headache. I was checking if you had any aspirin."

"Tell the truth."

"Paul!"

"You told me you didn't know Gerald Strupp."

"I swear I've never met him before."

"According to him, your name is Silverthorne." She glared at me. I waited until she spoke, but she said nothing. "On my first day here, Gerald told me he'd destroyed an academic career with a scathing review of S. Silverthorne's book manuscript. When I went to your room to find you, I saw your driver's license. I shouldn't have looked, but I did. It's Sharon Silverthorne's passport, but your photo."

"You had no right to go through my stuff!"

"And you're not who you say you are!"

"So, I know him. What's the big deal? He's a hideous excuse for a human being. He destroys everything he encounters." She averted her eyes. "This is humiliating, but I'll tell you because I trust you. As an assistant professor, I submitted a book manuscript to a publisher. I waited for months to hear the decision. When it came, I was devastated. While three reviewers were very positive, a fourth reviewer, who I found out was Gerald Strupp, strongly recommended not publishing my book. He cited sloppy scholarship, failure to cite eminent scholars (including himself), and merely repeating what other scholars had already written. Based on Gerald's credentials, they weighted his review heavily and rejected my proposal. I've never forgiven him."

"Wait a minute. Gerald told me that Silverthorne wrote an

aggressive review of his latest book before he rejected your manuscript. Was he right?"

"I didn't praise his wretched book, if that what you mean. I just pointed out some minor errors."

"Did Gerald just lie to me?"

Her face turned crimson. "He can rot in hell. My colleagues told me how good my book was and how it explored critical issues in archaeology. Gerald savaged my book because I dared to question the great and powerful Dr. Gerald Strupp." She burst into tears.

Her tears made her seem vulnerable. I put my arm around her and said, "I'm sorry." She moved my hand away.

"I don't want sympathy. I want to wreak havoc on Gerald's life as he did on mine. I want to drive a knife into his stony heart and twist it round and round. His screams will be music to my ears."

I've encountered hostile people, but none filled with as much hatred as she expressed. There was one big difference; I cared about the woman who, if someone murdered Gerald, would be my prime suspect.

She wiped away her tears and looked down at her hands. "I'm sorry." she said, "but I never thought he'd be at Armadillo. If I'd known, I never would have come here."

What she was saying didn't make sense. "Gerald told me that a young man, wearing a Bob Marley shirt, a dreadlocks wig, and sunglasses, visited his office and pumped him for information about his next writing project. You knew he'd be here, didn't you?"

"That was my attempt to sabotage whatever his next project was. And yes, I learned he was going to Armadillo. Then he kicked me out of his office. My disguise worked until he finally recognized me here. Shit!"

I took a deep breath. "Can I help you get out of here?"

She swayed her body back and forth as though trying to clarify her conflicting emotions. "I love being with you. If I can avoid Gerald, I can stay here. Just keep him out of my sight."

"It's too late for that. We're both on Gerald's payback list. But we agree about one thing: he'll show no mercy to anyone who gets in his way. I suspect he killed William, but I can't figure out his motive."

"I can't believe he trashed my book. No tenure and promotion committee will vote yes on me after what he's done. I'll never be able to find a job in academia again."

Pain and anger still consumed her, but I continued my line of questioning. "Did you know William?"

"No, but he tried to know me. Within fifteen minutes of arriving here, he groped and propositioned me. I quickly learned to stay clear of him. He was a creep, but I had no desire to kill him."

"Do you have a knife capable of plunging into a man's chest?"

"No, but if I needed one, I could get it from Doña María's kitchen."

"You're not the first person to say that."

"Paul, I need to be alone for a while. Give me an hour by myself."

"Whatever you want, Sharon."

Her head jerked back. "Say, you're a fast learner." She gave me a wink.

I headed to Doña María's kitchen for a cup of black coffee. Confronting Gerald and comforting an aggrieved Sharon had sapped my energy. Also, La Ruta's higher altitude was taking its toll. My body moved slowly; my head had continued to throb since last night. I looked at my watch and quietly cursed. I'd missed breakfast, and the board meeting started in ten minutes. I didn't want to go another round with Gerald. If Ruth appointed me to write Max's biography, all hell would break loose.

"I didn't see you at breakfast," Doña María said. "Have you stopped liking the breakfast I prepare?"

"No, I love your breakfasts." I did my best to explain my head hurt and that a cup of coffee would help.

"No, no. Your head hurts because you didn't eat the breakfast that I fixed for you. I don't want you to become as thin as Max. You must eat."

I thanked her for the coffee and pointed my feet in the direction of the library.

CHAPTER 29

The Elimination Round

By the time I entered the library, all the board members were gathered around the table. Closed curtains shrouded the room, giving it the feel of a funeral parlor. The yellowish glow of the table lamps enhanced the effect. Before taking a seat, I walked along the outside wall and drew the curtains open to the light.

"Thanks," Harriet said, "I couldn't stand another minute sealed in this casket of a room."

"Ruth, before we start," Roland said, "I have something important to share." Ruth motioned for him to continue. "My preliminary examination of Casa Armadillo suggests the stone foundation was once the base of a Maya temple. It's ludicrous to believe that Dr. Eicher employed thousands of locals to move massive stones to construct the current foundation. I offer two possibilities. First, over the last millennium, the local people have removed all the stones that once made up a pyramid resting on the foundation. The second possibility, which I believe is more probable, is that the Maya constructed the temple's foundation, and for reasons we don't know, never finished it."

I mentally applauded Roland for failing to consider a third and correct explanation: Armadillo's visible foundation formed the base of an inverted pyramid descending into the ground. But I chafed at the thought of him inspecting Armadillo. He had a sharp eye, and he'd keep asking questions.

Before I could comment on Roland's observations, Gerald jumped in and changed the subject. "Ruth, you're taking forever to make the biography decision."

Her mouth twisted into a ghastly smile. "Patience. I'll reveal all when I'm ready."

"You listen to me!" Gerald pounded his hand on the table. "Paul and I aren't racing to a photo finish to be Max's biographer. Because I possess compromising photos, you'll select me."

Ruth slumped in her chair as though his threat had sucked the air from her lungs. She recovered quickly and restored an unreadable expression. Only her glaring eyes hinted at a reservoir of pent-up hatred.

I sat back in amazement at Gerald's brutal efficiency. In a matter of seconds, he'd insulted me and stunned Ruth.

With fear hanging in the air, Harriet gave me a supportive look. "Can we get on with this meeting?" she asked.

"We're moving along," Gerald said. "We're talking about writing, which should be of interest to you."

Harriet wrinkled her brow.

"Come now; innocence doesn't become you. I analyzed your so-called research on Max's *Maya Magic*. It's all 'double, double toil and trouble, fire burn and cauldron bubble' to which you've thrown in a dollop of *Close Encounters of the Third Kind*."

"What you're saying is slanderous."

"Not if it's true."

Until minutes before, Ruth had run the board meetings with an iron fist. Now she'd relinquished control, or more accurately, Gerald had seized it. Nobody was standing up to him. *Enough is enough*. I screamed at Gerald, "Stop bullying women!"

"Oh, methinks it's chivalrous Paul riding to the rescue of two helpless damsels in distress. Well, forget it. They aren't helpless. I've probed for the truth about Max and Armadillo, and I've found quite a bit. As for you, Paul, I've given you ample chances to uncover Sandy Martin's identity."

I felt a wave of nausea as if he'd delivered a kidney punch. "That's the third woman you've attacked within the last minute."

"Calm down. Sandy—as you call her—is quite capable of defending herself without your assistance."

Now I knew why the board members in the room were quiet. Gerald had formidable weapons at his disposal to crush anyone who got in his way. The scariest part: he relished using them. I mimicked Ruth's posture of a few minutes earlier as I sank into my chair. I'd let Gerald believe he'd defeated me.

Ruth tapped on a water glass. "I have had enough! This meeting is over. We'll meet here at ten tomorrow, and I'll announce which proposal I've accepted for the restoration of Armadillo. I also will name Max's biographer."

Perhaps comforted with Ruth's promises or relieved that the meeting had ended, those gathered breathed a collective sigh of relief. I started for the door, but Gerald stood in my way. "No hard feelings, old sport. Just doing my best to make sure everyone understands my position."

I pushed past him, but Gerald grabbed my sleeve and didn't let go. "Slow down. I searched William's room, a man we'll memorialize as Armadillo's first contemporary Maya sacrifice, and I found nothing. You said he kept a journal. I want to see it."

"Let go of my sleeve!" I waited until he released his hold. "Are you searching for more blackmail material?"

"Meaning?"

"Gerald, feigning denseness doesn't become you." He flinched. "Last night, I overheard you threaten Ruth over photos, and you reminded her of them again today."

"And now you're eavesdropping on me? You're naïve, but you're getting to be a nuisance. Besides, you misunderstood. I didn't threaten Ruth; we were simply negotiating. But I propose a toast to us: 'May the most ruthless scholar lose.' I hope you caught the pun—it means if you don't have Ruth on your side, your biography of Max is toast. One way or another, she'll pick me."

"What's so important that you grabbed my sleeve?" I asked.

"What I can't figure out is *Maya Magic*. It's a masterwork, but infuriatingly obtuse. One scholar suggested that Max wrote it in a drug-induced state and that his purported findings were visual hallucinations. We know that some celebrities who came to Armadillo in the thirties got their kicks from cocaine. But despite many believing that Max drank himself to death, I can't find a bit of evidence he ever took drugs or drank any alcohol. What's your take on the book?"

I felt like scratching my head in disbelief: one minute, the man could bully people, and the next, ask their thoughts about something he was struggling to figure out. *Paul, keep your friends close and your enemies closer.* Still seething from his threats against Harriet, Ruth, and Sharon, I employed misdirection. "I'm not sure that when Max wrote *Maya Magic* that he used drugs." I modified my voice to sound more like a conspirator and leaned toward Gerald. "I suspect we have a potential Carlos Castaneda on our hands." I deliberately chose "we" and "our" to make it appear I was on Gerald's side. "Castaneda's *Teachings of Don Juan* makes for absorbing reading—after all, what young person doesn't aspire to be a shaman? But as you said about Max's drinking, there's no conclusive evidence. How do we know Don Juan ever existed? It's the same concern I have with Max's papers. I think Max wrote *Maya Magic*. Period. It was his sole contribution to archaeology. I find his book spellbinding fiction, but most likely bogus science."

I was hoping to throw Gerald off guard. I waited.

"That's good," he said. "Why not give up writing your biography of Max and help me locate his papers. I'll give you full credit for your contributions."

Sure, the egotistic fool will give me credit—in a footnote buried on page two hundred seventy-four. I bit down hard on my tongue to keep from laughing in his face.

"And just to show you I'm a generous scholar," he said, "I'll show you the photographs I found. That line of inquiry started when a Hollywood producer as old as Methuselah directed me to the existence of Ruth's infamous tattoo."

I delivered a neutral sounding, "Sounds like luck was with

you."

"Not luck, you schmuck. I work hard to track down every-thing for an intriguing story."

He worked hard, all right. He approached scholarship with a scorched earth policy, like Sherman marching to the sea, deter-mined to destroy anything standing in his way of writing an annihilating biography. "Look, Gerald, I have some thinking to do. I'll talk to you later."

"Don't forget my offer to give you credit in my biography of Max."

"Don't worry. I'll never forget." How could I ever forget the most insulting offer I'd ever received?

As to Gerald's photos, they could wait. An intriguing idea had grabbed me. I pivoted and returned to the library.

CHAPTER 30

Matching Wits

I n *Memoirs,* Max wrote vaguely about the burial chamber room of the Maya tomb, which Doña María's people called Armadillo. At times, Max seemed to drop clues that the library was the key to finding its entrance. Yet when I examined the clues more closely, they dissipated like smoke from a cigarette. I pulled the library's curtains closed. I rejected chairs with sagging cushions until I found a comfortable one. A recent disturbance in the library perplexed me, but I couldn't pinpoint what it was. I visualized each person at Armadillo. While several were disagreeable or worse, it wasn't people who baffled me.

The clock on the fireplace mantel struck eleven o'clock. *Amazing that old thing still works.* I sat back, closed my eyes, and listened to the room's silence. Board members had spoken their share of angry words, but the sound I heard now wasn't a language. Was it Gerald grinding his teeth? No—that was just irritating. Perhaps Ruth's incessantly tapping her fingernails when others spoke? No. I'd heard a short, unusual sound, quickly followed by a cacophony of voices. The unidentified sound, whatever it was, hovered in the canal that led to my eardrum.

And then in my head, I heard it—a hollow-sounding clunk. I imagined myself in yesterday's board meeting, and I reviewed the scene where I'd prevented Harriet from hurling a small onyx armadillo at Gerald. When the sculpture hit the wall to the left of the fireplace, it clunked. Most odd. Armadillo is a stable structure with massive, two-foot thick walls covered with thick plaster. When the sculpture hit the wall, it should've emitted a solid thud, not a hollow clunk. I stood where Harriet had been and picked up the onyx sculpture. I heaved it toward the wall to the left of the fireplace. The clunking sound matched the one in my memory.

To confirm my discovery, I tapped on the fireplace wall in different places using the onyx armadillo. To the touch of my hand, the plaster felt rock-hard, but when I knocked on the wall with the armadillo, it reverberated with a dull hollow thud. That wasn't right. I rapped on the wall adjacent to the fireplace, the one with the evenly spaced windows. Solid as could be— no hollow sounds. I tapped the other two walls with the same results. I returned to the fireplace wall and kept knocking as I walked both to the right and left. The entire fireplace wall sounded hollow.

If this was a false wall, what did it conceal? First, I needed to verify a hunch. I stood against the fireplace wall and counted my steps to the opposite end of the room. As I did so, I noticed to my right the asymmetrical arrangement of windows on the outside wall. The far-right window was jammed up against the fireplace wall, giving the wall with windows a cockeyed appearance.

Outside the building, I counted my steps from the far window of the library to Armadillo's right-angle corner. Even allowing for a slight error in measurement and thick masonry, the inside library wall was ten feet shorter than its outside distance. I walked out fifty feet from the building's corner. Despite the balustrade and vegetation partially blocking my view, I saw the library chimney arose from inside the house, about ten feet inward from the wall.

I reentered the library and locked the door. Having confirmed the fireplace wall concealed something—probably a secret room—I confronted another problem. Where was the room's entrance? Did the grand fireplace hide a passageway? In several pages of *Memoirs*, Max had described his childhood love of magic. When he was in fourth grade, his parents had taken him to Chicago for a performance by Harry Houdini. Max had watched in amazement as Houdini, chained and handcuffed, escaped from a securely padlocked, galvanized milk can that had been filled to the brim with water. Max had written that Houdini's escape "unconsciously convinced me that people could avoid fate if they used the magic that they possessed within themselves, that magic being imaginative thinking."

Houdini's performance worked its spell on young Max, who, from that point on, checked out every magic book in the Dubuque Public Library. By fifth grade, he'd memorized all the tricks and was forever pestering his parents and friends to watch his latest sleight-of-hand illusion. In eighth grade, he billed himself as "Eicher: The Maxifying Performer" and executed his magic with playing cards: "not that my hands were large enough to handle them deftly."

I reasoned that Max had applied the illusions of magic to create a fake wall. Perhaps the firebox held a hidden latch? A quick look convinced me I'd need to rent a power washer to remove a half-century of soot. Using the onyx armadillo, I systematically thumped each brick of the firebox. Real. Max had been a magician, but even he didn't possess the ability to pass through a solid wall.

Bookcases, with four-foot-length shelves, lined both sides of the fireplace. Yesterday, Sharon had marveled at how the shelves held an excellent collection of books on the early history of Mexico and Central America. The dustless books were a tribute to Doña María's fastidious housekeeping. I methodically inspected the bookcases. Nothing unusual caught my eye.

I crawled on my hands and knees and examined the tiles along the fireplace wall. I looked for signs of wear to indicate a shelf had been swung open over time. I'd almost completed my inspection when I noticed a faint arc on the tile. Looking up, I saw that ornately carved, six-inch-wide wood moldings separated all the bookcases. I pulled hard on the nearest one and tumbled back. In my hands, I held a long wooden strip of molding. On its reverse side, strong magnets appeared at one-foot intervals; the bookcase had correspondingly steel plates attached.

With the molding removed, I saw the bookcases weren't flush with each other but separated by a five-inch pitch-black gap. I pulled on a shelf from the right-hand bookcase, and it swung open a bit. I pulled harder. Slowly, the shelf followed the scratched arc on the floor. *Maxifying Performer, I applaud you.* I swung the bookcase closed and replaced the molding.

After retrieving my flashlight and loading it with fresh batteries, I returned to the library, locked the door, removed the molding, and pulled on the bookcase. It swung open. Cautiously, I stepped into the darkness. I felt like an intruder entering a sacred space. As I moved the flashlight around, its beam illuminated a Maya stone face staring at me. My heart almost stopped. I stood rooted in place as I gasped for air. Slowly, I swung the flashlight back and forth. More faces emerged from the darkness, taking my breath away.

I stepped back and moved the light up and down; a magnificent stone stela arose eight feet from the floor and dominated the room. Menacing figures covered the entire stela. My pulse again raced. I was sure this stela was the one that young María had shown Max. But how had they moved this massive piece from near the foundation to the top of it? I had no idea. Archaeologists would race to publicize the discovery of this stela. Not Max; he chose to hide his treasure from everyone.

Surely the hidden room had lights, but I couldn't locate a wall switch. A banker's lamp with a green glass shade rested on a desk at the end of the room. I pulled the chain and was amazed when light filled the room. Old wooden filing cabinets lined a second wall. All their drawers were empty. Large corkboards with pushpins decorated the third wall, but the boards held no papers. I was puzzled. This secret room had to be the office where Max worked and stored his projects. But apart from the stela, Max or someone else had removed anything of value.

I noticed my footprints on the dusty floor and realized that no one else's feet had stirred the dust on these stones in the recent past—not Gerald or any others gathered at Armadillo. If Gerald had found anything of value here, he'd have confided in me, his "promising scholar," even if he wouldn't reveal where he'd made his discovery. Gerald simply could not resist flaunting his most recent discoveries.

As I scanned the enormous, two-ton stela resting on a dark stone base, I had an insight. Just as Max had used the false fireplace wall as an obstacle to prevent anyone entering the tomb, perhaps he'd used the stela as a second obstacle. A tremor shook my body as I grasped that the stela might separate me from a chamber constructed more than a millennium ago.

Thick, small rugs surrounded the stela; I pulled them aside. This time I found the marks on the floor left by large ball bearings. Lying on my back next to the stone base holding the stela, I saw it didn't touch the floor. It was raised three inches. I scooted around the entire base, feeling into the small crawlspace. When I'd almost reached the place where I'd started, I suddenly felt a round knob. I pulled on it, a smooth metal shaft emerged. Although I wanted to scream with joy, I checked myself.

Am I ready for this? I pressed my shoulder hard against the stela. It slowly rotated in an arc, finally resting at a ninety-degree angle from its starting point. Then, my flashlight beam revealed a dark wooden trap door with a sizable, brass-ring handle. I deeply breathed in the dry air and exhaled slowly. *Oh, Max, you never did anything in a half-assed way.*

Suddenly, I worried that I might find a burial chamber as empty as the hidden room. My watch indicated I had an hour and thirty minutes until lunch, which meant I could explore the tomb and still have time to clean up. I didn't want to look as if I'd been moonlighting as a chimney sweep.

I pulled on the brass ring; its coolness transferred to my hands. Then, the trap door moved slightly up, revealing its hinged side. I rested the upright trap door against the adjacent wall. Shining a shaft of light into the blackness, I saw a steep, narrow staircase and low ceiling descending into a void. A recurring childhood nightmare surfaced in my memory, but the reality at my feet terrified me in comparison. The phrase, "I could hear my heart beating," had always struck me as hyperbole. No more.

At the height of their civilization, the ancient Maya had dug this passage into the earth. Carefully, I began the steep descent, keeping my head down. I knew enough to inch my way ahead, fearful of encountering snakes, scorpions, or—in this tropical environment—something far worse that I couldn't even name.

After descending for a couple of minutes, I calculated I was nearing...what should I call it since an inverted tomb's top was buried the deepest into the ground? The steps ended, and a short stretch of even floor loomed ahead. Other than Max's hand in the construction of the secret room and the swiveling stela, I hadn't seen any indication of his work since I'd begun my descent.

The tunnel widened, and I entered a stone chamber. I directed my flashlight toward an inner wall. Maya murals depicting figures in astonishing colors leaped out and assaulted my senses. My retinas felt fried. Moving closer, I beheld Technicolor versions of sights I'd seen before. I blinked several times to reassure myself that I saw the originals of the exotic drawings *Eros* magazine had published. On all four walls, Maya couples engaged in sexual positions, some of which defied my imagination. Centered at the top of each wall stood a three-foot glyph depicting a breathtakingly beautiful, painted armadillo.

I backed toward the center of the chamber to get a broader view and felt something hard hit me between my shoulder blades. Adrenaline shot through my body. I spun around, punching where I thought the person's face might be. My fist landed on nothing. I fell and struck the ground hard.

Looking up in the faint light, I saw something glowing. I reached for my flashlight—luckily, still working. The discovery would have skyrocketed me to the profession's pinnacle if I'd been a junior archaeologist. Before me, a gold armadillo the size of a storage chest rested on the lid of a sarcophagus. As I moved the light, the gold figure astonished me. Never in any museum had I seen such a magnificent sculpture. *Max, why in the hell did you keep hidden this world-class treasure?*

Looking past the armadillo, I saw another sarcophagus. This one was also lidded, but where a corresponding gold sculpture would have been, nothing appeared. Then I knew. Max hadn't told anyone about the gold armadillo, but he'd displayed his discovery with an enigmatic flair. One gold armadillo was in front of me; the other armadillo that had once rested on the lid of the second sarcophagus was in the courtyard, disguised by a thick coat of white plaster. Max had hidden one of the two in plain sight. That meant Doña María knew. She periodically gave the courtyard armadillo a fresh coat of plaster—likely following Max's instructions.

I longed to stay in the chamber and examine its contents, but others might notice my absence if I didn't return. Hopefully, I could slip into my room, wash up, and change clothes with nobody seeing me. I remembered Neumann admonishing me for hoping. But right now, no better word came to mind.

I returned to the library and looked back at the fireplace wall. Max learned skills from a second magician, Harry Blackstone, Sr., and a master at constructing grand illusions of solidity to conceal the Maya treasures. Max and Doña María had found the treasures but then hidden them. Why?

That was the problem. My re-discovery of Armadillo's priceless treasures—the unique stela behind the library hall, four burial chamber walls covered with ancient murals featuring erotica, and two gold armadillos—would be an archaeologist's crowning achievement. And while it was an intellectual challenge to match wits with the specter of Max and mind-blowing to chalk up my extraordinary success in finding his treasures, locating his papers eluded me. That's when I swore that I heard Max's ghost, an illusionist still at the top of his game, chuckling about his secret Maya world.

Before leaving the library, I opened the window curtains.

Drawing open the last one, I saw a figure move past the window. I peered out and saw Roland slowly walking along Armadillo's outside wall. Trailing behind him was the long blade of a tape measure. Since our first meeting on David's tour, I'd written Roland off as a pompous bore and Ruth's former flavor-of-the-month. But he was more; he was a serious competitor. I'd found Max's secret room after I'd finished pacing off the library's length and the outside wall. That meant that Roland had a fair chance of making the same discovery. I had to distract him from continuing his calculations of Armadillo's dimensions.

I called him from the front door. "I think I can save you from walking around on a hot, muggy day."

"How?"

"Would the original Armadillo blueprints help?"

"Sure would."

"I'll get them for you by tomorrow."

He retracted the blade. I didn't know where Max's blueprints were, but I congratulated myself on temporarily stalling Roland. On my way to freshen up, I saw David. "I just told Roland I'd let him see Armadillo's blueprints."

"Great. I've spent years looking for them. Where'd you find them?"

"Between the two of us, I lied to him."

David smiled. "Well, just between us, when at Ruth's request I invited him, I learned that his firm had filed for bankruptcy. His itchy wool suit may be the only one he owns."

"If he asks you about blueprints, refer him back to me."

"Gladly."

"By the way, David, while you don't have photos of Max, do you have some of Kate and Maurine? I'm curious about Max's taste in women."

"I'll leave some on the dresser in your room. You decide for yourself."

CHAPTER 31

From Blue Period To Rose Period

A ll my life, I've felt unlovable. Proof? The ugly birthmark on my face. And while I socialized with many acquaintances and cherished my close friends, I have always known that I didn't deserve a woman's love. But here I was at Armadillo, and for the first time in my life, a woman made me feel loved at the core of my being. I was loved; I was in love. I felt an overwhelming urge to belt out the "Hallelujah Chorus" like a Baptist choir.

Having located the Maya treasure, I wrestled with a choice. I desperately wanted to share the news with Sharon and others. Caution stopped me. With a killer still at large, euphoria induced by the discovery of buried treasure might blind people to the dangers they faced. But if I kept quiet about what I'd found and anything happened to me, archaeologists would remain unaware of Max's discovery, and it might be lost again—this time forever.

That wasn't quite right—Doña María knew about it, but she wasn't one to share her knowledge of Armadillo with others. As a young girl, María confided in Max, but never anybody else. Still, I was bursting to tell somebody, and Sharon was the one I thought I could trust. Max had given María a pendant, and in return, she'd given him a treasure. Sharon had given me the gift of love, and in repayment, I could give her the gift of a long look at breathtaking Maya art.

"I was hoping you'd get here," Sharon said as I sat down for lunch. "By the way, you've cleaned up rather well since your Blue Period last night."

"I've entered my Rose Period," I said quietly. "I've seen the vision of a lifetime."

She whispered, "Was it me?"

I believe in honesty, but sometimes, I can't bear to hurt people's feelings. I fudged the truth. "Who else?" She smiled; I felt ashamed.

"Sharon, I've got something to show you."

Once again, she excited me with her wink. While I was flattered, I knew she utterly misunderstood. I added, "in the library."

"Don't tell me that you found Max's papers before I did?"

"Better than that."

"You can't beat finding Max's papers."

"Yes, I can. Bring a flashlight."

"The library has lights."

"True."

On the way to the library, we stopped to pick up flashlights in our rooms.

"I'm curious when you washed off the paint on my body, did you happen to find a pendant?"

"No. Perhaps your would-be killer didn't have time to adorn you with one. But quit stalling, I want to see what you've got to show me."

We entered the library, and I locked the door.

While eyeing me warily, she smiled. "So what are we going to do? Never mind, I can guess. But couldn't you find a more comfortable place to make love? The sofa's too short, and its springs are broken. When it comes to being poked, I desire you over springs."

From a bookcase on the fireplace wall, I pulled off a strip of molding.

"Stop it, Paul! You're vandalizing Max's library."

"Watch." I yanked the bookcase, and it swiveled toward us.

She followed me into the secret room and moved her flashlight around. When it lit up the faces on the Maya stela, Sharon let out a terrifying scream.

"Pretty impressive, right?"

"I thought I was going to die."

"Welcome to Max's secret study, complete with desks, filing cabinets, and bulletin boards."

"This is awesome. Now with Max's papers, we can write his biography. Gerald will be the loser."

I pulled open a cabinet drawer.

She looked inside. "Empty. I'm starting to feel sorry for us."

"I was too, until...." I got down on my knees and fiddled around with one hand under the stela until I heard a click. "Now help me push this thing. And don't worry. Despite weighing several tons, it moves easily." We swung the stela aside. I lifted the wooden trap door and pointed down. "Want to go first?"

"Yes and no. What's down there?"

"I'll lead the way and show you."

"Okay, but I don't like enclosed places."

"What you're about to see will make you forget your fear."

"How did you figure out the stela would move and hide a tunnel?"

I put a finger to my lips to quiet her. I just about blurted out, "It's a guy thing." Instead, I said, "The stela was Max's way of hiding his secrets."

Upon reaching the burial chamber, she cried out, "This room is beyond my wildest dreams!" She hugged me. "You're incredible."

We spent an hour looking at the gold armadillo and the erotic murals. "Some drawings of the couples were the ones *Eros* published in the early sixties." I didn't mention Gerald's discovery of photos showing Kate and Max posed in the sexual positions the Maya had painted on the wall. I wondered why I wasn't telling her. "What do you think of Max's discovery?"

"It rivals the discovery of the Rosetta Stone. But why didn't Max tell the world?"

"I think Doña María knows, but she's highly protective of Max. I guess she'd never tell without his permission, and he died before he gave it. I'm sure that Max didn't tell Ruth or David about this place. I'm positive Gerald doesn't know."

"If, as you just said, Doña María is highly protective of Max, maybe she protected Max by burying his papers with his body."

"That's a strong possibility," I said. *Sharon's mind is razor-sharp. I should seriously consider her as a co-author for Max's biography—if we ever find his papers.*

Sharon clutched my arm. "Paul, I hate to admit it because I'm utterly enthralled, but I'm getting claustrophobic. I need to leave now. Is there a shorter way out?"

"Not that I'm aware of."

"The stela in the hidden room concealed the passage we took. Maybe there's another stela hiding a second stairway."

"If you find it, let me know."

"Nevertheless, I need to leave. This place is closing in on me. Let's go now."

"Sure, as long as Gerald didn't follow us and close the trap door and swing the stela back into place."

"Stop it!" With both hands, she pushed my chest. I landed on my butt.

"Now you're freaking me out," I said.

"Sorry. I'm getting the shakes and feeling nauseous. I need to leave now!"

As we left the library, Sharon touched my arm. "I apologize for my behavior down there, but I can't stand tight enclosed places. I'll feel better after a siesta." She winked and said, "Care to join me?"

"You're going to think I'm the most foolish man alive. So please don't be hurt that I'm taking a rain check. I need some time to think about William's murder and the attempt on my life." I couldn't believe I'd turned her down.

"That's strike one. I'm not hurt, but three strikes and you're out—of my life."

"Next time at-bat, I'll show you my Louisville Slugger. I'll stroke a single up the middle so fast that it will rip the cover off."

"You're a starry-eyed optimist. But I love you."

Instantly I knew that in rejecting Sharon's siesta offer, I'd screwed up big time.

CHAPTER 32

Floppy Disks

I walked to my room through corridors decorated with blackened-iron house crosses. What had Max's collection of crosses meant to him? The hope of salvation after an earthly existence that felt like a living hell? Or reminders of the unceasing suffering he endured? For me, the crosses evoked memories of William's death and the attempt on my life. The crosses also stirred fear of finding yet another corpse. Life was offering too many crosses to bear; I felt disheartened.

I'd planned to return to my room to think, but instead, I found myself standing at Gerald's door. Something rang false about Gerald's note to meet him in the chapel. Like the clunk sound in the library that I couldn't place, it was a persistent irritant. It struck me—that killers with any smarts don't put their signatures on messages to the people they intend to kill. On my roster of despicable people, Gerald topped the list. But begrudgingly, I gave him credit. However cruel and driven he could be, he was a meticulous and tenacious scholar as well as a formidable opponent. Our fight would be long and agonizing. *And one of us might end up dead.*

Remembering Gerald's stiletto pointed at me during my last visit, I knocked. I knocked some more. Soon I was pounding on his door—still no answer. I opened the door a crack. The curtains were closed, and the lights were off. I barely made out a human shape on the bed.

"Gerald, it's Paul. Can we talk?" No answer. I repeated my question. I opened the door, and silence met me. I took several steps toward the bed and stopped. Gerald lay on his back; his naked body wore a coat of blue paint. For the second time in two days, I felt a wretched gnawing in my gut. I staggered to the door and sucked in fresh air to stifle my gag reflex. The room smelled of death, but it mingled with another odor I couldn't place.

My stomach in turmoil, but my mind razor-sharp, I slowly approached his body. Once again, the murderer had imitated a Maya-style sacrifice. Gerald's sloppily painted skin looked like mine when I lay on the chapel floor. Not the meticulous work of the Rembrandt killer.

Gerald's chest was peppered with small stab wounds. In contrast to William, the paint on Gerald's chest covered the blood rather than the reverse. Someone had painted him after he died, not before. Gerald's body also lacked another signature of William's killer. As in my case, there were no rope markings on his wrists or ankles.

I noticed a gash, painted over with blue paint, on his right temple. Up close, I saw fragments of wood embedded in the wound. A gold armadillo pendant rested near his hairline. I picked up two index cards from among those scattered on the floor. Gently, I slipped a card under the pendant and removed it. I used the other card to flip it over. One raised dot—Doña María's pendant.

Near the bed, a one-foot-long fireplace log with dried blood stains near one end established it as the instrument that had knocked Gerald out.

As I looked around the room, I realized it had been ransacked. All the dresser drawers were out. Clothes, papers, pencils, and pens littered the floor. Where was Gerald's research on Max Eicher?

When I was growing up, my mom would chastise me when I rummaged for things. I ignored her voice in my head and did an exhaustive search of the room. Concealed in dark shadows under the bed, I located a TRS-80 computer and a dot matrix printer. *Wow, a state-of-the-art machine. I need to buy one of these. Golly, Paul, then a miracle will happen, and your writer's block will vanish.* Then I realized how ghoulish my train of thought was under the circumstances.

I checked out every possible hiding place but found no floppy disks. And no papers of any kind. If Gerald had kept a backup paper copy of his working biography of Max, it was gone—probably stolen by his killer.

I placed the computer on the desk and plugged it in. How much did Gerald's killer know about computers? Gerald was so compulsive about his research that I imagined he'd make backup copies, but where were they? I checked to see what was on the computer and discovered no files related to his book. No paper copies and no backup floppies?

Gerald was a careful scholar. Surely, he'd have backed up his files. Where were they? Fresh from guessing how Max's had concealed the Maya treasure, I sat and tried to put myself in Gerald's shoes. My body trembled involuntarily. I felt disgusted. Not a smart move. I asked myself what obsessed Gerald. The obvious answer—photographs.

To my surprise, David's photography studio, formerly Max's, looked like a photography studio. I laughed at my naiveté. *Did I expect it to look like a sauna?* On one wall hung a large photo of Ruth. Disturbed by the photo's fusion of sex, violence, and culture clash, I let out a gasp. Ruth's uninhibited sexuality made *Playboy's* centerfolds look like innocent cavorting nymphs. I leaned forward to take a closer look:

> Ruth lies on her back; her naked body follows the contour of a massive convex rock. She wears a peaked headdress. Two shadowy men in loincloths huddle in the lower right and left corners of the photo. One man holds her wrists; the other, her ankles. A figure wearing a Maya-like mask stands behind her holding

an obsidian, sacrificial knife with an eight-inch blade. He appears ready to drive it into her chest and remove her heart. Ruth's eyes are closed; her head is turned toward the viewer. Her face radiates a seductive look.

I remembered that Max had written: "The height of hypocrisy was the photo where she's poised to be sacrificed. She'd allow her mother to be a sacrifice, but never herself."

But why was this photo in David's darkroom? Since meeting him, I'd thought of him as a harmless individual. But to sacrifice a human is a bloodthirsty ritual. Did David have a dark side? Had he sacrificed William, Gerald, or both? I interrupted these thoughts and focused on the task at hand—finding the five and one-quarter-inch floppy disks.

Bottles bearing skull-and-crossbones warnings lined sturdy wooden shelves above the chemical baths. Hiding floppies too near the chemical baths was risky as David might spot them. Tables stacked with boxes labeled as prints or negatives hugged the second wall. If necessary, I'd come back to them, but I suspected Gerald wouldn't have hidden them there. They were the first place someone might look.

A large bookcase along the third wall held rows of cameras. A polished teak wood camera: a Zeiss Folding Tropica. *Impressive.* Next to it was a collector's fantasy: a Leica Elmar with a calfskin finish. Neither seemed large enough. Out of the corner of my eye, I saw a tripod holding a polished box crafted from exotic woods. I guessed it was a silent movie camera. The brass plate read "Ernemann E." I unlatched the panel and peered inside. *This is my lucky day—except for finding another dead body.* I removed three floppy disks labeled Eicher #1, #2, and #3, respectively.

On the way to my room, I passed Doña María in the corridor. She noticed the blanket I was using to hide Gerald's computer and the floppies.

"Why didn't you tell me you were cold last night? I'd have

given you more blankets."

I hugged the blanket closer to my chest. "I didn't want to bother you. By the way, please don't clean up Gerald's room just yet."

She shrugged and walked on.

I was relieved to be in my room rather than that of a dead man painted blue. For a half-hour, I unsuccessfully tried word after word as I searched for the password to open his files. *What password would a narcissist like Gerald use?* A bolt of insight hit. I typed the word *Gerald*, and Eicher #1 opened; the other two files rapidly followed suit. He'd been brilliant in many ways, yet incredibly stupid in others.

A glance through the files confirmed his thorough scholarship. When he went after dirt on someone, he found it. I yearned to spend hours looking at what he'd discovered, but a killer had struck again. I slipped the floppy disks between the loose pages of my copy of *Max Eicher's Memoirs.*

Two dead men. William Farrell, a threat to women, and Gerald Strupp, a menace to everyone. David, Roland, Father Lester, and I were the only guys left, and someone had already tried to murder me. But each person I'd interviewed about William's death seemed untroubled by an unsolved murder. I knew the reaction to Gerald's would be similar: Ruth would throw a party to celebrate, and everyone would attend. Those gathered would sing, "Ding dong, Gerald's dead...."

Solving these murders is a fool's errand. Why in the hell am I trying? Was I on an ego trip in believing I could solve two crimes? I couldn't even solve one. Perhaps my suspects were right, and I should, as one had suggested about William, "Let the dead dog lie." But now, there were two dead dogs. And while Sharon offered lukewarm support for me to continue investigating, I doubted she'd challenge my decision if I threw in the towel. But much as I despised Gerald, murdering another human being was inexcusable—even if the victim was Gerald. I wrote down the names of suspects and followed each name with a motive.

Ruth Eicher. Killed both men. William for perhaps violating her and Gerald for threatening to humiliate her in his biography of Max Eicher. Gerald also possessed pornographic drawings of her and threatened to destroy Max's legend. She had no motive for trying to kill me—she'd given me enough hints that she wanted me alive—in her bed. However, Sharon had suggested Ruth hated me for refusing her advances.

David Budman. Murdered both men to protect Ruth, but not likely given his reaction when he saw William's dead body. The photo in David's darkroom of Ruth on the altar indicated he was knowledgeable about human sacrifice. No known motive for trying to kill me.

Harriet Galveston. Killed William to avenge, however inaccurate, his raping her. Killed Gerald for publicly ridiculing her research. No motive for trying to kill me—unless my birthmark still bothered her.

Doña María. Helped kill William (with the assistance of others?) to avenge Harriet's supposed rape and because he endangered women when he visited. No known motive for killing Gerald or attempting to kill me.

Sharon Silverthorne (alias Sandy Martin). Killed Gerald for destroying her academic career. No cause for killing William. No possible reason for attempting to kill me.

Roland Westby. No motive for killing anyone. At Armadillo to avoid bankruptcy and renew his affair with Ruth. Given his failure with the latter, he might still kill Ruth.

Father Lester Sheehan. No way he deliberately killed anyone. If anyone had died, it would have been the result of his body-crushing embrace.

Most of my suspects had a motive for killing either William or Gerald, a few for killing both. With Gerald now dead, I couldn't think of anyone who would want to kill me. Perhaps I was deluding myself.

I possessed two pendants, and I'd failed to think about them. If I were a professional detective, they'd take away my license. It was time to engage in deductive reasoning. Max gave pendants to four women, with Doña María receiving hers first. Ruth's would have been the second pendant—with two raised dots. Kate's had three dots, and Maurine's had four.

The pendant with three dots that I'd found on William's body would be Kate's pendant—but that didn't make sense because she'd left thirty years ago. The pendant with one dot that I'd found on Gerald's body was Doña María's. But why would Doña María leave her pendant on Gerald's body? She had no discernible motive to kill him.

Back in high school, a teacher presented a logic problem to our class:

> *Jack is looking at Anne, but Anne is looking at George. Jack is married, but George is not. Is a married person looking at an unmarried person?*

I was the only kid in class to get the right answer. The answer is Yes, regardless of whether Anne is married or unmarried. In either scenario, a married person is looking at an unmarried person. Despite my considerable skill with logic problems, I was getting a splitting headache trying to logically solve the relationship of the four women who originally possessed armadillo pendants, two blue bodies with pendants, and killer/killers leaving pendant clues.

Mentally drained and discouraged, I leaned back in my chair. In my mind's eye, I saw the letter Theo had sent me shortly before I left Iowa City. The words on the envelope stated: *Open me when you are sick of Armadillo and thoroughly discouraged.* I tore open the envelope.

Dear Paul,

I searched through my files and found a poem entitled "Questions" that Max Eicher sent me a month
before he died. I don't know what he was trying to say,
but it might take your mind off the challenges Armadillo presents.

On your way home, send me a summary of your
experiences.

Warm regards,
Theo

Questions

How do I die when longing to live?
How tell the truth I so need to share?
How clutch the pain another must feel?
I'm risking all to make him aware.

Is this poem Neumann's idea of encouragement? While I felt like
crumpling the letter and pitching it into the fireplace, I decided
to reread it. Although poetry wasn't my specialty, I hazarded a
guess that Max was telling Theo that he was contemplating suicide, even though he wanted to live.

But what was the truth he needed to share? The Maya treasures in the tomb? Finding true love with Maurine?

And who was the other person in pain? Maurine—that Max
hadn't left Armadillo with her when he had the chance? Doña
María—for abandoning her by slowly committing suicide?

As to risking all, was it a confession of Max's love for Theo?

*Great! Now, my mind is distracted from Armadillo's challenges
and cluttered with four cryptic lines written by a suicidal man.
Thank you, Theo.* But it was time to get back to solving two
crimes. I knew for sure that unless William was the world's
greatest contortionist and could cut out his own heart, he
couldn't have committed suicide.

CHAPTER 33

Digging Up The Past

R uth received my news of Gerald's murder with indifference. For all she cared, I could've announced I'd killed a
mosquito. She leaned forward, but this time she didn't
touch my hand, arm, thigh, or other parts of my body. "I remember when Gerald first interviewed me last year," Ruth began. "In-
gratiation is an art when employed with skill, but with Gerald,
all I could see was a gifted sweet talker. First, he elicited the key
events in Max's life. Next, he went after details. He didn't press
me if I hesitated or looked uncomfortable, but he skillfully returned to those topics until I told him more than I'd planned to
say."

I gave an inward smile. Ruth's description of Gerald's interviewing style left no doubt that he possessed extraordinary
skills. That he employed it in such a destructive way was uncon-
scionable.

"But yesterday, Paul, you asked me to tell you about Max. I'm
no psychiatrist, but I believe he searched for a mother's love.
With me, he found lust. With Kate, perhaps a bit of intellectual companionship, but mainly a romp in the hay. With Doña
María, a close friend."

I had a difficult time keeping a straight face as she prattled on
about other women in Max's life. Best to listen and see what I
could pick up.

"You'd have thought Max was starved for sex on the home

front the way he went after Kate. On more than one occasion, I heard him call her Cupkate, his nauseating term of endearment. She was quite willing to satisfy his urges. Poor old Max, chasing after a woman half his age. Pathetic."

"Interesting," I said, "most women in your position would have been jealous."

"Well, as you know, I'm not like most women." She placed her fingertips together. "Max never grew up, and as we know, little boys need to play. Frankly, I found Kate's games amusing, even if she treated Max like a puppet."

Ruth had conveniently omitted a significant woman in Max's life, so I asked, "Was Maurine Madanes also a skilled puppeteer?"

Already mask-like, Ruth's face lost any remaining elasticity. "What about *that* woman?"

"Didn't she break Max's heart when she left Armadillo to return home?"

Ruth gave me a look of pity and emitted her high-pitched laugh. "You forget to mention how Max slowly pined away. Well, that's all a cock-and-bull story designed to entertain tourists. It gives Armadillo a romantic feel, keeps people coming here." She pointed her finger at me. "Want the real story, my dear boy?"

"Go on."

"Maurine was a scheming temptress. She flew here with the intent of snaring a famous writer for a husband. From the first time Maurine batted her eyes at Max, she controlled him. But I give her credit for quickly figuring out that Max wasn't the man of her dreams. After a brief stay, that rich bitch flew out of here all by her lonesome. But before leaving, she set Max on the road to ruin by drinking with him at every turn. After she left, he kept on drinking—only now more than before. All too soon, he was a blithering idiot—and even worse because he never heard from her again. If you'd asked Max, he'd have told you he was dying of a broken heart. I'm no doctor, but it was clear that mezcal killed him."

"What happened to Maurine?"

"Max didn't live long enough to hear about her fate, but I suspect he'd already figured it out. They say the Gulf is a big place; they never found her plane. But even in death, she grabbed the public's attention and sympathy. I get sick just thinking about her. People don't want to believe she miscalculated how much fuel her plane needed before running out. It's much easier to spread vile rumors that accuse me of sabotaging her plane."

"I haven't heard that one."

"Stick around, and you'll hear them all. I still detest Maurine for encouraging Max's drinking. From the moment she left Armadillo, he sat for hours at the piano playing tear-jerking songs. I'm the first to admit that Max had a soothing voice, but an hour of melancholy songs gets on anyone's nerves, especially when he slurred the words."

Here was my chance. "With Gerald's death, I guess you'll be naming me Max's official biographer."

"I want to revive interest in Armadillo. William had grand plans for a resort, which I found absurd, but he did want people here. Unfortunately, Gerald's book had a serious shortcoming— it was destined to destroy Max's legend and my reputation. He didn't reckon on my opposing him. I have ways to silence people who get in my way."

Ruth had missed her opportunity to name me Max's biographer. But more unsettling was her strong motive for killing Gerald. I decided to take a chance. "How did you silence him? Did you sweet-talk him into stripping down to nothing before you bashed him in the head with a log and repeatedly stab him? You have a talented mouth, but not that talented."

From beneath layers of makeup, I felt her hatred even as she soothingly said, "As you've suggested, my mouth could never be that persuasive."

"I'm convinced you successfully stopped Gerald from continuing his book, but how you did it is a mystery."

Her icy attitude transformed into prideful defiance, "I can't deny hating him after he threatened me. But your job as Armadillo's detective-in-residence is to prove who killed Gerald, not make baseless accusations."

I stood and made for the door. Ruth was right; I needed evidence. I opened the door but quickly turned to face her. "I suspect William and Gerald didn't put up a fight because you poisoned them. And I also think someone poisoned Max. Let's dig him up and find out."

"God, you're so naïve. Harriet believes all that Maya nonsense she's written. You have no such excuse. There never was an earlier Maya civilization near here. Max created that fantasy. If you've bought into it, then you're truly the fool of fools."

"No, Ruth, you're the one playing the fool. I'm not talking about Maya treasures, and you know it. I'm talking about Max. It's time we dig him up and determine how he died. I think his body holds the secret to how he, William, and Gerald died."

Routinely, Ruth had used her cunning powers to defeat her rivals. However, the woman facing me had ceased to be an adversary. Fear streaked her face. It was the scariest face I'd ever seen—the fear of a cornered animal who knows it's time to fight or die yet knows that to choose the former will inevitably lead to the latter. Her fear morphed into a moral imperative to bring down everyone around her. I faced a woman who reportedly had successfully conquered countless men. She was determined not to lose.

"You think you're so smart. You think a pile of bones will reveal secrets. Go ahead and dig up Max and listen to him flap his gums: 'Ruth poisoned me. She's a modern-day Lucrezia Borgia.' Oh, Paul, you'll have to do much better to be a real detective and solve whodunits."

"I want us to exhume Max's body. We'll let a forensic toxicologist determine if someone poisoned him."

"All you'll find in that wooden box are his bones."

"Bones tell stories."

"Even if you find traces of poison," she said, "it doesn't mean I killed him."

"If Doña María is correct, then only you and she saw him dead. Perhaps the two of you conspired together. Let's dig him up right now."

"Sure, Paul, if that will satisfy you, but Max died from alcohol." She laughed in her shrill way. "You'll find his body well preserved—pickled in alcohol. Since you insist on digging him up, we will. But prepare to be the world's biggest sucker."

Her last comment was ironic, given what I knew of Ruth's past as Lollipop. I let it pass. "Tomorrow morning, we'll dig him up."

My next suspect was Harriet. "When was the last time you saw Gerald?"

"This morning at Ruth's sad excuse for a board meeting."

"And where have you been since then?"

"Mind telling me where you're going with your questions?"

"I found Gerald murdered in the same manner as William."

Her head jerked back, but she rapidly recovered. "The Maya Murderer seems to prefer killing men. Coincidence?" Then the implication of her statement sank in. "I'm sorry. What I said was insensitive."

I couldn't tell if her apology was heartfelt or just words. "Thanks. And your alibi?"

"After the board meeting, I lingered over coffee at Diego's Mustache. Then, I stopped at the local hardware store to buy a paintbrush and a gallon of blue paint. They were sold out. I found out later that someone else got to him first."

"Harriet, don't quit your day job and go into improv comedy." She gave a silly smirk. "Let's start again with a different topic. This morning, Gerald cruelly mocked your book. That could be a reason to kill him."

She set her jaw. "Are you auditioning for Gerald's vacated role?" Harriet read my pained expression. "Sorry, I didn't mean to say that. But did I kill Gerald? No."

"Tell me why I should believe you."

"Let's turn the tables. Why shouldn't I believe that you killed Gerald because you want to write Max's biography?"

"Because I could never kill another human being."

"You're the most decent man here." *It felt good to hear her say that.* She continued, "Paul, I've seen the way Sandy looks at you. Be careful."

I debated whether to tell Harriet that Sandy's real name was Sharon Silverthorne and concluded that it was Sharon's decision. "She's the first woman I've been in love with, and she's in love with me."

Harriet bit her lip. "I'm sharing my woman's intuition."

I looked away. Was Harriet jealous of a younger woman?

It was an evening that surpassed my highest expectations. To enhance Doña María's feast of miraculous dishes, she offered margaritas made with your choice of tequila or mezcal. After dining, Sharon and I slipped away to her room. We made love by imitating several of the erotic positions we'd seen on the walls of the burial chamber. Occasionally, I wondered if the thick adobe walls of Sharon's room would sufficiently muffle our cries of ecstasy.

Returning to my room before sunrise, I saw a large envelope on the dresser: *To Paul from David.* The photos confirmed Max's taste in women. Maurine Madanes' makeup and attire confirmed that she possessed money. Max had been spot on in his description of her beauty: "Her face radiated a love of life, yet her dark brown eyes had a touch of melancholy that momentarily frightened me."

In David's photos of Kate Davis, her hair was wild, and her eyes were inviting. These were in sync with her body language that proclaimed, "I'm game for adventure. I always say yes to life." But what drew me to Kate was her electrifying smile that seemed to entice others in her photographs to smile also.

I could imagine Max being drawn to both women. Maurine's photos conveyed her depth and caring, while Kate's photos presented a high-spirited woman who energized others. Maurine offered Max a lifetime of love. Kate, a short-lived amusement. *I know that right now, I'd settle for either.*

CHAPTER 34

A Sign

A fter a hearty breakfast, I entered the kitchen. Doña María was stirring the contents of a large black kettle and giving instructions to the women preparing for the next meal. When I looked longingly into the pot, she offered me a spoonful. I was transported to heaven. When I asked for a second spoonful, her expression told me not to be greedy.

"Is this a good time to talk?"

"We can talk," she said but kept stirring.

I believed I'd go crazy with the tempting aromas if I stayed in the kitchen. "Let's talk where others can't hear."

"*Si, señor.* In my office." She asked the other women to excuse her and led me to a small, dimly lit room.

After she closed the door, I said, "Please show me the gold armadillo pendant that Max gave you many years ago."

She looked as if I'd slapped her. "Lately, you seem to know a lot."

"It was a story in Max's *Memoirs*. But I believe you no longer have the pendant that Max gave you because it's in my pocket."

As I reached into my pocket, she lifted a thin gold chain over her head and handed it to me. A gold armadillo pendant hung from the chain. I rubbed the pendant between my thumb and forefingers. It was identical to the ones found on the bodies of William and Gerald in size and shape. With one exception. The backside of the one Doña María had handed me was smooth. No raised dot. Every direction I turned, I found yet another detail that didn't make sense.

I looked at Doña María as if I were a simpleton. Doña María was Max's first love; therefore, her pendant should have one dot. In a flash, the ridiculousness of my assumption was obvious. I'd assumed that because Doña María was the first to receive a pendant, hers had a single dot. *What was I thinking?* When Max bought young María a piece of jewelry in the market, it didn't come with a dot on the back. My system of assigning numbers to pendants was off by one. The correct order was: María, no dots; Ruth, one dot; Kate, two dots; and Maurine, three dots. *I'm an imbecile!*

The no-dot pendant changed everything. My previous reasoning had led me to think that the three-dot pendant found on William's body belonged to Kate. Instead, it was Maurine's. Then just as quickly as my mind had cleared, it fogged up. My revised pendant order made no sense. Maurine had died at sea when her plane went down. Except in zombie movies, the dead don't kill people. But if Maurine didn't kill William, then who had access to her pendant? Ruth, David, Doña María, and possibly William were the only ones at Armadillo when Maurine was here.

I continued to follow the logic of my corrected numbering system. The single dot on the armadillo pendant I'd found on Gerald's forehead belonged to Ruth. But why would Ruth leave her pendant on a man if she killed him? "I apologize, Doña María, I've made a foolish mistake. I thought you killed him based on the pendant with one dot that I found on Gerald's body. Please accept my apology."

Her eyes focused on her hands in her lap. "I trusted you before. But now, I trust you even more because you can admit you made a mistake. I'll tell you a secret if you promise to tell nobody."

I didn't know what she might say. Maybe it had something to do with Max or where his papers were. I took a chance. "I'll tell no one."

She looked at me for a seeming eternity. "I sacrificed William."

I have endured people staring at my birthmark, but now I was the one staring. "Doña María, what are you saying?"

"Dr. Paul, I knew when you first arrived that you were the sign that I was looking to get my revenge. I'm sorry that I didn't thank you before, but I thank you now for freeing me from my long wait."

I had difficulty figuring out what to say next. Finally, my words tumbled out. "What do you mean when you say I was a sign? I don't understand."

"On the evening you arrived, I saw the birthmark on your face. My eyes aren't so good these days, and the light was dim, but it reminded me of an armadillo. I knew it was the sign that Max told me to wait for."

I was stunned. My birthmark had been a sign to Doña María that she could now sacrifice William. I struggled to catch my breath.

"Relax, Dr. Paul, and listen to my story."

I lapsed into silence, but I felt drained.

"In 1950, William visited Armadillo for the first time. Ruth was okay with him, but Max and I didn't like him. He was about twenty-five and in love with himself. As with many men who come to Armadillo, Ruth entertained William, but not in a too-friendly way.

"In the halls, William would press his body against mine and whisper sweet things in my ear. In my heart, I knew he was evil. I told him to leave me alone. He didn't. I complained to Max about him. Max ordered him to stay away from me and never touch me.

"One night, William came into my room before I'd locked the door. He started to say how much he loved me. I told him to leave because I wanted nothing to do with him. He held a knife to my throat and threatened to kill me if I screamed. He forced himself on me and threatened to kill me if I told Max. For two weeks, he stayed at Armadillo. During that time, I lived in fear, with my door locked every night.

"William arrived at Armadillo several days before Maurine arrived and left one day after she departed. After William left, I told Max what he'd done. Max was furious and said that William must pay. Not long after, we heard rumors that Maurine's plane was missing. Max was in shock. He ate little and began to lose weight. Shortly before he died, I told Max I was pregnant with William's child. He said, 'Wait for a sign, and then you'll know how to take your revenge.' He died one day later. I was sad, but I have waited for many years for a sign. I didn't know what the sign would be, but I trusted I'd know it when it came.

"Several years after Max died, William started visiting Armadillo each year. When he came, I hid my two daughters in the village. I didn't want them to see the man who was their father."

"Wait a minute," I said. "Did William force himself on you twice?"

"No. Only once. I had twins. A week ago, Ruth told me a young man was going to visit Armadillo, and he wanted to learn more about Max. He was a writer from the United States. I started to believe that the man might be the sign Max had told me to wait for. I remembered the stories I heard growing up, and I remembered seeing photos Max had taken that showed drawings of Maya sacrifices."

"You knew about them?" I asked, my voice revealing how troubled I was.

She held up her hand. "I'll tell you later. When I met you at the front door the night you arrived, I knew you were the sign I needed to get my revenge. I knew how William must die."

"You're telling me that I'm the sign you waited for all these years?"

"Yes. You are the sign."

"And you sacrificed William because of me?"

"Yes."

My head ached, and my body trembled. *She's telling me that my appearance at Armadillo set in motion William's sacrifice.* I felt wretched.

"After I greeted you at the door," Doña María said, "I went to my daughters and told them we must do something that might seem very wrong, but it was very right for me. I asked them to help me sacrifice an evil man who had hurt me very much. My daughters love and trust me. They said they'd do anything I asked because they wanted my heart to heal. I never told them that William was their father.

"My daughters and I prepared to sacrifice William. When he returned to Armadillo after drinking, I let him in and said, 'Señor, do you remember years ago when you forced yourself on me?'

"He was still as horrible as he'd ever been. He pulled in his big stomach and said, 'Sure, I remember you. Even in your silence, you put up one hell of a struggle.'

"In a soft voice, I said, 'My daughters are poor and beautiful. For the pleasure they provide you tonight, would you be willing to give them a gift of some money?'

"'How much?' He had a big grin on his face.

"I looked down. 'A gift is from the giver's heart. You must decide.'

"'I've never been stingy when it comes to first-class pleasure.'

"'Señor, my twin daughters will do their best to see you're pleased.'

"I saw his eyes open very wide. He said, 'I've hit the jackpot! I've had sisters, but never twins. Tonight's my night to die and go to heaven.'

"I thought he was half smart and half stupid. He was right about dying, but he was wrong about going to heaven. I told him we'd come to his room at midnight, and my daughters would do their best to satisfy him. I saw that lust filled his heart. Quiet fury filled mine.

"He met us at the door wearing a robe. He said, 'I'm ready for some action. Who's first?'

"I said, 'William, we must get you very excited before you find out what is to come. Please remove your robe.' He did and stood naked. I said, 'These two women want you to stand very still while they cover your body with blue paint.'

"'Oh, I love kinky sex,' he said.

"Very carefully, my daughters painted his body. 'Now, lie sideways on the bed. My daughters will put ropes around your wrists and ankles.' I didn't have to ask if he was getting excited because I saw he was.

"'I'm ready. Which woman's going first?' he asked.

"'Please daughters, pull the ropes tight.' They did. 'Now, William, we have a big surprise for you. Close your eyes, and you'll feel something you have never felt before in your life.'

"He said, 'I've got my eyes closed. Let me have it.'

"From a bag, I removed an obsidian Maya knife. I said, 'Keep your eyes closed. Now, remember your excitement long ago when you entered me. Tonight, I am going to put something in you.' With both hands, I lifted the knife above his chest. I said to my daughters, 'Hold the ropes very tight.' Then I said, 'William, open your eyes.' He did, and I plunged the knife into his chest as I said, 'This is my revenge.' In a flash, I watched the expression on his face change from lust to terror."

As Doña María told her story, I squirmed in my chair and breathed in short gasps. "Doña María, I pulled a gold pendant and chain from William's mouth when I found him. But now, based on the three raised dots on the backside, I know it was Maurine's pendant."

"I'll explain. The night that we sacrificed William, he wore a pendant on a chain. I was angry because Max gave them to people he loved, not people he despised. After I plunged the knife into his heart, I yanked the chain from his neck and jammed it into his mouth.

"I said to my daughters, 'Because his heart is still, now mine can be at peace.' We put a bedsheet over him, picked him up, and placed him in a wheelbarrow. We took him to the Maya sacrifice stone and lay him there where I removed his heart and put it in a stone bowl. We cleaned up his room and washed all the paint and blood from our bodies and clothes. I took the knife back to the kitchen and washed it off. My daughters returned to their homes in La Ruta. We haven't talked about it since. Now, I see their faces, and I see they're happy that I am no longer afraid for the women who come to Armadillo."

Doña María sat back. Her face radiated peace that transcended my understanding. She'd been the victim of William's sexual assault. Then, she patiently waited for years for the sign to execute her revenge. Ironically, I, who was committed to nonviolence, served as her sign to kill her tormentor. I looked Doña María in the eye and said, "I promised not to tell anyone. Your secret is safe with me."

"*Muchas gracias,* Dr. Paul."

"*De nada.*"

I asked, "Did you kill Gerald?"

"No. I had my revenge on the evil man who violated me—William. But Dr. Paul, you're a good man like Max was."

A question nagged me: Why had the killer painted William's body like a Rembrandt, while my body and Gerald's looked like the killer had used a paint-by-number kit? Now, I knew. Doña María and her daughters were artists. They'd painted William's body in the tradition of Maya painting in the same way Doña María had, many years ago, painted watercolor copies of the Maya glyphs in the secret room and murals in the tomb chamber. The person who'd colored my body and Gerald's body blue had tried to imitate Doña María's artistry but failed badly.

"One last question. How did William happen to have Maurine's pendant?"

"I think I know," she said. "An hour after Maurine and Ruth fought, Maurine searched all over the dining room for her pendant. She thought it had come loose during the fight. We looked thoroughly but never found it. I remember William watched the women fighting. He must have picked it up and not told anyone."

Walking out through the kitchen, I saw, for the first time, a drawing partially hidden in shadows behind the hanging cooking pots. It showed a Maya priest holding a knife above the chest of a prisoner stretched over a sacrificial stone. If the drawing were animated, in the subsequent frames, the blade would plunge toward the prisoner, and his chest would be cut open, and his heart removed. The gnawing feel of acid in my stomach was the same as when I'd first seen William's heartless body.

Doña María had said I was a good man. I thought it odd that two people had told me the same thing within such a short period. If it was true, why—now that I knew who'd killed William—was I not feeling utterly relieved? The answer came quickly: Armadillo still housed the second killer.

I started for my room, then turned and headed back to Doña María's kitchen. She and two assistants continued to prepare dinner. As I looked at the assistants, I knew I'd been blind not to notice how much they looked like their mother. "Doña María, let's go back to the room where we talked."

I sat in awe of the tiny woman sitting in front of me. I'd been so intent on hearing Doña María's story of sacrificing William that the significance of a framed watercolor of an armadillo on her wall hadn't registered. "Where did you get that sacrificial drawing in the kitchen? And this one? It's identical to the armadillos on the walls in the burial chamber."

Her face colored a bit. "I painted it soon after exploring the tomb with Max."

"You painted it?"

"Max told me that I was a very talented painter."

Unable to contain myself, I asked. "How did you know about the tomb that you showed Max?"

"For generations, my people have told stories about it. We knew that deep in the ground, there were Maya murals. Max had me do watercolor paintings of all the ones we found. They took much time."

"May I see them?" I said.

"Come to my room."

From a large trunk, she pulled out layers of clothing. Below were stacks of papers covered with exquisitely colored drawings from the Maya murals. "I painted all of these. But Max didn't want me to paint the ones from the Maya books we found in the sarcophagus."

I was speechless. Finally, I was able to get out, "Books? You mean Maya codices?"

"Yes."

"How many were there?"

"Max said a baker's dozen, but I figured out he meant thirteen."

"Where are they now?"

"Max kept them, and he wanted me to keep my drawings hidden in my room."

"Did he ever show these to anyone else?"

"Max asked if I'd show some of my mural drawings to Kate, but he said not to tell her about the codices. She gave them back to me after she finished studying them. Max made her promise not to tell anyone."

On a hunch, I asked, "Did any of the codices show couples making love?"

Doña María blushed. "One codex did. All the other images of lovemaking couples were painted as murals on walls. My Maya ancestors painted them. Even though I was embarrassed, I did the best job I could."

"Why did Max have you draw and paint them?"

She laughed. "Because Max drew like a child."

"Stick figures?"

"That is all he knew how to draw."

"One last question. Did you paint the Madonna and Child on the door of the confession box?"

"Yes. Two years before Ruth first came to Armadillo, Diego Rivera and Frida Kahlo visited. In 1932, I painted the door to honor them. They told me it was great art."

I was filled with amazement. I leaned back in my chair. Doña María had made drawings faithful to the stela's glyphs and the murals on the walls of the burial chamber. She possessed a treasure chest of information that might drive some Maya scholars to take extreme actions—perhaps even kill to possess the drawings.

"You didn't paint copies of the pictures in the codices?"

"No, no. Max photographed those."

One problem stood in the way: I'd found a stela with its many glyphs in Max's secret room. I'd discovered the erotic murals on the walls of the burial chamber. But where were the thirteen priceless codices and Max's photos of them? Had he destroyed them? Had they been buried with him in his grave? Were his other papers also in the grave?

"Please, where are the codices now?"

Doña María smiled. "They're with Max."

Her statement confirmed what I'd planned to do tomorrow—exhume Max's body. It would yield clues about his death, while, hopefully, his coffin would contain his missing papers and the Maya codices. I congratulated myself on finally putting all the pieces of the puzzle together—except for who killed Gerald.

CHAPTER 35

The Coffin

S tudents in my undergraduate classes will testify that I
enjoy giving theatrical lectures. In a scene I borrowed
from Agatha Christie, I gathered my possible suspects in
the library: Ruth, Doña María, David, Harriet, Sharon, Father
Lester, and Roland. I described how I'd found Gerald's body, and
how he'd met the same fate as William, minus the gaping hole in
his chest. The fear in the air was palpable. "We've talked about
the two people murdered at Armadillo. But I believe that thirty
years ago, Max met the same fate. Ruth has permitted me to
have his body exhumed to confirm or deny my suspicions."

I wasn't sure what I expected by way of reactions, but I hardly
anticipated silence. Finally, Roland said, "I hate this place!
Someone is going to kill us all if we continue to stay here."

"How do you think Max died?" David asked as his voice trembled.

I slowly scanned the room, taking the time to look at each
person in the eye. "I believe someone poisoned him."

Harriet's teacup fell from her hand and shattered on the floor.
Unrestrained gasps for air filled the room.

We all gathered at Max's grave. The two men who had dug
William's grave heaved out shovelfuls of red dirt. Finally, we
heard a thud as a shovel hit wood. Doña María told the men to
dig slowly and carefully. Fifteen minutes later, the lid of Max's

coffin was fully exposed. We gazed at it as though subjects in a mass hypnosis experiment.

Armed with a hammer and crowbar, I descended into the hole and stood beside the coffin. I pried loose the rusted nails on the lid of the coffin. Before I removed the lid, I asked Father Lester to say a few words. He spoke of the solemnity of the occasion and our need to respect the dead. He made no mention of the reason for the exhumation.

I glanced at Ruth. She looked right through me. I motioned for Father Lester to join me, and he did. Everyone watched as we lifted the wood lid and handed it up to Doña María and Harriet. The only thing in the coffin was a large burlap coffee bag, cinched with coarse rope.

"What the hell!" Harriet screamed. "You stuck Max in a bag. That's outrageous!"

I untied the knot, peered inside the bag, and gave a startled cry. I pulled out a stone the size of a cantaloupe. Then another stone and yet another. "Father Lester, lift your end of the sack." Additional stones tumbled out, but no bones, clothing, or papers. Ruth watched in silence, frozen like a granite statue.

As Father Lester and I climbed out of the grave, Doña María and David eyed one another. I asked, "What's the story? Ruth, Doña María, and David, you were all present at Max's burial."

One by one, Harriet pointed her finger at each of the three. "Which one of you is the grave robber?"

David spoke first. "Ruth insisted on burying Max here."

"He's right," Ruth said, "but I expected to find my husband's body in the coffin, not a sack of rocks. I was a grieving widow, and the last time I saw him, he was lying dead on the floor in his room."

"I swear," David said, "that Doña María and I buried Max, not rocks."

A barely audible voice said, "I filled the sack with rocks." All eyes turned toward Doña María. "I knew someday Ruth would die, and she'd want to be buried next to Max. But Max never wished to be buried next to her."

I felt like grabbing Doña María and shaking her. Instead, I quietly asked, "Where is Max's body now?"

"He's in a better place," she answered.

"Where?" I demanded.

Doña María moved her arm in a panoramic sweep. "Somewhere out there."

I'd had it with her vagueness. Perhaps I could get some straight answers out of Ruth—although I wasn't optimistic. I took her arm and escorted her away from the group. "I now know that the pendant I found on Gerald's forehead belongs to you."

"You're worse than Gerald!" Ruth screeched. "He never accused me of killing someone."

"Do you want to see your pendant?"

"Now, I get what you're up to," Ruth shouted. "Since we first met, you've been trying to seduce me. When I rebuffed your gawky efforts, you decided to get back at me. It won't work. I'm not turned on by a man with a devil's kiss on his face."

She attacked me at my most vulnerable place—my face. I felt humiliated and angry, both at her viciousness an at my vulnerability to her attack. I could barely contain my contempt, so I turned around and walked over to David. "Tell the men to put the dirt back in the grave."

Harriet came over and put her arm around me. "Are you all right?"

"I'm pretty sure I'm not."

Father Lester and David had been waiting for their turns. Father Lester put his arm around my shoulder, "Paul, I'm sorry this had to happen." He turned to David, "Gerald's body is in the storeroom. I'll work with the two of you to have another burial service. Any advice?"

David spoke up, "Yeah, have the guys dig another grave behind the Maya sacrificial altar in the other clearing. I'll have a carpenter make another coffin. When all is ready, we'll have another short service." We all nodded.

All the time we'd been at Max's grave, Sharon quietly

watched me. Now she came over and put her hand in mine. "Come, let's go to my room." She led me away from the empty grave.

CHAPTER 36

Return To The Tomb

I flopped down on one of Sharon's twin beds. "Two men are dead, and everyone is treating their deaths as inconsequential. They're in denial that a killer is on the loose."

"I agree. Can we go to the burial chamber again? I've steeled myself to deal with my claustrophobia."

People handle unexpected events quite differently. Some become emotional, while others act as if nothing has happened. "Sharon, did you hear what I just said?"

"I heard you. William and Gerald are no longer with us. Frankly, I'm relieved. But here's the most important fact: you've discovered an archaeological treasure for the ages. You'll be famous. Please, let's go again."

I vacillated between yes and no for a split second. I already had one strike for passing up Sharon's invitation to share a siesta last Monday. I wasn't about to rack up strike two. Then just like my impulsive yes to Neumann's offer to travel to Armadillo, I said, "Let's go."

Upon entering the library, we saw Roland with one arm reaching up the fireplace flue. I placed a finger on my lips to signal Sharon to say nothing. I called over to Roland, "What's up?"

"Just checking if the chimney draws well. Fireplaces clogged with bird nests are a fire hazard."

"We'll come back when you finish," I said.

Roland pulled down his arm, and we saw a newspaper still ablaze. "It draws well. I'm going now."

After he left, I locked the library door and closed the curtains. We entered the secret study, swung the stela aside, and lifted the trap door. I led us down the steep stairs. "This is still unnerving," Sharon said. The light from our flashlights bounced off the jagged walls and created ominous forms.

Two-thirds of the way down, my flashlight flickered. "Damn, why did I forget to put in fresh batteries?"

"That blow to your head in the chapel must have knocked out some common sense. But let's not stop now. I'll go back and get fresh ones."

"You sure that's okay? I know how much you want to explore the burial chamber."

"You think I'm going to take my sweet time? No way, I'll be right back."

"Make sure nobody follows you and be sure to lock the library door."

"Stop it! I'm an adult." She was right.

I listened as her footsteps retreated up the stairs, and then all was quiet. To save the batteries, I switched off my flashlight. Perhaps a minute or so later, I heard faint scraping sounds from above. Please, let it not be rats. While I hadn't seen any on my first visit, that didn't mean none existed. I poked the button on my watch, and a crisp blue light showed 4:15. The longer I waited in the dark, the more I lost track of how much time had passed. I looked at my watch again; seven minutes had passed. I told myself to calm down and give Sharon some time. At 4:34, my worries morphed into a panic. Surely nothing had happened to her. At 4:39, I climbed the stairs, lightly touching the walls to guide my way.

I guessed I was nearing the tomb's entrance. I pointed my flashlight upward, and the light danced across a wood surface. Why had Sharon closed the trap door? Bracing my feet on the stairs, I leaned my shoulder against the wood and pushed—no movement. I tried again—the same result. When I banged on the wooden exit with my shoe, the sound was muffled. Suddenly an image flashed in my mind. Someone had swung the stela back over the trap door. Nobody on the other side of the trap door would hear my pounding or my screams.

My chest tightened. Why had I sent Sharon up those stairs alone? We'd been careful to escape anyone's notice. But once she stepped into Max's secret study, someone must have seized her. It must have been Gerald, but then I remembered he was dead. Who then? Who benefitted if I were sealed in the passage to die? Harriet wasn't a likely suspect. I knew she didn't care for Sharon, but I felt that she liked me despite her sometimes-crusty attitude. She just seemed intent on disguising it.

It had to be Ruth. Those killed or nearly killed had all been men who thwarted her plans. Both Gerald and I couldn't wait to write Max's biography, but she didn't seem to trust us, especially Gerald. And if dead men tell no tales, neither do they write malicious books about Max. Accusing Ruth of poisoning Max turned her against me, too. In retaliation, she locked me in a tomb to die.

I tried waiting, but my imagination kept getting the best of me. I'd give Sharon another fifteen minutes. Time crept, but she didn't return. The trap door wasn't a formidable challenge—it was an impossible one. Even if I succeeded in breaking through the wood with a flashlight, the massive stela imprisoned me in a Maya tomb. I was doomed to die.

How could I possibly escape? My breath came in short gasps. How long before I used up all the oxygen? How much longer could I last? Hours? Days? Horrible thoughts engulfed me. I had neither food nor water. I tried to remember how long humans could go without each. The flashlight batteries might last an hour at the most—if I stumbled around in the dark.

Only Sharon and the person who'd sealed me in knew I was trapped down here. Incapacitated or dead, Sharon couldn't help me. And Ruth *wouldn't* help me because she wanted me dead.

Bleak visions danced before my eyes. I saw horrible images of my mouth as dry as a desert, my lips cracking and bleeding from lack of water, and a pile of my bones discovered years in the distant future. I ordered myself to stop imagining a hopeless future and think about how I could save myself from certain death.

Without turning on the flashlight, I inched my way down the stairs and back into the burial chamber. The optimistic part of my brain kept telling me there had to be another exit. What do I remember about pyramids? Not much. Then I remembered that mazes of tunnels wound through Egyptian pyramids. If this tomb contained another tunnel, inevitably it would lead out from this chamber. But even if it existed, where was it?

When I'd been in the library searching for Max's secret room, I'd painstakingly examined its nooks and crannies. I turned on my flashlight and tried the same approach in the burial chamber, but I only found solid walls with no levers to pull or buttons to push. My hopes faded. In my head, I heard Neumann again telling me that hope wasn't a strategy. *Shut up, Neumann!* I'd located Max's hidden chamber and all its treasures. I'd found a woman I cared about who also cared about me. But now I was destined to die—and sooner rather than later.

The only places I hadn't looked were inside the two sarcophagi. Perhaps Max had designed a latch for the stela. I lay on my back next to the gold armadillo sarcophagus and worked my way around it—nothing I could see or feel suggested a latch. I checked out the second sarcophagus—again, no luck. I dusted myself off and quickly realized I was wasting energy. I didn't need the archaeologist who found my body in the distant future to say, "Very unfortunate that the poor guy starved to death, but he sure kept his clothes neat and tidy."

Perhaps a tunnel emerged inside a sarcophagus. After considerable effort, I managed to push the lid off the sarcophagus with no armadillo. I faced a dark void.

I turned to the sarcophagus with the gold armadillo on its lid. How much did the armadillo weigh? I pushed on it as hard as I could. It moved slightly. By the time I moved the armadillo and the lid off, I'd be weak and frantic for water. But what choice did I have? Gathering all my strength, I pushed on the gold armadillo. And kept pushing. Slowly it inched across the top of the sarcophagus until it teetered on edge. I gave one last push, and the armadillo crashed to the floor. Its long tail broke off. *Great, now I can add Vandalizer of Antiquities to my vita.* Could anything worse happen to me? Nothing, except dying in this tomb. This time, I imagined an angry archaeologist in the distant future as he kicked and scattered my bones.

To prevent more damage to the armadillo, I pushed the lid of the sarcophagus in the opposite direction. It fell and shattered into two large pieces. Inside the sarcophagus, the bones of a human lay stretched out. A jade mask covered the face side of the skull; a ten-inch gold, armadillo medallion rested on the ribs. The figure's jewelry matched the level of the highest craftsmanship of any civilization. Feeling like a monstrous vandal, I removed the bones and jewelry and gently placed them on the floor. I could see legions of future archaeologists condemning me and giving me an infamous name: Dr. Paul Seawrong. I searched the bottom of the sarcophagus until I touched what felt like a wooden panel with a large metal ring at one end. I'd bet on hope before and knew better than to let it unduly influence me now. Just as I reached for the ring, my flashlight began a constant flickering.

Time was slipping away. Focusing all my strength, I pulled the ring, and slowly one end of the wooden bottom rose above the lip of the sarcophagus, then slowly sank as my muscles tired. So much for all those years of pushups and pull-ups. The adage "work smarter, not harder" floated through my brain immediately followed by "figure it out or die!" I needed a lever to raise the lid and an object to hold it in place. Glancing around the room, I saw nothing I could use.

I stepped into the sarcophagus and conducted a second inspection. Then I saw it. Located near the large metal ring was a much smaller one. Glimmers of hope flirted with my emotions. I pulled, and this time, the hinged wooden lid lifted with little effort. The opening measured at the best three-foot square. By this time, my dying flashlight barely penetrated the darkness of the steep stairs.

My mind rebelled at the thought of yet another descent into the earth. My heart rate increased; my mouth felt crammed with cotton. One level down, someone might find my body. But down there? Forget it! There had to be a way out because going down was counterintuitive. Taking a deep breath as though it might be my last, I dangled my feet in the new tunnel and slowly lowered my body. Finally, my foot touched the first step. I turned around so that I could back down the stairs.

I lowered my foot until I felt the next step. In this way, I continued into the abyss. As this tunnel tapered, the tunnel leading to the burial chamber seemed like a stately staircase. My flashlight died, my foot slipped, and I missed the next step. My arms flailed and grazed the walls. I felt weightless as I fell backward and down.

CHAPTER 37

A Rock And A Hard Place

I lay stretched out on the stone floor and opened my eyes. I saw nothing, total blackness. The cold from the stone had crept into my bones. Shit! Compared to the pain in my head now, the blow I'd suffered in the chapel barely hurt, like a minor irritation. I reached around and finally found the flashlight. Flicking the switch back and forth produced no light. What time was it? My watch showed 9:30. I'd been unconscious for about four hours. Then I noticed the tiny a.m. and realized I'd been out for more than sixteen hours.

I felt around for the stairs. Wait, what was I thinking? Going back up to the burial chamber wasn't the answer. I raised my arms above my head and slowly stood up. Good thing, because given the low ceiling, I'd have gone down for the count.

Hunching over, I staggered forward. My foot hit something, and a sharp pain radiated through my body. I knelt as my hands explored the height and depth of ascending stone stairs. Despite the coolness of the tunnel, sweat poured off me like I'd been in a sauna for hours. My labored breathing scared me. With my head aching and my foot throbbing, I inched up the stairs. As time ran out, I became convinced that the passage led to a dead end. Vanished were my earlier fears of snakes, scorpions, or whatever might harm me. I felt mortal terror.

To protect myself from bumping my head, I kept one arm raised above my head. My hand touched a hard surface, and I jerked back. That precaution saved me from ramming my head against a flat board. The object felt solid like wood. I pushed it, but it didn't move. Then I remembered how Max had painstakingly secured the opening into the tomb's passage.

I ran my hands along the board's edges and felt cold metal. Two sturdy latches locked the board in place. I released the latches and pushed again—this time, it moved. I lifted it quietly, and that was when I saw a sliver of faint red light. *Am I in Hell?* Raising the board higher, I peered into a room bathed in red light. A man, half turned away from me, was pouring something into a shallow tray. I knew where I was. Ecstatic at escaping from my death sentence, I bellowed, "Top of the morning to you, David."

He shrieked, and his arms flew up, as did the chemical bottle. The liquid splattered across the floor, giving the room a pungent odor. "You scared me to death!" His body was shaking, as was mine.

I climbed out of the passage. The top of the wood board had a stone veneer so that the tunnel's entrance blended flawlessly with the floor. I fully understood that Max could magically conceal anything he didn't want others to see.

I steeled myself and mobilized for action. "We need to be extremely careful. Someone tried to kill me by sealing me in a burial chamber below us."

"What chamber?"

"An awful place with snakes and scorpions! But there's no time to explain. If Sharon isn't already dead, I believe she's in real danger of being killed."

He looked skeptical. "Are you kidding me?"

"David, someone has killed two people and twice tried to kill me. We need to protect ourselves and others. Find a weapon to take with you." I unscrewed one of David's cameras from its tripod and headed for the door, armed with a tripod.

David stood, unable to move.

I shouted at him. "Move it, or more people will die!"

Before my eyes, I watched David morph from an adorable

Golden Retriever into a snarling Rottweiler. "Yes, sir."

I bolted from the darkroom, determined to save Sharon. I called back to David, "Follow me to Sharon's room." Along the way, we passed Doña María, who was pushing a laundry cart toward the kitchen. "Doña María, alert the guests that the killer has tried to kill again. Grab a weapon to protect yourself." She gave me a thumbs up and rushed off.

David and I slowed our pace and listened as we approached Sharon's room. Birds chirped, but other than that, Armadillo was eerily quiet. David peered through a window, but curtains blocked his view. I knocked loudly—no answer. I threw open the door and opened the curtains. On a rug in front of the fireplace lay a woman's body.

David let out an ear-piercing scream, "No, not Ruth!"

My body slumped in relief. Thank goodness, it wasn't Sharon.

David knelt beside the body; I looked around. *Where is she?* I checked the bathroom. Not there either. I looked under both beds and in the armoire. *Where is the woman I love?* I stood motionless in the middle of the room; my mind went blank. Armadillo had become a slaughterhouse.

David looked up and wiped tears from his face. "Who would want to kill Ruth?"

"Where's Sharon?" I asked him. But I didn't wait for his reply before I raced to my room. It was a mess. My scholarly notes and the materials I'd brought to Armadillo were missing, as were Gerald's papers. Someone had tried to kill me and then stolen everything. I sat on my bed and reviewed my thoughts. Who would benefit if Gerald, Ruth, and I were dead, and the killer possessed all the source material on Max Eicher? In answer to my question, the final pin in the tumbler aligned, and the lock, which had prevented me from thinking clearly, sprang open. I'd wrongly concluded that Ruth was the killer. In truth, it was Sharon. I winced in repulsion.

Instantly, all became clear. Sharon, the woman who'd helped me begin to accept myself, had twice tried to kill me and succeeded in killing Gerald and Ruth. With me dead in a tomb and never found, Gerald sacrificed, and Ruth dead and no longer alive to authorize Max's biography, Sharon could write the book herself. She now possessed all the source materials that belonged to Gerald and me. Also, Sharon now possessed Max's invaluable manuscript, *Memoirs*. All she lacked were Max's papers—assuming they even existed.

Now, she could become the sole author—not a second author in Max's biography or only acknowledged in another scholar's footnotes. All credit would go to her. She and I had loved each other; I couldn't believe she'd try to murder me. But the irrefutable evidence all pointed at her.

I returned to Sharon's room. David had lifted Ruth's lifeless body and cradled her in his arms. His tears flowed, and his piercing wail filled the room. "David, I know you're grieving Ruth's death, but I need to examine her. I must point out that this room is a crime scene." He scowled at me, then gently lowered her body to the floor and sat down.

The gruesome scene sickened me and added to my anguish. I touched the blood-matted hair on the back of Ruth's head. I ran my finger along a straight, three-inch-long indentation. In death, I thought she looked better than in life—possibly because I didn't have to fight off her attempts to seduce me or resist her attempts to control me. As I studied her, my body trembled at the thought of how close I'd come to dying deep in the earth.

"David, any idea where Sharon went?"

He looked at me, but I'm sure he didn't see me. Who is Sharon?

"Sandy Martin's real name is Sharon Silverthorne. Any idea where she is?"

"I don't know." All David could think about was Ruth.

"David, this is important. Sharon killed or tried to kill people who prevented her from being the author of Max's biography. William, Gerald, and now Ruth are dead."

"You're sure it was Sharon?"

"Sharon's gone. All the research materials on Max are missing."

"I guess that makes sense," David said in a lifeless voice.

Before my eyes, I watched his face age. He was in shock and useless. I needed people who could help.

After checking Harriet's room, I found her sitting on the bench outside of the dining room. She greeted me with an exasperated look. "I slept in and was hoping one of the staff was around to make some coffee. Have you seen Doña María?"

"I saw her a while ago, but I've got terrible news. Last night, Sharon sealed me in a tomb below the library—from which I just escaped. She murdered Ruth."

She looked at me as if I'd spoken a foreign language she didn't understand. First, David couldn't follow me, and now Harriet. Was I garbling my words or talking gibberish? I told her Sandy was Sharon Silverthorne and repeated what I'd told David.

"Sweet Jesus!" She hugged me tightly. "I'm glad you're safe."

"Sharon's on the loose. We need to find her."

"Let's get Doña María, David, and Father Lester to help us," she said.

"David's with Ruth's body. What about Roland?"

Harriet waved her hand dismissively. "Forget about him. Yesterday morning, I spotted him leaving with his suitcase. When I asked where he thought he was going given the roads' condition, he sneered and said, "I'd rather risk washed-out roads than certain death here." When I asked if he'd told Ruth he was leaving, he said no. He added that he'd finally realized Ruth was lying to him. She had no money to pay for any architectural restoration. "Oh, and David told me later that Roland was a deadbeat who conveniently forgot to pay his bill before leaving." Harriet sniffed the air. I think I smell fresh coffee. Doña María must be back." Aware of the aromas of a meal cooking on a wood-burning stove, we headed to the kitchen.

Harriet poured herself some coffee. Doña María sat down on a small stool, and after I told her about finding Ruth's body, she cried. Her daughters comforted her.

"Listen, everybody," I said. "We must find Sharon, who tried to kill me and killed Ruth and Gerald. Itzel, please check in La Ruta if a taxi has picked up anyone at Armadillo since yesterday. Harriet, please search the rooms facing the front courtyard, including the library. Also, find Father Lester and ask him to check the chapel. Doña María, please check all the rooms off the central courtyard. I'll search the rooms bordering the back courtyard. We all need to be extremely careful."

"No problem," Harriet said, "I'll take this." She reached into her purse and pulled out a handgun.

"What's *that*?" I asked.

"Officially, it's a SIG-Sauer P220, but I call it The Equalizer."

Doña María took the tripod from my hand and handed me a wickedly sharp knife from a kitchen drawer. On my way out, she flashed me a sly smile and waved her largest knife.

I'd been worried that the women at Armadillo were vulnerable. Talk about underestimating people's strengths. Perhaps, Sharon was still on the property. I first determined that she wasn't in the back courtyard or hiding in the storeroom with William and Gerald's bodies. Then I walked out of Armadillo's back door. I took the path leading to Max's grave and the sacrificial stone. But instead of turning to the right, I turned toward the sacrificial stone. A waning crescent moon hung in the humid, morning sky.

I walked closer to the sacrificial altar. Empty. Mercifully, there hadn't been another sacrifice.

Thirty minutes later, our search party gathered. Doña María informed us she'd seen no sign of Sharon in the central courtyard.

"She's not in the front," Harriet reported.

"Nor in the library," Father Lester said.

I thought back to Sharon's room. She'd taken all her things, and she wasn't at Armadillo. In all probability, she took a cab to Tuxtla, where she caught a plane to Mexico City and then home. Because she'd killed Ruth and Gerald and buried me to die in the tomb, she'd have known that someone would try to pursue her. Most likely, David. Almost eighteen hours had passed since

Sharon had killed Ruth. Sharon was long gone. Those still living were now safe.

My head throbbed, my body ached, and I couldn't think straight. Exhausted from all that had happened, I went to my room and collapsed on my bed.

CHAPTER 38

A Presence

I fell asleep and was rapidly trapped in a nightmare, the second since I'd arrived at Armadillo. Dead Gerald taunted me about how even as a ghost, he'd won a Pulitzer for his biography of Max Eicher. He reached out his hand and touched my shoulder in his patronizing way. Even as my body jerked back, I swung my fist hard at his face.

He screamed in pain. I opened my eyes and saw Harriet holding her hand over her bleeding nose. "Oh, great!" she said, "I hope you didn't break it."

"What happened? What did I do?"

"I came to comfort you, but thanks to you, I'm going to have a black eye and a crooked nose. The unfairness of it all." Melodramatically, she tilted her head back and placed the back of her hand on her forehead.

"Bravo! That's a brilliant imitation of Ruth's acting in her silent screen days," I said. Harriet's mouth twisted into a grimace. I added, "Okay, no more wisecracks from me. My lips are sealed."

"Like my eye will be in a few hours. But enough of this. I've come to say I'm sorry that Sharon wasn't the person you thought she was. You cared a great deal for her." She placed her hand on my shoulder.

Insights raced into my awareness. Growing up with a mom who wouldn't touch my birthmark and a distant alcoholic dad, I'd played the role of a man who refuses to be hurt. I'd tried to project a persona of strength against a world where people feared my face. I couldn't let others think I, who displayed an unforgettable birthmark, was vulnerable. I offered the world a hard armadillo-like shell.

I don't know how long Harriet's hand rested on my shoulder, but as time passed, I felt the comfort she was offering. After her opening words, she remained silent. But her genuine words, "I'm sorry," continued to reverberate in my head. They eased my hurt.

"Thank you, Harriet."

"Come to my room. Let's talk while I apply an ice pack to my nose and eye. I suspect you might like some tequila."

"It's early, but yes."

I sat back in a chair. In a few minutes, Harriet returned with an ice pack, two glasses, and a tequila bottle. "Pour yourself one while I work on my swollen face."

I felt drained. I sipped my drink while she attended to the red, swelling area I'd left on her face.

After several minutes of applying the ice pack, she said, "You've been through a lot this week. Stand up." She reached her arms around me and gave me a reassuring hug. Her perfume lingered in the air. "It's a shame Sharon hurt you as much as she did."

I swallowed hard. "Sharon is incredible. Even though she'd lost her husband in Vietnam, she could still reach out in a caring way."

"What husband? She was never married."

"She said she was. At the end of her sophomore year in college, she married Ken, an African American who served in Vietnam. A local newspaper ran a photo of her posthumously receiving a Purple Heart in her husband's name. He was killed in action in 1966."

"That's nonsense. I knew Sharon Silverthorne, whom you call Sandy Martin, as an undergrad. She took one of my archaeology classes at UMass. One of the most brilliant students I've ever taught. She wasn't married."

"Maybe she didn't tell you."

"No. Sharon was never a grieving widow. On the contrary, she always had a man in tow and never the same one twice. Anyway, it will be easy to verify if she was married or not."

"Perhaps she didn't tell the truth about that," I said, "but I know one thing for certain." I heard the tremor in my voice. "Gerald killed her career with a savage review of her first book manuscript and all because she negatively reviewed his latest book."

Harriet bit her lip to refrain from speaking, then blurted out, "Paul, she lied to you. I read that venomous review she wrote. Even my colleagues who despised Gerald believed he could win a libel suit against her. The editor was out of his mind to publish it."

Now I bit my lip. "Sharon told me that Gerald strong-armed her faculty to deny her tenure. She was terrified that she'd end up working in a fish canning factory."

"There's no easy way to tell you this, but that's not why she'd end up there. Here's what a senior administrator at her college told me. Sharon completed her doctorate at The University of Texas." I nodded because that part was correct. "In record time, she became a tenured associate professor at a small and very prestigious college nearby."

"You're sure? She told me that she was an assistant professor, and the faculty would deny her promotion and tenure."

"About a year ago, the President of The University of Texas received an anonymous parcel—perhaps sent by Gerald—but that's speculation. It contained a thorough analysis that con-clusively demonstrated that Sharon Silverthorne plagiarized large sections of her dissertation. After verifying the evidence, her degree-granting university rescinded her doctorate. The college where she was teaching—not wanting to blemish its sterling reputation—proceeded quietly to fired her."

I closed my eyes and then slowly opened them. I set my jaw and raised my voice. "Why didn't you tell me sooner?"

"Because around her, you looked like a lost puppy who'd finally found a home."

"I did?"

"You did."

"Harriet, you've been telling me "the truth" about Sharon. Isn't it time you told me the truth about being in Gerald's room the morning he died?"

She eyed me with a cautious look. "You're good. I didn't think I'd left any clues."

"You didn't leave a thing. You left a presence—your distinctive perfume."

"Oh, yes, my favorite. Tatiana by Diane von Furstenberg." Harriet paused before saying, "As you surely guessed, I was furious about Gerald's mocking my research. I went to his room and to ask if I could borrow a copy of his latest book. He laughed at me and walked over to his desk. When his back was to me, I picked up a small log from the stack near the fireplace. I concealed it behind my back and walked over to him. 'Are you looking for an example of real scholarship?' he asked. 'Your research can certainly use a lot of help.' For a second time, he laughed at me. I swung the log and hit him on his temple. His eyes rolled, and he fell back on his bed—absolutely still."

"Dead."

"No, just unconscious. I checked his pulse. He was breathing normally, and his body wasn't painted blue. I left his room filled with joy."

So, Harriet left Gerald's room satisfied after rendering him unconscious. In those circumstances, I'd have felt the same. And she admitted hitting him with a log and knocking him out. All I had was her confession that she'd been at the crime scene. But that didn't account for the knife wounds in Gerald's chest or the blue paint job that I'd seen.

CHAPTER 39

Colorless Tears

My brain was fried, and my stomach rumbled. I needed a break from Casa Armadillo. It took no effort to persuaded Father Lester to join me for lunch at Diego's Mustache. As we ate, he entertained me with stories about the eccentrics, villains, idealists, believers, and charlatans who populated the world of Spanish religious art. I told him I was impressed by his calm nature considering the three deaths that had occurred. He gave me a saintly smile. "I've read all the Father Brown short stories by G. K. Chesterton. In one, Father Brown says, and I paraphrase: Hasn't it struck you that a man who does little but hears confessions is fully aware of human evil?' Father Brown is my role model for taking life in stride." By the time dessert arrived, I was relaxed and able to think clearly.

The moment I returned to my room at Armadillo, I knew what I needed to do. I stuffed my shaving kit and a change of clothes in a small bag and jogged around puddles of water into La Ruta to catch a taxi. Jorge flashed a friendly smile. *Of all the drivers in all the towns in all the world, I end up with him again!* I hardened myself, and he stomped on the gas pedal. The road was a muddy mess. After I offered Jorge an obscene number of pesos, he kept the taxi racing at half the speed of sound.

Was I on a wild-goose chase based on a crazy hunch? Perhaps. Sharon was a quick-thinking killer, but she'd also shown herself to be quite strategic. Most people would head to the airport in Tuxtla. But if Sharon had wanted to throw us off her trail, I had a hunch she'd hide out temporarily at Trudi Blom's Casa Na Bolom before catching a plane home. If I were right, I'd confront her and take her back to Armadillo; if wrong, she'd be long gone now.

Several hours later, Jorge and I arrived in San Cristóbal, and he dropped me off at Na Bolom. I told the desk clerk that my friend had checked in last night. I described Sharon but didn't give her name.

"Yes, we have a Sharon Silverthorne staying in Suite Jataté."

"If you don't mind, I'll take a room far away from hers. We work together a lot. Sometimes, I need time for myself. Please don't tell her I've checked in." I slipped him enough pesos to ensure his silence. Considering Sharon's striking beauty, the clerk must have thought I was out of my mind.

A tall stack of firewood and piles of blankets at the foot of the bed promised protection against chilly evenings. I looked at the lamp on the nightstand and predicted it held a fifteen-watt bulb—I was right. That wasn't a problem; I wouldn't be reading tonight.

Shortly before they served dinner at Na Bolom at seven o'clock, I knocked on Sharon's door.

"Paul!"

"Not expecting me, Sharon?"

"No, no. It's just that you surprised me."

"I bet I did." I waited. "Going to invite me in?"

"Of course. I've been thinking a lot about you." She gave me a lingering hug. My arms hung at my sides.

"Did you think about me a lot after twice trying to kill me?"

"That's mean! What are you talking about?"

"And did you also think a lot about Gerald and Ruth after you killed them?"

The color bleached from her face. "That's crazy talk. I love you."

"Sealed in a Maya tomb, I found it impossible to feel your love."

"Why are you twisting what happened? When I went back for your batteries, Ruth lay in wait at the top of the stairs. I didn't see her before she knocked me out. She's the one who sealed you in."

"Right."

"When I awoke, I was lying on a large sheet of plastic on the bed in her bedroom. She'd tied my arms behind my back and bound my ankles. She was sitting in a chair and watching me. A knife lay on the bedroom nightstand; a bucket of blue paint and brush were beside it." Sharon paused.

"Yeah, sure. Go on."

"I struggled to get loose. I'll never forget Ruth's hideous smile as she said, 'Well, pretty girl who stole Paul from me, you're next.' I screamed, but nothing came out. She'd stuffed a wad of cloth in my mouth. 'It's time for another Maya sacrifice. But first, I thank you and Paul for leading me to Max's secret room. I'd never have found it without you. I haven't descended the stairs yet, but I'm sure there's a chamber holding treasures beyond my wildest dreams.'

"She picked up the knife and walked toward me. 'Since we met, I've thought of you as a heartless seductress. When I'm finished with you, you'll truly be one.'

"I twisted and struggled. Ruth touched the point of the knife with the tip of her finger and smiled. 'I wanted to cut out Gerald's heart, but I didn't want to replace a bloody mattress. You're lying on a plastic sheet because I want to cut out your heart and not ruin my bedding.' She laughed horribly at her gruesome joke.

"I was terrified as she approached. I pulled my knees to my chest, and as she leaned toward me, I kicked at her with every ounce of strength I could muster. My feet rammed into her stomach. When she doubled over, I kicked up hard. She fell back, hit her head on the corner of the fireplace, and crumbled to the floor. I rolled off the bed and inched my body over to the knife.

After what seemed like ages, I was able to cut myself free."

"You have quite the imagination," I said. "Now, give me a break and tell the truth."

"Paul, I was scared. I love you more than you can know."

I crossed my arms. "Then why leave me in a tomb to die a gruesome death? How did you so conveniently forget to come back to save me?"

"I swear I was out of my mind after freeing myself. I panicked. I felt I couldn't trust anyone. I ran back to my room, grabbed everything, and fled here. After I got here, I tried to call Armadillo, but the lines were down. Please forgive me. You and I can go back to Armadillo in the morning and tell everyone what happened. Otherwise, they're going to hate me, but worst of all, you're going to hate me."

"You're right about us going back to Armadillo."

She reached out her arms. "Paul, I love you. I'm ashamed of leaving you to die. Please forgive me. Hold me."

I stood with my arms folded across my chest. "Where are the research materials you stole to write Max's story?"

"I never stole anything."

"Then step aside, while I look around. Toward the back of the lowest shelf was a briefcase with the embossed initials G.S. —Gerald Strupp. Inside were Gerald's notebooks, my copy of *Max Eicher's Memoirs* (containing Gerald's three floppy disks I'd slipped between its pages), my notes, and an envelope containing one photographic negative of Max and Kate. "And you were going to return all this to me?"

"I have no idea why I took your stuff," Sharon said. "I panicked and just grabbed everything." She ran her fingers through her hair. "Let's go out for dinner but not to paint the town. I need to talk."

"Not tonight. Besides, my appetite's gone. And you need your sleep to be fresh when you tell your story to our friends at Armadillo. We'll take a taxi back in the morning. I'm not taking that road at night. Goodnight, Sharon."

I picked up Gerald's briefcase and returned to my room. After carefully sliding the door's wooden security bar into place, I sat down to think things through. Several hours ago, I'd finally grasped that Sharon was the most pathological liar I'd ever encountered—an extremely dangerous psychopath. She'd killed Gerald and Ruth, two people who stood in her way. I now fully understood why twice Sharon had tried to kill me. She didn't love me. I was just another obstacle blocking her path from writing Max's biography.

So why are you letting Sandy out of your sight? I raced to Sharon's room. Her door stood open. Everything of hers was gone.

Sitting on her bed, I asked myself if I'd let her slip away? Possibly. But I knew I could never prove she was the killer because too much of my case against her rested on circumstantial evidence. Even with irrefutable evidence, no male juror would ever convict Sharon. Her wide-eyed innocence added to her dazzling beauty hid her deceptive empathy and caring—all the right words but none that she meant. She could effortlessly persuade a jury that she told the truth, even as she shamelessly lied.

And you think because you're an expert on Freud that you understand people? With no warning, I broke into laughter—at myself —for spewing forth so many rationalizations. I, who'd written Freud's biography, had been blinded by my need for Sharon's love. Consistently, I'd ignored the signs that she took advantage of me to get what she wanted—sole authorship of Max Eicher's biography.

I walked into the bathroom and stared at my face in the mirror for the first time without turning away. In the depths of my being, I now understood the tragedy of Max's life. He'd fallen in love with a faithless woman, but he was bound by his religious faith to stay married until one of them died. In one way, I'd been more fortunate. I was suffering from a broken heart, but twice I'd lucked out when Sharon attempted to kill me. In another way, I'd been less fortunate. At least Max had found—if even for such a short time, Maurine, the love of his life. In hindsight, I clearly understood that Sharon had never loved me. I had no one.

In the dim light of the bathroom, I studied my face. I watched as colorless tears rolled down the left side of my face and picked up the pink tones of my skin—the tears on the right side, the burgundy tones. And yet despite my pain and sorrow, I suddenly realized that I'd made a colossal mistake.

CHAPTER 40

An Explanation

T he breakfast at Na Bolom was filling and tasty, but I still longed for one prepared by Doña María. After ensuring that my driver wasn't Jorge, I caught a taxi back to Armadillo. I found David in his darkroom and told him that Sharon escaped after I caught up with her. He took the news stoically, as though Sharon didn't matter because nothing would bring Ruth back. "We need a meeting to update everyone," I said. "I'll inform Doña María, Harriet, and Father Lester and let them know we'll meet in the library at two o'clock. David, as the senior person at Armadillo, you should run the meeting." He agreed.

The atmosphere in the library was somber but decidedly more relaxed than during recent meetings. Father Lester asked for a minute of silence to remember those who were now absent from our lives. He added, "And let's especially remember those who lost someone close to them." I glanced at David's swollen eyes. Despite Ruth's egotistical and controlling ways, I grasped how much he'd loved her. During the silence, I thought about Sharon and felt a sour churning in my stomach.

David ended the remembrance by calling on me to reiterate the sequence of events of the recent murders. I presented my rehearsed statement. "Though Gerald and I each wanted to be Max's official biographer, I was unaware that Sharon harbored the same ambitions. She told me Gerald had destroyed her career, but she'd begun their feud by writing a potentially libelous review of his latest book. The night before last, I received a note to meet Gerald in the chapel. Sharon, not Gerald, had written it. When I went to the chapel, she lay in wait to kill me. I nearly went the way of William and Gerald, but Harriet showed up and foiled her plan.

"I can speak to what came next," Harriet said. "When Sharon heard me, she quick-wittedly screamed, 'Oh, Paul, you can't die." She fooled me into believing she'd arrived just in time to save you."

"After our final board meeting," I said, "I discovered Max's secret study and a passage to the treasure buried deep below us."

Harriet shouted, "What secret study? What buried treasure? You found Max's writings?"

"I've been here forty-five years," David said, "and you're saying that the treasure was below me all the time?"

A clamor ensued. "Hold on! I'll answer your questions shortly. Before noon two days ago, Sharon met with Gerald. She knocked him unconscious, stabbed him, and painted his body blue. Then, she stole his material related to Max Eicher. At that point, Ruth and I stood in Sharon's way. After dinner on Tuesday, I made a critical mistake. For a second time, I took Sharon to see the treasure. She seized her chance and sealed me in the tomb to die. Then she killed Ruth. I suspect she told Ruth that she possessed all the materials she needed for Max's biography since Gerald and I were dead. She most likely demanded Ruth's endorsement. Ruth had many facets to her personality, but letting another person control her wasn't one of them. Can't we all hear Ruth's likely response to Sharon?" All four nodded. "Sharon killed Ruth and fled with research materials belonging to Gerald and me. Now here's the good news: all the stolen documents are now safely in my possession. The bad news: Sharon escaped before I could bring her back to Armadillo."

I looked at David and saw the puzzlement on his face. He was perhaps wondering how I'd retrieved the documents if Sharon had escaped. I kept talking. "In summary, I offer the following as the official explanation of what happened. Initially, Gerald killed William because William's plan for Armadillo might prevent Ruth from endorsing Gerald's proposal to write Max's biography. Sharon tricked me into thinking she cared about me. In reality, she desperately wanted to write the book herself. She knew if Gerald, Ruth, and I died, she'd be free to write it. I suggest we bury Ruth in a grave next to Max's grave—the one with a sack of rocks, although given their glacial relationship, perhaps several yards apart."

David stood and said, "I propose we accept Paul's explanation." The group gave its consent. "As the senior person at Armadillo, I authorize Paul to write Max Eicher's biography. He has assured me he will write an honest account that respects the lives of those in this room. Paul, we look forward to reading your next book." The group joined David in a round of applause. I grinned and thanked them. *I wonder how David thinks I can write Max's biography without his papers.*

"But there is more," I said. "Lying beneath our feet are archaeological treasures. You'll see magnificent Maya murals, the remains of a Maya king, a jade death mask, a sizable gold armadillo pendant, and a gold armadillo sculpture. Everyone who has visited this place has already seen a gold armadillo sculpture, but not recognized it. *Armadillo 1930,* Max Eicher."

Harriet let out a shriek. "When I first saw that plaster armadillo in the courtyard, I thought it was the ugliest thing I'd ever seen."

"It's ugly," I said, "but we all know Max's love of magic. For fifty years, art lovers have shaken their heads and pitied the talentless Max.

"That explains a lot," Harriet said. "I was tempted to tip over that hideous sculpture. If I had, I might have discovered the gold armadillo. Too bad I didn't act on my impulse."

A bemused look graced David's face. "I'm embarrassed to say this, but as I held Ruth's lifeless body in my arms, I thought I could finally pitch that eyesore."

During the meeting, Doña María had stayed silent, but now

she spoke. "I helped Max get that armadillo up the stairs and out to the courtyard. We mixed plaster and covered the entire animal. Soon it looked much bigger. I offered to paint it, but he said I'd make it look beautiful. He liked it ugly because then people didn't look at it too long."

"Doña María is right," I said. "Max was an expert at concealment. He hid his study behind the fireplace wall in the study. And he hid the stairs that lead to a Maya tomb under a stela weighing tons. And now, it's tomb tour time. Doña María, would you please get five lanterns for our exploration? Harriet, would you mind helping her?" Harriet gave me a look that seemed to say, "Hey, buddy boy! Doña María and I aren't your domestic help."

CHAPTER 41

A Second Explanation

As soon as the lanterns arrived, I yanked off the strip of molding to the fireplace's right. David, Harriet, and Father Lester gasped; Doña María smiled innocently. I swung open the bookcase to more gasps and a smile.

"I can't believe it," David said. "It's been right in front of me all this time."

Harriet wagged her finger at Doña María. "You've known about this all along, yet you never told anyone."

"Yes, I knew. Max and I worked to make sure nobody would find it. Paul is smart. He figured it out."

I blushed at her compliment. "We have Harriet to thank for my discovery because of her wild pitch at the board meeting." She looked puzzled. "Gerald provoked you, and you responded by throwing a small onyx armadillo at him. I heard a sound that wasn't quite right, but it didn't register at the time. Later, I threw the onyx armadillo at the fireplace wall. Sure enough, I heard a hollow thud." I wanted to share additional details of my discovery, but the group was getting impatient. Before I led them into the secret study, I grabbed a thick book from Max's bookcase.

"I don't think that's going to help us," David said.

"No, but it might get us at the truth," I answered.

Harriet scurried around the secret room. "It's set up like a study, but the bookshelves and the filing cabinets drawers are empty. Where's Max's work?"

"This is how I found it."

"Any clues to where the papers might be?" she asked.

"Not a one." I showed the group how the stela swiveled to expose the trap door. "Doña María, please light the lanterns." Although my memory of imminent death inside a sealed tomb tightened my stomach, I forced myself to sound calm. "David, you've been living above this treasure for a long time. I suggest you lead us to it."

"But Paul, earlier, you told me there are snakes and scorpions down there."

"Sorry, that was my fear talking; I saw none. I'll hand you a lantern as soon as your feet are secure on the landing." He descended into the passageway. When he touched the landing, I placed the thick book on the floor and let it lap over the opening a bit. "David, watch your head!" I closed the trap door and sat on it.

"Hey, what are you doing?" David called out. "I can't see a thing!"

"Your eyes will soon adjust. And because of the small opening, you're not going to run out of oxygen."

"Paul, let him out," Harriet said. "That's a cruel thing to do." She winked at me.

"Now, David, you and I need to talk. In the library, we agreed on an explanation of events related to the killings. There's one big problem: I lied. I want you to tell us the accurate version of what happened."

"What are you talking about? You said Sharon killed Gerald and Ruth and tried to kill you."

"My version sounded reasonable, and everyone agreed. But there's a problem: it doesn't hold together. Sharon didn't do any of the things I said she did."

"So, you think I killed them?" David asked. "That's a lie!"

"David, I agree with you. However, we'll release you after you tell us the real story."

Father Lester smiled at me. "David, it's in your best interest to own up to what happened."

"I'm not confessing to anything."

"I'm not after a confession, David," I said. "I'm after the truth."

"Paul," said Harriet, "he's been trapped down there long enough. He can talk to us in the library. Can't you tell he's suffering?" Once again, she winked at me. Our good cop/bad cop routine was proceeding nicely.

"Harriet, let me handle this." I leaned my head close to the small opening. "David, you'd have gotten away with it, but you overlooked two things: the indentation on Ruth's head and the rug."

"Lift the trap door and let me out! What do an indentation and a rug have to do with anything?"

"They point to how Ruth died," I said. "When I caught up with Sharon in Na Bolom, I was convinced she was the killer. But she told me Ruth knocked her out as she emerged from the tomb. She awoke bound and gagged in Ruth's bedroom and lying on a plastic sheet. When Ruth approached with a knife, Sharon kicked her. Ruth fell back and hit her head on the edge of the fireplace. She described Ruth lying unconscious on a rug. David, when I examined her wound in your presence, the area on the back of her head was swollen with a three-inch, straight indentation."

"Lift the trap door and let me out! A damn indentation means nothing!"

"There's more. You and I found Ruth's body in Sharon's room. That was puzzling. Why would Sharon describe all the events as if she'd been in Ruth's bedroom? If Sharon had moved the body, she'd have incriminated herself.

"When I returned to Armadillo after talking with Sharon, I examined Ruth's bedroom. Her Art Deco fireplace, including its corners, has the straight, sharp angles and edges of that era. Two feet above the floor on a sharp-edged wood pillar, I found bloodstains. By way of comparison, Sharon's room has the traditional round-cornered, adobe fireplace found in all rooms except Ruth's. None of the traditional fireplaces would have left a straight indentation. Ruth died in her bedroom when she hit her head on the Art Deco fireplace."

"Pure fantasy," David said. "Now, end this charade and let me out."

"No such luck, David. Another detail in Sharon's story didn't make sense. She described Ruth as lying on a large fireplace rug after she hit her head. Shortly after I arrived at Armadillo, Ruth, in her seductive way, showed me her bedroom. Thanks to my photographic memory, in my mind's eye, I can see the Art Deco designed rug on the floor in front of Ruth's fireplace —without doubt, the same rug that we found Ruth lying on in Sharon's room. But it's not the one I saw days earlier in Sharon's room. Doña María confirmed that Ruth's rug was now in Sharon's room."

Silence ensued from below the trap door.

"David, let's make this easy. You tell us what you know, and we'll let you out. Play games with us, and you're going to get very hungry and very thirsty."

During another long silence, I began to wonder if David had suffered a heart attack. "Let me out of here. I can't breathe," said a trembling voice from beneath the trap door. "I'll tell you everything."

"The true story?"

"I'm ready to talk."

I swung open the trap door and gave him a hand as he climbed out of the passage. "Father Lester, would you please take notes of the conversation that David and I have?" We moved to the library. Father Lester readied his pen.

David let out an eerie moan. "I've known Ruth for years," he said, "but lately she'd started behaving strangely. She believed that raising money for Armadillo would be easy. Complications arose. Intent on destroying both Ruth's and Max's reputation, Gerald blackmailed Ruth with compromising photos." On the verge of throwing up, David paused, his face pale. Father Lester retrieved a small crockery pot from the library shelves and arrived in time for David to halfway fill it. David wiped his wet lips with his handkerchief.

"Ruth killed Gerald. I know because she led me to his body. There were small, but numerous knife wounds on the front of his shirt. A knife, a can of blue paint, and a brush were in the corner. Ruth demanded that I help her by cutting open Gerald's chest, removing his heart, and painting his body blue to appear identical to William's body. Then she left us." David paused and threw up some more. "I hated the man, but I couldn't cut out his heart. I took off his shirt and applied the blue paint—the whole time, my stomach churned. Once I knew she'd killed Gerald, I assumed that she'd killed William, too. And now it makes sense that she'd twice tried to kill you—once in the chapel and once in the tomb."

"Wait a minute, David. Was Ruth strong enough to knock me out and drag my body behind the altar?"

Doña María spoke up. "I often saw Ruth lifting weights when I cleaned her apartment—probably for an hour, four times a week. She worked in vain to maintain a young woman's body."

I breathed more easily. David had helped Ruth in her effort to make Gerald's body look like William's sacrificed body. But David had made a mistake: he'd jumped to the false assumption that Ruth killed William. I knew from Doña María's confession that she'd sacrificed William because he'd long ago raped her. Before she'd confessed, I promised not to tell anyone. I'd keep her secret.

Father Lester cleared his throat. "One thing puzzles me, Paul. When you and Sharon visited the burial chamber, wouldn't you have locked the library door from the inside? If so, how did Ruth follow you and Sharon into the library and the secret room?"

"I can answer that one," David said. "Ruth carries keys to every lock in Casa Armadillo."

I changed the subject in my next question to David. "What do you know about Ruth's attempts on my life?"

"Nothing conclusively. She considered herself irresistible—always had. She believed if she went after a man, he was hers.

You incurred her wrath because you repeatedly spurned her advances. And she hated Sharon because she stole you from her. On the night before last, I went to Ruth's room and found her on the bedroom floor. There were ropes, paint, a brush, a wadded-up cloth, and a plastic sheet. I concluded that Ruth's plan had gone deadly wrong."

"So, you moved her body to Sharon's room."

"I figured if her body were discovered in Sharon's room, people would assume that Sharon killed her. It would also divert attention from Ruth as Gerald's and William's killer. I hid the paint and other stuff in a back storeroom."

"And the pendant I found on Gerald's forehead?"

"After I'd painted Gerald's body—ugh, just thinking about it makes me sick—Ruth summoned me to her room. She handed me a pendant and made me go back and put it on Gerald's forehead. She said, and I quote, 'it will provide another silly clue for Paul's pointless investigation.'"

I cringed. Ruth was unaware of the dots on the pendants and didn't realize that the single dot on the back of the one she left pointed to her. "One last question. Why cover for Ruth?"

"Because I'd do almost anything for her. When I first arrived at Armadillo, I thought I loved her and that she might love me. Over time, I realized she only loved herself. But as I fell out of love with her, I fell in love with her image. I covered for her because I thought I was protecting her name." He covered his face in his hands. "How does a man make such a fool of himself over a woman?"

I thought of Sharon and shook my head. *Don't get me started on that topic.* "Here's the deal, David. Father Lester's going to write up his notes and then read them aloud to us. If the account of your actions is accurate, you'll sign the paper, and the four of us will witness it. I'll keep the paper to ensure you do not change your story. Agreed?"

David looked exhausted, but I also detected relief. "I agree."

We waited while Father Lester wrote the document. After everyone had signed it, I said, "A few hours ago, I proposed a story that we'd tell the world about this last week. We all agreed. But given David's account of events, we know my previous story was wrong. Ruth appears to have killed William, killed Gerald, attempted to stab Sharon, and twice tried to kill me.

"But a bit ago, you told us that Sharon killed Ruth," Harriet said. "I'm confused."

"Sharon kicked Ruth to protect herself from Ruth's knife. Ruth fell back and died when she hit her head on the fireplace; there were no other marks on her body." I didn't add that while Sharon hadn't killed anyone, she was still a thief, a compulsive liar, and the woman who broke my heart.

David had been quiet but suddenly said, "I think we should face the facts and accept them. Ruth snapped and tried to kill anyone who got in her way."

For several minutes, the grandeur of the Maya murals left everyone speechless. Harriet and David finally raised questions about how to understand the murals. I said nothing, but I thought it was obvious: they are couples engaged in coitus. David went into an ecstatic state over the jade mask and the large, gold armadillo pendant next to the Maya king's bones.

I knew it was coming and wasn't surprised when Harriet said, "That sarcophagus has been disturbed and its gold armadillo damaged. Max should never have removed the body and the invaluable treasures from that sarcophagus." I kept silent. "Wait a minute, Paul," Harriet continued, "how did you escape from this burial chamber?"

I paused, knowing that what I was about to disclose was sure to get me in trouble. "I explored this room, looking for a second tunnel. I found none. Next, I looked inside the lidless sarcophagus. I removed the bones and objects of art to survey the bottom of it. I found nothing. I removed the gold armadillo and lid from the second sarcophagus."

"But the armadillo's tail is broken off," Father Lester said.

I watched as he grappled with the problem of the damaged

armadillo. He quickly found the answer. "Paul, you damaged a priceless treasure!"

"Father Lester, I had two choices. Damage the armadillo or die."

"I get your point." He thought for a second and added, "I suggest we think of the armadillo as having acquired a patina." The expressions on the rest of the group's faces indicated they didn't buy his reframing of the damaged artifact.

I showed them the metal ring, the trap door, and the stairs descending into an abyss. Nobody wanted to exit that way. We lingered in the chamber room for an hour.

Before leaving, I asked Doña María, "Do you know what happened to Max's possessions?"

"I like this room." She grinned. "For many hours, Max and I looked at everything we found here. I spent a long time in this chamber painting copies of the murals."

"Where's everything now?" I asked. "And where are Max's bones?"

She pointed at a sarcophagus. "I put them in there after the flesh was gone."

A storm cloud gathered on Harriet's face. "Tell us the truth, Doña María. When Paul removed bones from that sarcophagus during his escape from the chamber room, were the bones the Maya king's or Max's?"

Doña María smiled a sweet smile. "I think of Max as a great king. I took out the Maya king's bones and dressed Max in his jewelry."

"Wait, what happened to the bones of the Maya king?" David asked.

"Dogs love chewing on them."

Father Lester gasped; Harriet and I let out prolonged groans, and David laughed. "Max would have loved the irony of having a king's burial. After all, he called his wife, the Ice Queen." Once again, I groaned, but this time Harriet rolled her eyes.

"Looking on the bright side," I said, "I'll be writing the biography of a man who was buried like a Maya king. That fact alone might boost book sales."

Father Lester smiled at me. "I like the way you think. But it might be best if we reassemble Max's bones in the sarcophagus and arrange the jewelry. Now *that* would be a great photo on the cover of the book jacket."

I thought if I wanted monster sales, the cover jacket should feature Max and Kate having sex Maya style. I stopped myself from sharing that thought.

Doña María's eyes took on a faraway look. "One thing we all know. Max was a man of mystery."

CHAPTER 42

Safe In Iowa City

On my journey home, I wrote to Neumann with an update about the events at Armadillo. I presented the facts about the murders and my role in solving them. Then, trying to sound as if I weren't seeking pity or seething with anger, I described falling in love with Sharon—and how she'd deceived me. Finally, I thanked Neumann for pushing me to write Max's biography. The book was my highest priority, and I'd begin writing it, if, and only if, we found Max's papers.

Arriving home was bittersweet. Spring was a week away, but after the warmth of southeastern Mexico, Iowa City was far too chilly. Classes would resume on Monday. I'd be teaching undergrads who'd returned begrudgingly, as I had, from midterm break. That said, I was relieved that in Iowa City, I wouldn't find sacrificed bodies painted blue.

I had nothing to write, so over the next two weeks, I avoided my typewriter and talking with my department chair. When one of my favorite students asked me what was wrong, I told a white lie and said everything was going well. But I knew my lie wasn't white.

On the last Friday night of March, David Budman called as I enjoyed a glass of wine. He went straight to the point. "Doña María and I just found Sharon Silverthorne's body."

Relief raced through my body, followed by a sickening image

of yet another corpse. I felt nauseous and took several deep breaths. "Go on."

"Before you left Armadillo, you led us on a tour of Max's secret room and the Maya burial chamber. After you started home the next day, I began worrying that we'd left the burial chamber's entrance open. Anyone could get in. When I entered Max's secret room, I saw the stela was swung open, and the trap door was up. I shut the door and swung the stela closed.

"This afternoon, Doña María and I decided to inventory the jewelry in the chamber. At the bottom of the steps, we discovered Sharon's twisted body. A dead flashlight lay beside her."

I struggled for words. "I thought she'd headed back to the States."

"That's what we all thought. She must have sneaked into Armadillo after you showed us the chamber. Father Lester, who stayed on at Armadillo to document the chapel, will officiate at her service. We'll bury Sharon next to the sacrificial stone, near the graves of William and Gerald."

"Good choice." I instantly regretted my harsh sounding words. Internally, I felt like I was being offered numerous emotions on a multiple-choice question. Right now, the correct answer was all-of-the-above. I hung up and topped off my wine glass.

While the news about Sharon was unnerved and depressed me, I also felt restless. Something was all wrong—one mystery persisted. *Figure it out, Paul. You paid your dues as a detective at Armadillo.*

I sat in my favorite Stickley rocker and thought hard. Two hours later, I'd finished off a bottle of good wine. I'd also solved a mystery that had haunted me all my life.

CHAPTER 43

A Visit

A month after arriving home from Armadillo, I made a trip I'd been dreading. As I drove a rental car through a neighborhood of low-slung Hollywood bungalows built in the thirties, I wasn't sure what I'd say or how to say it. Eventually, I turned right at a private drive and made my way up a steep incline. Ahead of me, a massive, red-brick Victorian mansion crowned the hilltop.

I grabbed my briefcase from the car's backseat and climbed the fifteen steps to the front door. I took a deep breath, rang the doorbell, and waited. Because the man who opened the door wasn't wearing sunglasses, it initially took me several seconds to recognize him. Without his shades, he looked older than I'd remembered him.

"Hello, Theo. I made a special trip here to see you."

For a few seconds, he appeared confused. Then he offered a broad smile and invited me in. The hallway was pure Victorian: a Thonet bentwood hat and coat rack, and an iron umbrella stand lent stylish touches. "What a spectacular Victorian home," I said.

"It's a replica of my childhood home in Dubuque, Iowa."

"That was my guess." *It's easy to exchange pleasantries, but how do I tell him what I came here to say?*

He motioned me into the living room. It was a museum filled with late nineteenth-century furniture, none of which looked comfortable. "I'll show you around later. Have a chair. I received your letter about falling for Sharon and how badly she treated you. It pained me to hear that."

I'd spent considerable time trying to forget Sharon, which, filled with anger at her, was even harder after her death. Theo's attempt at comfort felt a bit like pouring salt on my wounded heart. "You probably haven't heard. Shortly after I left Armadillo, Sharon died when she fell down the stairs leading to the burial chamber." I thought I was in control, but my words blurted out. "She wasn't what she appeared. I thought she was a woman who cared for me—birthmark and all. I didn't realize how starved I was for love. All that lay hidden from me, beneath my strong desire to learn about Max Eicher." *Paul, stop blathering on about Sharon and tell Theo why you're here.* I paused and gathered my thoughts. "I came to share the solution to a mystery I've solved. As you were aware, but I wasn't: you and Max Eicher are the same person. And that person is my father!"

The man facing me paused, then slowly nodded. "I thought I'd covered my tracks rather well. How did you figure it out?"

He's treating this as a puzzle to figure out—okay, I'll play along. "To your credit, you almost succeeded. Then I pieced all the nagging details together into a coherent story. At our one-and-only meeting in Iowa City, I felt disoriented. So, I asked myself questions. Why would Theo, a gracious, warm-humored gentleman at the reading and signing, abruptly become abusive in the Hotel Washington? Why point out my birthmark, call me a dishonest coward, laugh at my writer's block, and then turn around and offer me five thousand dollars to spend a week in Armadillo? Why put me through a silly silo of emotions and make my world spin? Two weeks ago, I arrived at the simple answer: you wanted to keep me off guard by stirring up my emotions so that I wouldn't question your intent. You didn't want me thinking about why a famous screenwriter had contacted me out of the blue and given me such a strange assignment."

"So far, you're making sense," he said. "Go on."

"I did some detective legwork. I checked the flights out of Des

Moines, Iowa, to Los Angeles on February fifteenth. And sure enough, Theodore Neumann was on a plane, not a cross-country bus. So much for Theo's alleged heart condition. I quizzed the desk clerk at the Hotel Washington. After I gave him twenty dollars, he confessed that you'd taken the room for that evening, but you hadn't stayed there during your visit to Iowa City.

"Finally, Jim Harris at Prairie Lights Bookstore confirmed that you contacted him about doing a reading and signing. That hadn't bothered Jim because he was delighted to have a distinguished presenter."

"Your work ethic is most impressive."

"There's more. After returning to Iowa City from Armadillo, I carefully reread *Max Eicher's Memoirs.* The manuscript was typed on old paper with an antique typewriter, but one sentence struck me as peculiar. Max, who died in November of 1950, wrote that 'Ruth wanted to be the head honchō at Armadillo.'"

Theo shrugged his shoulders. "What's wrong with that?"

"Honchō is the Japanese word for "squad leader." The term was picked up by the U.S. military after WWII but didn't appear in common usage in the States until the mid-fifties. It certainly wouldn't have been in use at isolated Armadillo five years earlier."

Theo sat back in his chair. "Congratulations. Your research is as exhaustive as it was with *Freud.*"

"There was one last piece of evidence that confirmed your identity: Maurine Madanes' obituary in the *New York Times.*"

"I'm not following you."

"I reread the photocopy of Maurine's obituary and studied the accompanying photo. Suddenly I saw it for what it was—a David Budman photo. His style is in a class by itself. But David has never left Armadillo, so the photo must have been taken when Maurine visited Armadillo in 1950.

"That's when I trusted my intuition. Max wanted her picture, so he had David take it. But according to all sources, Maurine was Max's equal. I bet she'd have wanted his picture in return.

And perhaps the two wanted a photo of themselves together.

"I called David and told him I needed the photo he'd taken of Max for my biography of him. This time he didn't give me the runaround. He cooperated without hesitation and sent me these photos." I withdrew separate photos of Max and Maurine from my briefcase and a photo of them together. "You're thirty years older, but you and Max are the same person."

Theo looked through the photos. "She was a beautiful human being. We were so in love. I still feel the pain of her loss." Theo's eyes became moist. He sat without saying a word for some time.

"Theo, I'm sorry for your loss. Will you tell me why you have always avoided having your picture taken?"

"It's a simple story. I see myself in a way that others don't. From birth until I entered adolescence, I was quite chubby. Growing up, I always hated looking at photos of myself. When I was thirteen, I destroyed all my childhood pictures. My parents were furious but also deeply saddened. At that time, I also decided never to let anyone take my photo. However, after Maurine and I fell in love, she persuaded me to have David take photos of us."

"When did you write *Max Eicher's Memoirs?*"

Theo's eyes twinkled. "Six months ago. I located the typewriter in an old MGM warehouse. A colleague happened to have a functioning typewriter ribbon."

"That means if Sharon had succeeded in stealing it, she'd have possessed a worthless forgery?"

"Some parts are accurate; other parts are the product of my active imagination."

"The penny jar story?"

"Sadly, that one's accurate," Theo said.

I was on a roll. "In 1950, when you transformed yourself from Max Eicher to Theodore Neumann, the absence of Max's photos —these being an exception—made it harder for people to remember what you looked like in the past."

"You've become quite the detective."

I acknowledged his compliment, but as we talked, I'd felt my anger build up in intensity. "Why didn't you just write your autobiography and stop playing games with me?" *It's time to stop withholding my anger.* I pointed my finger at him and said in a loud voice, "What makes me furious are the games you've played at my expense. How many years have you known I was your son and not told me? You once called me a dishonest coward. What about yourself?"

CHAPTER 44

Accidents

I had finally let out how I felt. Drained and relieved, I sat back in my chair. After a minute or two, Theo exhaled slowly. If my confrontation troubled him, it didn't show. Quite the contrary, his face looked relaxed.

"To answer those questions, we'll need to go back in time a bit. Since 1927, Doña María has been a trusted confidant. We've corresponded continuously since Max "died" in 1950. But in 1966, one of her letters contained a bombshell. She wrote that her two daughters were soon to celebrate the *fiesta of quince años*. Then, she added, 'If your child were a girl, she also would be celebrating her fifteenth birthday.' What did Doña María mean? I nearly had a heart attack. Don't worry, Paul, that was a figure of speech.

"I wrote back for an explanation. The answer was quite simple. Doña María cleaned Kate's room during her stay in 1949. On many days in November and December, Doña María smelled vomit in her bathroom. Also, Kate no longer placed sanitary pads in the wicker basket beside the toilet. Since Doña María was also experiencing the same symptoms, she concluded Kate was pregnant, and I was the father. Not wanting to embarrass me, neither Doña María nor Kate said anything to me at the time. I suspect Kate didn't want to give birth to our child at Armadillo, knowing Ruth would make her life a living hell—just like she'd made mine.

"After receiving Doña María's explanation, I searched for our child. I started by trying to locate Kate. Tragically, Kate died in a car accident in 1963." Theo nervously rubbed his hands together. "I was persistent in tracking you down. I remembered Kate said in a letter that she'd delayed her trip back to New York and had stayed with her aunt in Santa Fe, New Mexico. I had a gut feeling she'd given birth during her stay and placed the baby up for adoption. I was right. I found your birth certificate, which described a dark birthmark under your right eye."

"That describes me all right." *Amazing! I'd just reacted as though my birthmark was a fact, not an indictment of who I am.*

"It took some doing, but eventually I located you, the baby with the birthmark. Then, right before your adoptive dad died in your senior year of high school, I decided to intervene."

"And I know how," I said. "You're the anonymous relative who established a trust fund for me."

"Right. I've followed you at a distance for fifteen years. I'm very proud of you."

"I know I ought to thank you for that. But what the hell, when we met in February, even then, you didn't reveal who you were? I even told you about my adoptive parents, and you offered only sympathetic words. Why not tell me? Why make me figure it all out?" As he pondered my questions, his eyes widened; I saw his fright.

"That's your hardest question. I don't have an acceptable answer except to say—and this is hard—that I was afraid. I feared you'd reject me and never let me get close. Part of it was my ego telling me to forget my painful past and focus on what I now had —a successful career in Hollywood. In truth, I don't know. Part of me wanted to reach out to you, and that's when I dreamed up sending you to Armadillo to write Max's biography."

"I don't get it," I said. "Why not tell me who you are in Iowa City? Why send me to Armadillo and subject me to such danger?"

"I never imagined your life would be in danger. Now I regret that I didn't reach out to you much sooner—whether years ago or in Iowa City. I kept making the same mistake of thinking this isn't the right time. I regret hurting you, and I apologize."

"Thanks for saying that. It helps. But back in 1950, you led everyone to believe you'd died, although there are numerous accounts of how that occurred."

A grin spread across his face. "Ah, you're talking about the great escape that Maurine Madanes and I planned. We faced an insurmountable problem. I was then and still am a devout Catholic. Notwithstanding how nightmarish my marriage, divorcing Ruth was never an option. Given the love Maurine and I shared, we planned to change our identities. Like phoenixes, our new lives were to arise from the ashes of our former selves. But it wasn't to be.

"According to our plan, Maurine would appear to die in a plane accident. The day she left Armadillo, I stood by the plane looking forlorn. In stark contrast, Ruth smiled and treated me as though we were the best of friends. Maurine planned to fly along the coast of Mexico until she reached a spot where the Gulf waters were the deepest. She was to set her plane on autopilot to fly over the water. And while still over land, she was to parachute out. I'll never know what happened, but something went wrong—and she and her plane were never found."

"I'm so sorry that happened to the love of your life."

"Maurine was always so confident that I believed nothing could go wrong with our plan. I was devastated when it did."

"Yet, you arose from the ashes of your prior life."

"Yes. Back at Armadillo and before Maurine left, I'd shipped, with Doña María's help, all my papers, photos, and other possessions to a trusted friend in Hollywood."

I pointed at Theo. "I struggled with how in the hell I was going to write Max's biography if I didn't have his source material. And which, incidentally, I began to doubt existed."

"After Maurine left Armadillo, I commenced my acting career. In my first starring role, I played a man sinking into suicidal depression. Although I'm highly allergic to alcohol, I carried around—but never drank from—a mezcal bottle. I deliberately slurred my speech and began speaking abusively. I had a lean frame, but I intentionally ate less to lose weight. My body looked like a Day-of-the-Dead skeleton. When Doña María and Ruth came into my room on that last night, they saw me lying on the floor. Doña María held up my arm. Ruth took my pulse and detected none."

"How'd you do that? An ancient Maya drug? Curare?"

"Nothing so esoteric, just a magician's trick I remembered from my childhood. I placed a three-inch wooden ball in my armpit. When Doña María held up my forearm, I squeezed hard on the ball. Presto! My heart rate became undetectable."

"You amaze me," I said.

Theo's eyes twinkled. "While Ruth rejoiced, Doña María sneaked me out of Armadillo and made arrangements to get me to the States. Then she had a local carpenter build a wooden coffin. Doña María added stones to give it weight." Theo gave a fake shiver. "Over the years, many visitors have paid their final respects to an empty coffin."

"But Doña María said she removed the bones of the Maya king from the sarcophagus and replaced them with yours."

Theo slapped his thigh. "She told you that? That's a good one!"

"She lied?"

"Let's just say that both she and I occasionally employ misdirection. Paul, I'm dead serious. I want you to write a biography of Max and my story. Your mind is razor sharp and effortlessly cuts to the quick. I hope you're still game?"

"Theo, I acknowledge you as a master trickster. But before I give a definitive answer, I'll have an attorney thoroughly study the contract's fine print."

"With that statement, you've just shown me you're my son. Let me get us some drinks, and we'll toast to that.

Theo poured me a glass of wine and a 7-Up for himself. I raised my glass. "I propose a toast of thanks that you finally acknowledged that you are Max and my father." We clicked glasses and smiled at each other. "I'm curious. What else was in the burial chamber? Doña María mentioned thirteen Maya codices. Did she also make that up?"

"Doña María told you the truth. Come, I'll show you the codices."

He removed a book from a shelf and pressed a hidden button. I watched in amazement as a set of bookcases slowly retracted and then moved to the right. Theo stood in the doorway as I circled the faintly lit room, bordered with display cases. Above me hung large color photographs depicting couples illustrating Maya sexual positions. I pointed at them and said, "They have the makings of a *Maya Kama Sutra.*"

"That's a great book title, Paul. But if I'm not mistaken—and I'm not—you aren't the first to suggest that title. It's first mentioned in Max's *Memoirs.*"

He was right. I quickly diverted his attention from the photos by pointing to the various control boxes that monitored temperature, humidity, lighting, and motion. Theo followed my gaze. "When the company installed state-of-the-art conservation and security for rare objects, I told them I was preserving classic films made with cellulose nitrate, which were susceptible to fire. Made sense to them."

I wasn't ready for what I saw in the display cases. The codices, unfolded like stretched-out accordions, were written in a hieroglyphic script. Theo said, "The Maya used wild fig tree bark to make the paper. Study the serpentine drawings of human figures, small blocks of symbols, and numbers composed of shells, dots, and bars."

"The colors in the drawings pulsate," I said.

"Doña María and I hit the jackpot. These codices cover a gamut of topics—history, astronomy, economics, politics, and agriculture."

"As well as, it appears, sexuality," I added.

"Yes, one codex was exclusively devoted to sexual positions. I'll show you that one tomorrow."

"Any luck in deciphering the codices?"

"Glad you asked. Next month, Random House will publish

a thirteen-volume set of books with full-page, color photos of all the codices and my translation of each. As to the codices themselves, I've spent the last year in secret negotiations with the Mexican government to return them. In exchange for the codices, the government has broken ground on a new building to house them in Mexico City. They also agreed to my non-negotiable condition: restoring and preserving the Armadillo temple as a national treasure."

I groaned. "Theo, I agreed to write the biography of Max Eicher. If I must also write the biography of Theodore Neumann, then you've just lengthened the book by adding thirty more years."

"I haven't begun to tell you stories about my years as a screenwriter. You must include them."

"I don't remember giving you control over what to include."

"That's because your bargaining position is weak." Theo watched as my face sagged. "But because I trust you more than any other possible biographer, I promise not to interfere. I'm through hiding who I am. You're free to write a warts-and-all biography, which I'll state in our contract."

"I have one last question before I go to bed. How did Ginzburg come to publish the erotic drawings in *Eros*?"

"That also puzzled me. So, I contacted Ginzburg and pressed him for the truth. He said that Kate, as was typical of New York artists, needed money, and he, as a publisher, needed sensational articles. I assumed she'd photographed Doña María's mural drawings that Max had showed her. She permitted Ginzburg to publish the drawings in exchange for a considerable sum of money and a vow of silence about the source."

"I'm glad he broke his vow. By the way, I'm planning to sleep in tomorrow morning. But after breakfast, I'd really like a tour of your home."

"Good, that will give me the chance to show you the boxes upon boxes of archival materials from the lives of Max Eicher and Theodore Neumann."

That evening, I lay awake for hours. I had—in the words of Theodore Neumann—found, cherished, and embraced my passions. I knew my writer's block was behind me, and I looked ahead to writing the definitive biography of my father.

CHAPTER 45

Prairie Lights

Upon returning to the University of Iowa, I finished teaching my 1980 spring classes. Then, I took an extended leave of absence from the university to write Max/Theo's biography. I lived in Theo's home, which contained collections of everything a biographer might want. The hardest part of writing was reconciling the two aspects of the man. But as I soon discovered, Max's change of identity didn't result in a man who ceased being Max. Following his "death" in 1950, my father doubled his energies and his output. By day, he wrote screenplays; at night, he deciphered Maya codices.

Our most serious dispute was whether to include a 1949 photograph of Kate and Max having sex. My father championed the idea. I knew I'd matured based on my experiences at Armadillo, but including a nude photo of my biological parents making love—even if they were wearing masks—made me highly anxious. I had a disconcerting feeling that one of those photo shoots had resulted in me!

Theo wasn't about to let up. "We can pick a discreet photo. After all, John Lennon and Yoko Ono appeared nude on a cover of *Rolling Stone* in 1968. I know Kate would have wanted to include a photo of the two of us. After all, she believed her body was the Eighth Wonder of the World. Remember, I was the sheepish one who wanted to wear masks to disguise our identities."

"Excuse me, Theo. I believe you initially suggested taking those shots." I stepped back and thought a moment. "Here's the deal. We already have David Budman's 1950 photo of you when you were Max. Sooner, rather than later, David should take a photo of you as Theo. The two photos will go on the book jacket of my forthcoming biography, *Max Eicher/Theodore Neumann: Revealed for All to See.* In exchange for this cover, I'll allow you to have one nude photo of you and Kate, i.e., my parents, in the biography."

"Paul, I acknowledge your gifts of deduction and investigation. But before I give a definitive answer, I'll have my attorney thoroughly study the contract's fine print."

We both laughed for a long time. Then we rose from our chairs and embraced each other for an even longer time.

Almost three years after my first meeting with Theo in Iowa City, I sent Theo and my friends the following invitation:

Paul Seawright invites you to a reading
and signing of
Max Eicher/Theodore Neumann:
Revealed for All to See
Prairie Lights Bookstore
7:00 p.m., February 14, 1983

I stood beside the podium as Jim Harris introduced me. "On Valentine's Day three years ago, I had the honor of presenting the screenwriter Theodore Neumann, while Paul Seawright sat in the audience. Only Theodore knew that Paul was his son —now we all know their true relationship. In the intervening years, Theodore's work has been acknowledged and acclaimed. His thirteen-volume set of Maya codices won the International Book Award for Science two years ago. The thirteenth volume —nicknamed the *Maya Kama Sutra*—made the *New York Times'* bestseller list. Theodore was also honored as a McDermott Fellow for his pioneering work in helping to crack the Maya code. But enough of an update on Theodore. Tonight, our focus is on his son, Dr. Paul Seawright.

"Last week, Paul's book was published to reviews that give new meaning to the word glowing. I'll give but one example: 'More fascinating and enlightening than Seawright's *Freud*, this biography includes nods to the genres of mystery, suspense, adventure, and romance, but brilliantly transcends them.' This evening, I have the honor of presenting Paul, while Theodore sits in our audience. Paul, the stage is yours."

My special guests sat in the front row of the standing-room-only crowd: my father, Doña María, David Budman, Harriet Galveston, and Father Lester Sheehan. To my astonishment, Doña María and David were holding hands. My former students sat in the second row and waved. Near the back of the room, my department chair, who'd given me such grief over publish-or-perish, smiled and gave me a thumbs-up as if he'd known all along that I'd eventually publish my next book.

I was acutely aware of the absence of six people who were no longer living: William Farrell, Gerald Strupp, Ruth Kelly Eicher, Sharon Silverthorne, Maurine Madanes, and Katherine (Kate) Davis. I'd never met the last two, yet I missed Maurine, the love of Max's life, and Kate, my mother.

"When a person's life is as memorable as my father's, the biographer's task is a joy to write. Thank you, Father, for all your support." I thanked my friends and concluded, "Special thanks to Doña María, who, as a young girl, showed Max Eicher an inverted Maya tomb in appreciation for his giving her a gold armadillo pendant."

During the next thirty minutes, I read excerpts from my book and shared anecdotes. During the question-and-answer period, a former student asked if there was any truth to the rumors that I'd solved some murders at Armadillo.

Without skipping a beat, I said, "In a place as mysterious as Armadillo, all sorts of rumors proliferate." In unison, my special guests rolled their eyes.

After the applause, congratulatory handshakes, and book signing, I excused myself. As I washed my hands in the restroom,

I looked in the mirror and noticed for the first time how my face combined distinctive features from each of my parents. I shared Max's elongated face and Kate's winsome smile. But I was ecstatic that I'd seen my face before I saw my birthmark.

Filled with confidence and a sense of inner peace, I returned to the large room. I signaled to Theo, Doña María, David, Harriet, and Father Lester. "This place is too public for an intimate celebration. Please be my guests at the Hawkeye Bar and Grill for dinner and drinks. I've reserved a room."

Before falling asleep that night, I reflected on the journey that my father and I began three years ago when he was eighty, and I was twenty-nine. Then, I was often naïve, self-deprecating, and obsessed by my birthmark; thank goodness my father believed in me when I didn't believe in myself. Since I first met him, I've found my father unpredictable, exasperating, and provocative. Over time, I've learned to feel compassion for him, which after waiting far too long, I've been learning to give myself. Despite the obstacles, we have persevered. Neither of us can know how many years together we have left. But it doesn't take a detective to discover what we both know: our mutual love will sustain us across our time remaining.

ABOUT THE AUTHOR

John Littrell

John Littrell began writing Death at Armadillo so long ago that no memory traces of its origin survive. On the other hand, he fondly remembers being a Professor of Counseling with expertise in short-term therapy. Drawing on his understanding of human psychological strengths, flaws, and perversities, Littrell creates intriguing characters. His skill in rendering exotic settings draws on his extensive world travel. Formerly, an author of academic books, Littrell is now a mystery writer. He and his wife live in Santa Fe, NM.

ACKNOWLEDGEMENT

I offer my heartfelt thanks to Mary Littrell, my long-time editor. Wearing the hats of many types of editors, i.e., developmental, structural, copy, and proofreading, she has continually convinced me of her invaluable contributions to my writing.

Two friends stand out as indispensable in their comprehensive editorial critiques of this manuscript. Carol Eastes and Elyse Demaray offered encouragement but pulled no punches when their sharp eyes spotted holes in the plot, implausible coincidences, and other embarrassing writing errors.

Special thanks to Brian Cassidy, Bill Frank, Bill Leeman, Rich Meenan, and Benita Vassallo for their invaluable assistance in improving this novel.

Others offered feedback that enhanced this book. I thank these people for their support: Rick Bohn, Jim Boyd, Mary Cassidy, Dan Friedman, Karen Kleeman, Kelly Koepke, Marquisa LaVelle, David Littrell, Stephen Littrell, Noreen Perlmutter, Deb Valentine, and members of the Santa Fe Writers' Group (Sonni Cooper, Marty Gerber, Richard Perk, & Victoria Varley).

Grammarly's algorithms flagged potential issues in my manuscript, which I might never have spotted. All too often, its suggestions were dead-on, which is most appropriate in a murder mystery.

I much appreciate the cover art direction by Larry Vigon and the cover design by Larry Vigon and Barbara Leung Larson.